Johnny Kelly

6tHouse

First published in 2011 by
6tHouse
an imprint of
Wordsonthestreet
Six San Antonio Park,
Salthill,
Galway, Ireland.
web: www.wordsonthestreet.com
email: publisher@wordsonthestreet.com

ISBN   978-1-907017-09-4

Cover design, layout and typesetting: Wordsonthestreet
Cover images: Front - Štěpán Kápl/Dreamstime.com
              Back - Michaeldb/Dreamstime.com
Printed and bound in the UK

Banjaxed

Johnny Kelly is from Co Mayo.
He is 25 years old.
He lives in New York.

To my mother, Maureen;

you're some Mam for one Mam.

Chapter 1

Do you know something, it's a right pain in the bollocks being a ciotóg. Christ above. I'm fit to eat iron with these scissors. Would it kill them to make a few thingamajigs with us lefty loosys in mind? Crack, you bastard, crack. What good is it buying a new pair of gloves if they're imprisoned inside the packet? Throw-in is set for one o'clock. Anything else to get out of the way? The prayers are prayed. Three Weetabix swallowed. Is the bowl in the sink? It better be or the Weetabix will be welded to it and Mam'll get cross. My gear bag is packed: boots, togs, towel, banana, agus a bottle of Lucozade.

--Seanie Carolan, centre halfback, sticks to a good forward like shit to a blanket.

The county final, we're up by a single point, one of their forwards breaks free from his man with a clear path to the goal. Looks like this is it, game over for Ballybar Crokes. Just as he belts the ball, out of the blue dives myself, arms outstretched like Superman. I somehow, miraculously, block the would be killer shot. The crowd let out a slow sigh in relief as we retrieve the ball and run out the remaining minute. When the ref blows the final whistle, everyone roars and legs it onto the pitch as happy as Larry. My team-mates hoist me up over their shoulders and chant,

--THERE'S ONLY ONE SEANIE CAROLAN! ...ONE SEANIE CAROLAN...

Flash-Flash-Flash. The photographers snap like mad, bedazzling the bejesus out of my eyes. Next thing I'd be giving the victory speech, in English agus Irish, thanking the fans for their unwavering support throughout the roller-coaster ride of a season.

--Three cheers. Hip, hip, HOORAY! Hip, hip, HOORAY! Hip, hip, HOORAY!

Bingo. The fecker of a packet finally cracks. A good pair of gloves are hard to find, I'm a fan of these ones though, they're a perfect fit and have a savage grip when the ball's all wet. Christ, I can't wait. The pre-match nerves are going full tilt, not the shit your trousers type, the good ones, the zippy nerves. I just have to put a bit of blue Dax Wax in the hair and I'm ready for off. Jesus, look at the cut of me, to the right of my fringe I have a rebellious enough oul cowslick. I won't let it get the better of me. No siree. The blue Dax Wax will put the skids under it.

"Mam, are you right?"

Kililea Park, here I come. Tis a fine size of a stadium so it is. If it was pushed, I suppose it would seat a good twenty thousand arses. The majority of under-twelve matches are played on a smaller pitch, but we get to have at it on the full size for the final show-down. A few weeks ago some hardware shop or something painted their logo onto a couple of the seated stands. After a match it was gas altogether, when the supporters rose up, they had yellow arses from the paint. I nearly died laughing so I did. There was a big article about it in the Connaught Post with the yellow arses on show for all to see.

Mam pulls the car over and lets me out near the clubhouse side of the pot holed car-park. She's only able to wait for the first half before she has to go back to work above in St Teresa's nut-house. Southport GAA, a shower of bastards if ever there were, mosey on down to the far dressing rooms acting like they're the hard men. We call them Port-holes and they call us Mullets. Back in the Famine, Southport were sitting handy on the coast and could catch plenty of fish to stall them over during the tightest of times. The poor crowd here in Ballybar had neither spud nor fish to fill their bellies, so the lads in Southport gave us the Mullets to chomp on and stave off starvation. I follow the concrete grey corridor to the dressing rooms, that healthy stench of soil and sweat hits the back of my srón. Most of the lads are already togged out. The duffel bag of yellow and red jerseys lies in the middle of the floor.

"Howya, Conor, how's the craic?"

"Seanie, how's the form?"

7

"Mighty."

Conor's the team captain, he's from one of those big footballing families, the whole lot of them are mad into GAA. I wouldn't be surprised if someday he ended up playing for Mayo. Packie Quinn, our manager, traipses into the dressing room, the crease between his eyes is tightened, his right hand rests on his hair challenged scalp. Whenever Packie's right claw is placed on top of his head like this, something is awry. Usually he has his right index finger buried deep within his schnoz.

"Okay, lads, listen up. A bit of bad news. Vinnie had a bad oul spill and can't play today. He fell off his bike and broke his shaggen collar bone."

Oh God no. Packie throws his bobbing head over my way.

"Carolan, you'll play in goal, won't ya?"

"Yeah, no bother, whatever you want."

Feck! I hate playing in goal. Shite! I'm the only one who has played in goal before. The time I minded cool, Ballinward were missing a few of their best players, making me look way better than I actually am. Blast it anyways. I should say no. Is it too late to say no? Why did I say yes? Why didn't I at least try and talk Packie out of it? Same old, same old. Say nothing, and nothing will be said. It's like my cousin Kathleen, she always cooks her mashed potatoes with onions in them, I can't stand onions, she may as well serve dog shite and custard as to put onions in the mash. Do I complain? Do I feck.

--Seanie, are you certain you don't want me to give you the mash without the onions?

--No, no, it's grand.

--Are you sure, loveen?

--No, no. No bother.

Packie steps out of the dressing room into the hallway, his crown shining like a hound's balls. Feck, feck, feckedy, feck. I hate going in goal. Feck. Packie pops his head inside.

"Let's hurry it up lads."

Alright, suppose I better get togged out. The only under twelve jersey left is the keeper's long sleeved number 1.

The Port-holes are already on the pitch warming up, jogging back and forth in their green and white gear from sideline to sideline. We emerge from the tunnel, the cogs of our boots clack on the concrete till they meet the grass. The black clad referee stands in the middle of the field, he calls captain Conor and the Port-hole captain over to decide the toss. A couple of turns in mid-air and the coin returns to the ref's hand. Conor looks happy. Yes. We won it. Lovely hurling. We'll be playing with the wind for the first half. Packie empties a blue net filled with O'Neills footballs and fires them out onto the pitch. I go for goal.

"Here, take plenty of shots so I can get a good feel for it."

Balls galore are lobbed into the square. A couple of shots fall short before the crossbar. To practice a kick out, I set the ball on a small mound of pitch.

Kick...

Not great so it's not. I might be better off taking them out of my hands. It's grand having the long sleeved goalie jersey, it's a fair bit warmer than the others and thankfully there's a strong smell of washing powder drifting off of it. The short sleeved jerseys always have a powerful pong of lad no matter how many trips they make to the washing machine. To warm up, we jog and sprint, fist passing to a team-mate as we go from the goal to the half-way line.

"Bring it in, lads," shouts Packie.

We head over towards our dugout. Southport, the pack of wankers, do the same. Both teams line up, the supporters in the stands rise, here we go, the National Anthem. I'm sure most of them are well versed at miming the hell out of it. Not me. I know it like the back of my hand. Proud as a peacock so I am. The speakers beside the scoreboard blare in and out of tune for a second or three.

Sinne Fianna Fáil,
Atá faoi gheall ag Éirinn,
Buíon dár slua,

9

Thar toinn do ráinig chughainn,
Faoi mhóid bheith saor
Seantír ár sinsear feasta,
Ní fhágfar faoin tíorán ná faoin tráill.
Anocht a théam sa bhearna baoil,
Le gean ar Ghaeil, chun báis nó saoil,
Le gunna scréach faoi lámhach na bpiléar,
Seo libh canaig amhrán na bhFiann.

Applause and whistles drown out the last line like always.

"Come on Ballybar!"

"Up Southport."

Sixty minutes to decide the under-twelve County Mayo champions. I'm going to knock forty shades of shite out of any Port-hole who comes within ten yards of the square. Even if I'm not in my ideal spot, it doesn't mean we're losing the flipping match. No way. Packie huddles the starting 15, arms on shoulders, close together.

"Alright lads, this is it. We have to give everything we got tofuckenday. Remember, backs, stay tight to your men. Forwards, take the points and the goals will come. Do ye hear me?"

We all scream, "Yeah!"

"A great man once said, would you rather live a thousand years as a sheep? Or a day as a lion?... Today, lads, let's be lions."

"AAAAAAHHHHHH!"

We bout it onto the pitch ready to give it fecken waskey. Mam waves to me in the stands, I hope she can stay long enough to see me kicking Port-hole backside. A good lock of other parents and familiar faces stand next to her. The umpire leans against the goal posts, he sports a white coat and a smirky puss, the white and green flags are on the ground beside him. Captain Conor, wearing the socks up high, bangs off his Southport counterpart in anticipation of the ball being flung up between them at centre field. The ref blows the whistle and throws in the ball. Conor wins it. Game feckin on.

"Good man yourself."

Conor, with a solo, steps away from his man and creates some space, he sends a low kick pass skidding up the left side to the half forward line. Our number 12, Gary Mangan, scoops it up with a defender on his arse. Mangan steadies himself, faces the halfback and tries to side-step him with a solo and ball fake. The ref whistles and the action freezes. Looks like the Port-hole tackled Mangan too high. Free to Ballybar.

"Well up, Gar."

Mangan's a brilliant free taker.

"Come on, Gar, over the bar with it."

He moves back a few steps. The ref gives him the go-ahead. Mangan straightens up, bounces the ball once and with a running kick boots it high. The ball hangs near the inside of the left post then goes over the bar. The umpire waves his white flag. A point to the Mitchels.

"Up Ballybar!"

"Go on the Mitchels."

By Jesus, we're sucking diesel. Packie stands on the sideline, arms folded, pleased with the start. The Southport keeper hits a short kick to their right cornerback, he takes the pass and leaves it off to a team-mate, they then move the ball around the back line with a number of short fist passes. One of them, with an awkward hoof, sends the ball hovering towards mid-field. Captain Conor tries to intercept the pass. He misses it badly. A Southport mid-fielder breaks the ball down, controls it, and peers up at his half forward line. He belts the ball high into the sky. Near the 45 meter line our backs and Southport's forwards cluster around the middle. The ball looms overhead, waiting to drop. Christ, who's supposed to be marking that number 13? Bounding towards the middle so he is. Everyone jumps for the ball, but number 13, with a running leap, hangs in the air like a snake taking a shite and comes away with it. Two of our halfbacks try to force him to give up the ball.

"Get on him, will ye."

Number 13 stays poised, with a nifty solo he turns both of them and plows down the centre of the pitch.

"Stop him."

The fullbacks intervene. The centre back and right fullback close him down and shift him towards the sideline.

"Lads, the middle!"

Unmarked, Southport's number 12 bursts down the centre. Number 13 notices him and quickly fists a pass over to his sprinting team-mate. He catches it. Shite. He's coming straight for me. Unchallenged. One on one. Stay on the line? Run out to meet him? Quick. I scamper out to stall the ball. We make eye contact for a split second. Number 12 has great ball control, he solos and bounces with ease. Palms up, hands out wide, I make myself as big and broad as possible to psych him out. He tries to get me to bite on his left and right fakes. I'm bang smack in his face now. No way are you getting around me, ya bollocks ya. The ball falls to his right foot. He hits it low. Where's it gone? No. Through my legs. It rolls over the white goal line into the back of the net. No. The umpire waves his green flag. Goal for Southport. No. Packie goes bananas on the sideline next to the dugout. The Southport fans go ballistic.

"Go on Southport," shouts someone behind the goal.

Through the legs, Jesus Christ Almighty.

There's only ten minutes left in the second half. Thanks be to God. My eyes are tearing like feck, I want this match to be over something shocking. Four goals in the one match. In the county final. Christ. Why didn't Packie sub me off at half time? A good lot of the supporters were even roaring at him to substitute me.

--Take him off, take him fucking off!

I wish he did instead of embarrassing the skitter out of me. A right shitehawke so I am. Southport know they have it won, their faces shine with glee. The ref better not play any extra time or God fecken help me I'll decapitate him. Vinnie, the lucky whore, sits in the dugout near the end of the bench with his right arm in a sling. Why couldn't I have broken my collar bone? I'd have snapped both my legs off if I knew this massacre was in store. Four goals. Mother of God Almighty. Look at all the cog marks around the square. The place is half destroyed, the Southport forwards more or less set up shop around me for both halves. Everyone will be yapping about the match on the drive home as they wipe the condensation from their windscreens.

--Jesus, Carolan was useless. He lost it for ye so he did.

I can see the report in the sports section of next Wednesday's Connaught Post. Something to the effect of:

Ballybar Crokes, obliterated off the face of planet Earth.

That'll be just the headline, I'm sure they'll name names to add insult to injury:

Seanie Carolan lets in four, yes folks, that's right, four goals in the under-twelve final. As far as we are aware, The Guinness Book of World Records will be entering it in their latest edition for most goals in a county final.

I'll probably be named eejet of the month for my troubles as well. Above the column, there'll be a nice happy picture of myself with the blue Dax Wax in the hair:

This month the award for greatest eejet among them all goes to Seanie Carolan, for his diabolical display of goal-keeping in last week's county final against Southport GAA. In fact, he was so atrocious, we here at the Connaught Post have decided to name the award after the great fool.

Southport are running out the clock now, they've used up all their subs and haven't been as aggressive for the last five or so minutes. The under-fourteen final is on after us, both teams wait on the sidelines to get warmed up. The ref checks his watch, he puts the whistle to his lips and blows it three times with emphasis on the third blow. Match over.

Final score: 0-7 to 4-8.

The Port-hole crowd are delighted, the supporters rush the pitch while the Southport players hug and celebrate victoriously. Most of our lads are bawling their eyes out with their chins welded to their upper chests.

Someone shouts, "Heads up, Ballybar."

I wish we could hold our heads up, it would be great if this was a match where we fought the good fight and lost. You can live with

13

that, but this was not one of those matches. We have just been annihilated. People might question our mental health if we were able to hold our heads up after this God awful game.

--Up to St Teresa's with them.

Especially me, I'm the fall fella. Four goals in the county final. The Lord save us. As we walk off the pitch the under-fourteen finalists run on and begin warming up. The Southport forward who scored the first goal sneaks out of the crowd and comes over to shake hands with me.

"Hard luck," says he, giving his condolences.

Never again am I wearing a fecking football jersey.

There is no,

--Maybe next time.

Or,

--Oh well, let's have a laugh about it.

Never. It's not worth it. To hell with a silver medal. I'm too fed up. Someone stops at the dressing room door, it's one of the lad's fathers.

"Hard luck, lads. Hard luck."

Luck my bollocks. Here comes Packie, this time his hand's not on his head nor is he picking his nose, both claws rest in his track-suit pockets. Packie glances round the room, disappointed, he sighs and begins his eulogy.

"Tough match, tough match... Sometimes to learn how to win ye have to learn how to lose. The match was one of those lessons. Southport were the better team, they got all the bounces. On another day it could have worked that way for us, but you never know how things will fare on the day. Ye were good, in spurts. But they were good all the way and that's why they won and they deserved it, so fair play to them. We have to take this and learn from it. A lot of ye'll be moving up to the under-fourteen squad, and experience like this will stand to ye so it will. Overall, we had a great year and we should be proud of that, alright... I don't want any player thinking it's their fault we lost the match. It takes a team to win and a team to lose."

Packie's not gawking at me, but that's definitely directed at myself. Feck Packie, the gobshite, this is his fault. He's the manager. The buck in charge. It was his idea to put me in goal. Not mine. I just did what I was told.

I didn't say goodbye to any of the lads, I'm not arsed, they're probably all blaming me anyways. The shouting and roaring of the under-fourteen final catches my lug, hopefully one of the teams gets hammered to high heaven so they can know how it feels. Outside there's a couple of oul pairs doing a post-mortem on the match. I step out. They see me and go silent, I can feel their eyes on me, after a second or two they go back to their gabbing. I'm going to keep the head down and belt on home. I've no time for any of them. At the bottom of the car-park, there's a bunch of loud lads on bikes, I remember seeing them on the sidelines watching the match. Don't look at them. Chin to chest. Eyes to ground.

"Hey you? Come here, hey," shouts one of them.

They snigger and sneer among themselves.

"You're shite, hey."

Feck the lot of them. Dickheads. The moment I get home to the gafe I'm going to curl up into a nice small ball on the couch. First though, some tasty treats are in order. I deserve a bit of comfort after the day I've had. I'll stop off at the shop and get some chocolate biscuits and a bottleen of Club Orange. Sunday bloody Sunday, there'll be rakes of people out and about the town for pints and dinner, I'll have to take the scenic route home to make sure I don't bump into anyone I know. Otherwise, I'll have to recite the whole flipping fiasco. I'll go down past SuperValu instead of walking through Flax Street, then head up Monument Hill and I should be grand.

Home, safe, sound and showered. One bit of good news is that the biscuits came with 33 and 1/3 percent extra. At least the chocolate came up Carolan. Now, it's time for a video to chill the beans, something light-hearted, I doubt there's anything on telly anyways. The Sunday Game is probably on and that's the last fecking programme I want to watch. What will I put on? Something good. Let me see. I have it. Back to the Future, you can't go wrong with Marty Mc Fly and Doc Brown, a sound pair of lads so they are. Wouldn't it be mighty to have Doc's DeLorean. I could've gone back in time, saved Vinnie from breaking his collar bone and let him be the sacrificial lamb, then I'd be one of the lads blaming him for the cat display of football. What else? I could have gone back and told myself to fake an injury and not play in the game at all at all. Then people would say,

--Sure it's a different team without Carolan in the line-up.

The power button glows red and the graphics on the little monitor do a little dance. I give the tape a quick blow in case of dust. Into the machine's gob it goes, after the machine swallows the tape, play-back begins. The new video machine is working sound, our old one was chewing up tapes and breaking the whole time. I was fiddling around with it myself trying to get it to work, but the yokes in it are fecked. The whatdoyoucallthem? The heads. That's them, they're the ones. We were told they're fairly expensive if you have to get them repaired or replaced. Sometimes if you use a video cleaner it fixes the machine for a while, this time though they were too far gone. No amount of cleaning solution would get them working proper. The fella in the video shop said the best job would be to buy a new machine and save ourselves the hassle. Mam agreed. Sure we've had it for long enough anyways. The other day, I tried hooking it up to the telly in the kitchen, but the bastarden thing wouldn't work at all at all. Tis just totally and truly banjaxed.

Chapter 2

S hite. That's the bell now. I take a quick glance downward to make sure the end of my right trouser leg is still tucked tight into my sock. Grand so it is. At Marian Row, peddling like a mad yoke, I swing a righty tighty onto the Oldport Road. There's a fair bit of traffic clogging up the way. Tis quicker to cycle on the footpath, only a couple of people to dodge instead of fifty cars. White hair and a black gown appears at the school's main entrance. Brother Leary. Ready to kill. Mr. Kenny pulls into the car-park ahead of me. I guide the front spokes into a wheel-space at the end of the stand and click the combo-lock lickety split. Brother Leary, frowning, checks his watch. I bout it up the small slant towards him, a couple of stragglers follow behind me, their school-bags bouncing off their backs. Leary looks down at us, those two square white thingys like blank copy-pages dropping from his collar.

"Come on, come on, we don't have all morning," says he, in his highly annunciated manner.

One by one he takes our names in his big bad book of lateness. Brother Leary is the head honcho around these here parts, the last of the Brothers at Saint Patrick's. Leary hates first years, and the years above us, and most other people in general I reckon. Last week he went spare altogether at a lad in my class for not wearing his school tie. Everything else was in sound order: sky-blue shirt, navy jumper, grey trousers, but no striped navy and sky-blue tie. The penalty for lateness is a sceal two. Overall, there's three types of sceals: one, two, agus a trí. If you get a combined sceal six, it means you have detention on Saturday morning, besides lateness, teachers give out sceals if you act the goat in class or don't do your homework.

"Next."

"Sean Carolan."

Leary adds me to the list. Inside I go, time to head to assembly. Before normal classes we have assembly, where roll is taken and the

Class Head takes care of housekeeping. Our Class Head is the very mammyish Miss Keogh, she teaches us religion as well. The name of our class is 1A1. There's four classes altogether in first year with around thirty pupils per class. The foyer is quiet, only a few other late lads getting books from their lockers. One of the things about secondary school is that they don't force you to cover your books and copies in wallpaper. We're big boys now. We can fuck them up any way we please. Room 0-3. Miss Keogh's door is open wide.

"Well?"

"Late Seanie," says she.

"Yip, Brother Leary nabbed me on the way in."

I rest my arse next to my best pal Chris Conway. Chris is Irish-Canadian, his oul fella's from here and his mam's from Toronto. The Conways moved over when Chris was about ten, they found a nice gafe down the road from me in a new estate. I remember when he first came over, the poor bastard took so much abuse so he did. Given he spent the first ten years abroad, it's only natural he'd have a Canadian accent. Unfortunately for Chris, to the untrained lugs of Ballybar, his accent sounds American. Which means he might as well be American because everyone is going to call him a Yank whether he is one or not. From the very get-go, Chris said it was a huge culture shock, he wasn't used to getting the piss pulled out of him by his friends 24/7. People were forever trying to fix him about the fatness of Americans.

--Seven cheeseburgers, please.

Some of the lads would invent blatant lies and say them to him in brutal American accents to rile him up. The type of cheesy things you might see on American programmes.

--Hey, Chris, dude, I saw you and your family riding your BMXs to the park on the weekend. Pretty sweet, man.

Chris says it still vexes the shite out of him when people pull that shit, he knows well the cynicism towards the image of a picture perfect happy family. It's not a proper family without a drink problem so it's not. Anyways, the so-called Yank's been here over three yonks now and is well able to give it as good as he gets it.

18

The twenty-five past nine bell rings. Inside my jumper, I check my left shirt pocket for the oul timetable. Bollocks. Forgot it.

"Hey, what's first?"

"French," says Chris.

"Très bien."

French isn't too stressful. My brain doesn't work awful well early in the morning, something like maths for instance won't go into my skull till well after small break. The hallway is jammers with uniforms, all moving around the school in an anti-clockwise fashion. One of the serious rules is the one way system, everyone has to go anti-clockwise, it's supposed to be more efficient. Big Brother Leary is planted in the middle of the foyer, making sure there's not too much messing and jigacting. If you don't shift your arse the right way, Leary will shift it for you.

--Play up and I'll bum you into the middle of next week.

At big lunch a rake of us Saint Pat's buckos head up town to the Arcade, it stretches from Tobin's car-park through to Main Street. The Moore College crowd stall around SuperMac's or in the alley beside the Humbert Inn. Tis beyond me how the lads in Moore College get anything done with women in class, I'd be on a horn all day so I would. I haven't a notion where the girls from the Convent go at lunch, you never see many of them about the town, they must stay good and close to the Sisters.

"Mc'Hugh-cumber, ya whore ya?"

"Arra howya horsebox?"

The Castlevary man himself, Cathal Mc'Hugh's not in our class, but we always have a chin-wag at lunch time. He's a gas ticket altogether.

"I seen your oul lady on Parrish's corner yesterday, Mc'Hugh."

"Would ya go away, the tide wouldn't take your oul lady out."

"Oh yeah, well, a sniper wouldn't take out Mrs. Mc'Hugh."

"Yours would run rats from a haystack."

"Your oul lady has a face on her like a dog trying to chew a wasp."

"Mrs. Carolan has a look on her like Shane Mac'Gowan's liver."

19

"Oh Jesus, I give up. Good one."

He takes a bow.

"Thank you, thank you."

"What's the craic?"

"Not too much, looking for a fight."

"Yeah?"

"Yeah, a conker fight."

Mc'Hugh unveils a black lace threaded with shiny dark brown conkers.

"Unbeaten so I am."

He slides his king conker to the end of the shoe lace.

"That's a big fucker, where'd ya find it?"

"On our land, there's loads of horse chestnuts around the gafe."

"You have it varnished?"

"I do indeed. A cracker of a conker so it is, but they're all afraid of me, Seanie boy."

"No man has the nuts to compete."

"Not one between them."

"What else is going on?"

"Did I tell ya about last Friday on the way back?"

"No."

"Wait till ya hear. My cousin and a bunch of his cronies threw me in the stream."

"Will ya stop."

"I was drowned'd for the rest of the day, the bus driver thought I pissed the pants on the way out home."

In first year, it's a rite of passage to get thrown in the stream beside the school. You have to be careful if you have any older relations knocking about. They'll always turn on you.

"Are you going to hit the Townhall on Friday?"

"I'm not sure yet. If I can squeeze a few spondoolies out of the oul pair for the taxi home, I might be able to drop in for a gurch."

"Sure you will of course, share a taxi with that ride of a sister."

"We'll see how's she's cutting."

20

It's bad oul tack to land yourself on Brother Leary's shit list twice in the one day, I said I'd get my arse back in good time before two o'clock. We have a double class with Mr. Neill, our English teacher. Mr. Neill seems sound enough, but he can't control the class for love nor money. He's an older sort of a gent and his diction is absolutely dire, when he gets flustered he speaks in bursts, it's like his gob can't keep up with his brain. Some students call him,

--Mahill.

That's what it sounds like when he says the name Michael. On a hook outside Mr. Neill's room, I hang my jacket as the bell rings. The room isn't looking the best. There's a few paper airplanes poking out of the bin and some snapped elastic bands on the floor. Students saunter into class in dribs and drabs, there's no rush for Mr. Neill's. The man himself bumbles in with his battered brief-case and dark grey blazer. A lot of older teachers sport blazers like Mr. Neill's, leather elbow patches must have been the height of style ages ago. What was so appealing about them? I haven't a notion.

"Okay, okay, settle down now."

The class looks fairly full. Chris is the last man in, he usually goes home for big lunch. Mr. Neill shuts the door, then steps to his desk and opens his notebook. The class whispers while he peruses it for a few seconds until he arrives at the correct page.

"Do ye all have your books? If ye don't, share with the pupil beside you."

Fittttlllllleeeettttt.

"Ah, guys," says Chris.

"Eggie."

"You won't get that out in a cold wash," says one of the lads.

The messing has begun.

"Quieten let ye," says Mr. Neill.

"Ah, Chris."

I always blame Chris when someone opens the lunch-box, even if he's absent.

"Chris, God," says Rasher Corrigan.

Chris has his jumper pulled up over his srón. Mr. Neill's already

21

worried.

"Here, you, open the window there."

Rasher rises from his desk, the windows are large panes with three linked vents at the top. They have to be pulled open with a long hooked stick. He opens two windows. The class, although a bit giddy, settles somewhat.

"Today, we're going to look at Swift's-"

-Fittttlllllleeeettttt.

Guffaws galore follow the fake fart.

"Ah, Chris."

Everyone blames Chris.

"Chris, put a cork in it."

"It's not me, I swear."

Mr. Neill tries to ignore the flatulence, he belts on with the class.

"Jonathan Swift's-"

-Bahahahah, Bahahahah.

It's a fecken sheep bleating. The sound's too manufactured to be an impression. What was that? Nobody seems to be guilty, it's not Rasher, I can see under his desk. Nothing there. False farts and baaing sheep.

Bahahahah, Bahahahah.

"Whoever's doing that cut it out immediately. I'm warning ye."

Mr. Neill goes around the class wide-eyed. Where's the sheep? The desks are great for hiding things, they're creaky oul yokes with a shelf underneath for books, or sheep.

Bahahahah, Bahahahah.

Mr. Neill turns quickly, but no sheep in sight. I notice something passing hands between Rasher and Alan Flynn, it's a small box with a sheep on it. Rasher hides it under his desk.

"I'm warning ye now, anymore messing and it'll be a thousand lines."

Mr. Neill retreats to the blackboard, he picks up a piece of chalk and begins to write something.

Bahahahah, Bahahahah.

Everyone laughs. Rasher, with the sheep box in his possession,

22

passes it on to the next lad.

"Alan, where did you get that?"

"Up in Galway, I was there the weekend and seen it in the joke shop."

"It's gas, man."

"Class isn't it."

Mr. Neill roams the room again looking for the phantom sheep.

"Who is it?" asks Mr. Neill.

"Sir, it's a ghost," says Rasher.

"Non corporeal, I doubt it."

He's getting fierce flustered now, the words leave his gob fast and hard.

"Where is it?"

Fittttlllllleeeettttt.

Mr. Neill catches Rasher's fake fart.

"That's it. What's your name?"

"What, sir?"

"Don't think I didn't see you, ya pup ya. Name?"

"Give him a phony," whispers Chris.

"...Tommy Rourke."

Mr. Neill writes Rasher's false name on the board, but the instant his back is turned,

Bahahahah, Bahahahah.

Mr. Neill blames Rasher.

"Keep at it, Rourke."

He has a set on him now.

"Sir, I didn't do nothing."

Mr. Neill strikes a mark beside the name Rourke on the blackboard.

"My good name is being ruined," says Rasher.

Chris fires a paper ball from one side of the room to the other. Mr. Neill, mad as a wet hen, notices the paper ball, he picks it up off the floor and puts it in the bin.

"Sir, Sir, someone stole my pen."

"Hah? What?"

"Sir, someone stole my pen. My grandfather gave me that pen on his death bed. Seriously, whoever has it give it back, I'm not messing."

"Whoever took it, hand it over immediately, come on now."

"Come on lads, give it back, it has sentimental value," says I with a half smirk.

"Come on now, own up."

I gawk at Mr. Neill in the face, then glance down at his right blazer pocket, reaching into it, to the amazement of the class, I yank out my stolen pen.

"My pen, you stole it!"

Incredulous so I am.

"Maaaaaa."

Gobsmacked so he is.

"You're off your tits," shouts someone.

"Maaaaaa."

The poor bollocks sounds like a sheep himself. I sneaked the pen into his pocket when he was weaving through the desks in search of sheep.

"Sir, why would you do that?"

"Maaaaaa."

A knock at the door. Shite. Quiet.

"Shhhhh. Shhhhh."

"Come in," says Mr. Neill, regaining his composure.

Mr. Corley, the Vice Principal, enters. Another buck who has been around for ages, he's a hardy enough oul fella, I wouldn't be inclined to test him. Even his face is tough, a scowly, scrunched, whiskey puss. He used to teach science, but now he's too busy with the Vice Principal stuff. Everyone has the gobs firmly shut. Corley carries a large ledger under his arm, Mr. Neill meets him at his desk as they go over some papers. We're all skitting our arses off. Whenever you're not supposed to laugh, it's always way harder not to burst your hole. Mr. Corley slowly glances up at us, you'd swear he can sense the divilment in the class, keep still, look straightforward and serious. The two of them finish up, Corley fastens the ledger and closes the door behind him. We better cop-on for a bit in case Corley returns. I'm sure he's well aware of the fuckacting that goes on in Mr. Neill's. We'll quit while we're ahead.

Last class of the day. Geography. Bored to tears so I am. Mr. Lydon should get a job at putting babies to sleep, he'd be unreal at it, the dreariness and monotony of his voice would have them out for months. Mr. Lydon is a good bit different than Mr. Neill. He's all bite and no bark. Neill goes daft trying to get the class to behave, he'll write names on the board, make out that he's going to have someone suspended, but never follow through with it. Lydon on the other hand, mess in his class and detention is definitely in the near future. What can you do? Clock-watch. Scratch your bollocks. Look at the floor.

"Urban sprawl occurs when cities and towns begin to spread outwards to the..."

Christ, he'd sicken your shite. You can't even gaze out the windows, they're too clouded with condensation. I wonder what he'd do if someone wrote: 'Fuck you,' on them?

--Who did that? Ten page essay for everyone on watching paint dry.

Mr. Lydon doesn't open the windows at all at all. The close room and high levels of CO_2 in the air are perfect to keep pupils placid in the afternoon. Outside, a faint hammering can be heard, they're building a new extension on to the back of the school. State of the art apparently. They're also developing a football pitch, but it's not going to be full size. The owner of the next field over won't sell the land. I don't know why, I'm sure the Brothers would give him a fair enough price. If I were him I'd sell it for a bomb and take off like fecken Gulliver so I would. To have a load of spons would be savage, you can do anything as long as you have the spons in your pocket. I'd build a big roof over Ireland. Stop all the rain. A massive glass yoke so the odd time the sun does decide to show its shy face it could shine on through. It'd be useless to build it out of galvanize, the roof would be rusted red in days. Friday's going to be a good one, down the lake on the lush, then in the Townhall on the pull. I've the feeling it'll be a brilliant night, not many other first years will be let out. Pioneers, myself and Chris shall be. Chris' cousin better sort us out though, he was acting all Fonzie like the last day.

--Yeah, sound as a bell, boys. I'll get ye lush no bother.

Vodka doesn't give off a heavy smell like cans, a helping of curry chips afterwards will provide adequate cover, so long as we're not too fecken steamed. I wouldn't want to be carried out of the Townhall for a stomach pumping above in casualty. Mam would hit the roof, I wouldn't be let out again till the Leaving Cert if that ever happened. The women will be looking lovely so they will: high-heels, short skirts, tight tops and loose belts. They'll dress nice and conservative leaving the gafe, a pair of denim jeans, then change on the way into a miniskirt. Whatever it takes to convince the oul pair that their little angel's a good Catholic, instead of traipsing about the town like an English girl on holidays. I doubt there will be an awful lot of first year birds out. We'll have to go older. We might even try a few third years. Sure why not? Chris can put on the accent good and thick and we'll say we're in third year ourselves. Play it cool and they won't have a clue, we don't look that young for first years, not like some of the lads, sure they're still only gossures.

God, is class ever going to be over? It's been pulling and dragging forever. The desk here has seen its fair share of biro, covered in it so it is: black, blue and red. I should make my mark. Grunge seems to be the main inspiration for this table's tattoos. The lads were probably bored shitless listening to Mr. Lydon like myself, doodling away to pass the day. I may as well add to it. Grunge. Let me see. I need something angst inspired. My cousins would know what to write, they're mad into Nirvana. I'd be surprised if there's much grunge in the Townhall, it'll be all dance, hard house and trance. Giving it loads. Think about what it's like for a grunger on a Friday night in Ballybar. Where can they go and lament? Where can they feel down? Where can they unleash their rage? Nowhere. That's where. How alienating. How morose. How would I feel?

Life is a big cake of shite and I have the largest slice.

Four o'clock, thank fuck.

"Seanie?" Chris asks, pulling the puppy dog routine.

"Yeah."

He stares at my bike, then turns his attention to me and cants his head sideways.

"Backer?"

"Pretty please."

"Where's yours?"

"I got a puncture at lunch, when I came out the tyre was as flat as Miss Keogh's chest. My dad had to give me a ride back at two o'clock."

"Alright, come on, but you're walking up the hill."

"Cool."

I twiddle with the combination lock on the front wheel, it takes a bit of fiddling to free it from the spokes and stand. The school side of the road and footpath is wedged. School buses and parents are parked along the way in a fine long line. We make for across the road. Chris hesitates when crossing, I stall the digger at the opposite curb. A couple of cars are holding up the show, Chris waits for them to shift, while I reach down and stuff my right trouser leg-end snugly into my sock. One of the days I must buy a chain guard for the front gears, then I won't have to be worrying about my pants all the time. Tis a miracle they haven't got torn up in the crank yet. Chris crosses.

"Ready?"

"Yip."

I've left shoe waiting on the curb and right shoe on the right pedal. He grabs a hold of my shoulders to balance and swings his left leg over the saddle, he sits down and steadies himself. Someone on the saddle is a nuisance when you have a bulgy school-bag on your back. Chris, legs dangling near the ground, helps me push off with his toes.

"And they're off."

I go for the footpath. It's safer with all the traffic on the Oldport Road. My front and back tyres hit the curb good and hard, it's killer

27

on the balls if you're getting a backer.

"Ahhh, my sack," says Chris.

"Whoops."

"That's how you'll warp your wheels."

Even though Chris is as thin as a lath, the extra weight makes cycling more difficult than normal. I click my grip shift and put the back gears into fifth, I leave the front gears be in third. We start to pick up pace on the path.

"What are you going doing for the evening?"

"Not sure, got no wheels, what you at?"

"Thinking of going looking for conkers. Mc'Hugh has this massive one and nobody's beat him yet."

"Where are you thinking?"

"Not the Square everyone goes there, maybe around the Hospital or Flood House."

"Down near the Church might be good."

"Yeah, at the Brother's gafe, around there."

"Defo."

"You going to come?"

"Ah... I'm not taking backers all evening."

"Have you no puncture repair kit?"

"Nope."

"I've one at home, I'll drop over to yours at five."

"Make it six, I don't want to rush my homework that much."

"Sound, I'll be round at six, but be ready, don't be saying you have to stay for dinner."

"My mom's working late tonight so she left food for us."

"Grand so, six it is."

"Cool."

"Actually, shite."

"What?"

"Did you bring your maths book?"

"In my bag."

"Good, I forgot mine. I might borrow it off you, save me coming in early in the morning trying to get maths done in assembly."

"That works. Bring it home tonight and you can give it to me in the morning."

"Sound job."

Chapter 3

Dolled up nice so I am. The four S's are well taken care of: a shite, a shower, a shave and a swank. My face wasn't really shouting out for a shave, but I gave it the once-over for luck. The stereo is going full whack to get me in the form for shape throwing. A good dose of white scuff-coat wouldn't do my Adidas runners a bit of harm, they're a little faded around the sides. Fuck them. Sure they'll survive for one night more.

A banging from below.

"Turn down the music!" shouts Mam. "I'm on the phone."

The kitchen is directly under my room so too much of a racket is easily heard. Mam takes full advantage of this, she always bangs the ceiling with the end of a brush handle in the morning. It drives me mental when all I want is a little more kip in the cot. I lower the volume and take a good gander in the full length mirror, this top will look class in the disco, across the middle and on the forearms are sets of reflective strips. They'll shine all sorts of ways in the Townhall so they will. On the banister, at the bottom of the stairs, my good jacket hangs on for me. I head down to throw it on and tell Mam I'm off.

"Mam?"

She opens the kitchen door with the phone pressed against her lug.

"Come-here-to-me, Sean is heading to the disco tonight so I'll have to let you go..."

Christ. Hurry it up will ya? I rush her by pointing at my watch.

"I know, yeah, yeah, it's great for them. Listen, tell Dick I said hello... Alright, Ann, bye, bye."

At last she hangs up.

"Right, do ya have everything?"

"Yeah, sound."

"Do you have your key?"

"I told ya I have everything."

29

"Okay, okay, there's no need to eat the head off me."

She clicks open her purse and hands me ten pounds.

"That's for the chipper afterwards."

"Thanks."

"You're meeting Chris?"

"Yeah, I better go now. I told him I'd meet him at the bottom of the road."

Mam walks me to the front door. I can tell she's a biteen nervous, this is only my second Townhall disco since starting first year.

"Be careful."

"I will."

"And let me know when you get home."

"Yeah, yeah, see ya."

"Alright, enjoy it."

At the bottom of the road, Chris leans against the small wall beside the stream. Bane's Hill is behind him. It's fierce steep altogether, the top of it is lined with big bunches of whin bushes.

"Howya."

"Bad news," says Chris.

"What is it?"

"Vodka's gone."

About a month and a half ago we got our mitts on a litre bottle of vodka from Chris' cousin Mark. We hid it up the hill in a bush only we knew how to find and tonight we're supposed to be polishing the bastarden thing off.

"Fuck it anyways, are you a hundred percent sure?"

"Pretty sure."

"Well, we're in good time, we can double check in case you missed it."

"Yeah, let's. I might have missed it, but I'm pretty sure it's gone."

Chris was bang-on about the vodka. Some bollocks definitely stole it, myself and himself have a couple of conspiracy theories about who might've done the deed. No hard evidence though. This leaves us with one goal and one goal only, get lush, get lushed and get into the disco. The two of us are on the look-out in the alley beside Heneghan's Butcher on Flax Street, straight across the road from the Townhall. The town has a mighty buzz to it on Friday and Saturday nights, there's people galore out gallivanting around the place. Chris has a rake of older cousins, we're hoping we'll bump into one and see if they'll go into Sloyan's off-licence just down the block from us.

"Well, look who it is," says Chris.

I glance up the way, it's Rasher Corrigan. Flax Street is chock-a-block with cars. Between two bumpers, Rasher crosses over to us with a big smiley head on him.

"Howye lads?" asks Rasher.

"Not good, Rasher, some bollocks stole our drink. What are you up to?"

"Getting lush."

"No way, who's getting it for you?" asks Chris.

"My cousin Nicky."

"Do you think he'd go in for us?"

"Don't know, I'll have to ask him. Come on sure if ye want, I'm meeting him now in Boland's Alley."

Rasher leads the way through Tobin's car-park and up by the back of Stauntan's sports to Rolland's Alley.

"I reckon if ye give him a tenner he'll go in for ye."

Good job we brought some extra spons in case of an emergency. Me and Chris wait near the back while Rasher has a look down Main Street to see if his cousin's coming.

"That's him now," says Rasher. "Do ye have the spons?"

Fast as we can, we hand Rasher our money.

"Two naggins of vodka?"

"That's the one."

The man himself strolls in under the arch. Rasher greets his cousin and starts gabbing away, the back of his head bouncing all over the place as he does. Nicky's a tall fella with a whispy beard, by the looks of him I'd say he's a sixth year. Rasher's a charming oul whore when he wants to be, he's a lot cuter than he lets on half of the time. Nicky squints at us for a second or two.

"God, I hope this works," says Chris.

"Do you think we should offer him more if he says no."

"No harm in trying, right."

"Right."

"Here we go."

Yes. Looks like Rasher's plamausing has done the trick.

"Lads, this is Nicky."

"How's the craic?"

"Hey."

"What do ye want, lads?" Nicky asks.

"Could you get us two naggins of vodka?"

"Don't know, I have a fucken bitch of an order already, they'll think I'm opening my own offie if I buy any more vodka."

"Yeah."

"I'll tell ye what, how about two bottles of Buckie?"

"Yeah, yeah, sound."

Buckfast's a type of tonic wine with a rep for driving people a bit mental in the head. Neither of us have tried it before so we're well up for giving it a lash. Fuck it. Sure even if it tastes rotten, tis better than no lush at all at all. Nicky heads in next door to Boland's off-licence.

"Rasher, nice one altogether."

"No worries."

"Yeah, you're a life saver, man."

"Seriously, we owe you one, big time."

After what feels like an hour, Nicky returns with three plastic bags bulging with lush. He hands Rasher one of the bags.

"Alright lads, have a good one," says Nicky.

"Thanks a million, hey."

Nicky bolts off for Main Street, the other two bags clinking with drink.

"This is unreal," says Chris.

"Buckfast gets ya fucked fast."

32

"Come on to fuck, boys."

Rasher hides his flagon of cider up his bomber jacket and holds it in place with his left hand. Chris and I are able to conceal the Buckfast bottles in our jacket sleeves.

"Right, we all set?"

"Let's do this."

The lake isn't too far from us, through Tobin's car-park, down by Flood House, then either under the bridge or across from the Sports Hall. We'll stall the ball where the craic is ninety.

The lake's the spot to be, there's a fire-log burning yellow and plenty of people drinking away. What more could you ask for? The bridge was fairly dull, only a couple of lads lushing on the far side. The three of us manoeuvrer our way through the crowd, bottles out. I know a couple of people to see from around the town, no one we know to chat to though. Time to hit the bottle. We lean up against the broad green railing that stops people from tumbling into the lake. Chris and I crack the seals of our Buckies, Rasher's cider hisses at him as he loosens the lid.

"Alright boys, cheers."

We three take good gulps of our lush. The Buckfast is fairly strong and sweet, but drinkable enough.

"Not too bad," says Chris.

"I could get used to it, bejezze."

"How about you, Rash?"

"Bulmers goes down easy so it does, it tastes kind of like Cidona."

"I bet it does."

Rasher searches through the left breast pocket of his bomber jacket. After a bit of foostering, he uncovers a packet of Benson & Hedges.

"Do ye want a fag, lads?"

"Go on, sure."

"Chris?"

"Yeah, why not."

Fuck it, we may as well have a couple of puffs. Normally we never

33

touch the cigarettes, but it's a Friday night down the lake. If we're going, we're going full tilt. Rasher puts one on his lips and lights it up with a small plastic gas lighter. He holds the lit lighter steady for Chris and myself to spark up our fags. We both sputter a few times after inhaling.

"They're strong fuckers," says Chris.

"Yeah, they are alright."

"You're Silk Cut Blue, boys."

Rasher with his wrist curled inward, holds the fag between the tips of his right index finger and thumb. He takes a long slow pull. The lit cigarette glows brighter as he sucks, but the aficionado himself doesn't even bother to inhale properly. The eejet keeps the smoke in his gob instead of taking it into his lungs. I'm not going to bother getting on to him about it, he did sort us out with lush after all.

"Boys, do ye want to leave me sound arses of the Buckie and I'll leave ye a good arse of the Bulmers?"

"Yeah, cool," says Chris.

"I don't know, you know what they say?"

"What?"

"Beer before wine is fine, wine before beer is queer."

"Good one."

"Rasher'll be grand, but me and you, Chris, might get fucken locked altogether."

We're putting the final touches on Rasher's cider as he sucks back the last of our Buckies and duckarses a fag. The lush is working its charm grand, I was a biteen cold earlier, now the wine has me warmed up lovely. Oul Rasher is getting fairly locked, his eyes have a glassy glare to them, same craic with Chris, the drink agrees with him though, he didn't get thick or anything when a couple of lads asked him where in America he's from.

"Do ye have teenage discos in Canada?" some randomer asks.

"Nah, we have ice hockey."

"I know that, but what about, like, going out?"

"Yeah, we drop the booty."

Chris starts doing some mental hip-hop dance, dropping his arse to the ground.

"Ha, ha, will ya go easy before you mill yourself."

Out of the blue, a rake of people start booting it in our direction.

"SHADES!"

A Paddy Wagon darts into the Sports Hall car-park. Four Guards leap out sporting the usual luminous jackets with their flashlights in hoof. Everyone drops everything and bouts it across the skinny bridge leading to the other side of the lake. The ground bounces up at me, it's like I'm seeing things through a fecking hand-held video camera.

"Guys, up here," says Chris.

A bunch of us leg it up the wet grassy slope trying not to skid down on our arses. As soon as we reach the top, we hop the wall at the old graveyard. Staying low, and panting like fuck, we make it as fast as we can towards the middle of the graveyard where there's some cover.

"Fucking hell, the cops," says Rasher.

I peep over the top of the wall, trying to catch my breath. Farther down from us there's a good lot of people sprinting towards the diving board. God, I'm as high as kite from the adrenaline and Buckie so I am. On the other side of the lake, the Guards' flashlights wander around in the darkness searching for people in hiding. The other side is dodgy enough. It's a cul da sac, so you could get cornered awful easy.

"At least we got most of our drink drank," says Rasher.

"True enough," says Chris.

"Come on, it's fucking spooky here."

"What time is it?" asks Chris.

"Time for the Townhall, boy. Come on to fuck with ye," says Rasher.

Back to the alleyway beside Heneghan's Butcher and a final prep before we enter the Townhall.

"Here's some tune-gum lads," slurs Rasher.

He holds out two sticks of chewing-gum.

"How lushed do I look?" Chris asks.

"You look grand, I'm telling ya."

"Do you think they'll notice?"

"Just have the spons ready and they won't cotton on."

"How are my eyes?"

Chris, trying to be helpful, squints into Rasher's eyes for a second or three.

"A little red."

"Are they?"

"Yeah, but they won't cop it in the dark."

Across the road we go, there's a small queue of four girls at the Townhall entrance. The three of us are well oiled and a biteen nervous of being turned away by the bouncers.

"Just stand straight and look serious."

Before you're let into the disco you have to be frisked to make sure you're not trying to sneak lush or knifes inside. A fella and a girl stand by to do the frisking. The girls ahead of us queue up at the girls station, leaving the fella who frisks fellas free. Rasher's first. His bomber jacket is puffy and has a fair few pockets. The frisker takes his time with him, he's being extra frisky.

"Next."

My jacket, like Chris', is light enough so the frisker flies though us. At the pay window I hand in a five pound note, the woman behind the window takes the spons and stamps the back of my wrist with a red Townhall mark.

"Nice one," says Rasher.

We're all in sound. Strobes and coloured lights flicker and shine all over the gafe, to the right and left are the men's and women's jacks, they're not too packed yet. Through the wooden floor-boards, I can feel the vibrations of dancing and trance tunes. Jackets and jumpers are strewn across the chairs all around the hall. The Townhall itself is a good size with high ceilings and at the very back a stage where the DJ spins the decks. A small dark extension, with a slight step up to it, is to our right.

"Careful."

36

The extension wall is also lined with chairs, it seems like a grand spot to leave the jackets.

"What do ye reckon?" shouts me, over the beats.

"Grand."

Chris and Rasher agree, we put our three jackets on the back of a chair nearest the far step of the extension. On the dance floor people are throwing shapes like there's no tomorrow. Rasher points to the floor. Chris and I follow. Now's a good time to dance before it gets too thronged, I hate when there's too many people and everyone's all over everyone. You feel like throwing a jab to clear the way. The three of us are fairly steamed, I've been slurring my words like fuck since the lake. A bit of bopping is a good way to burn off some of the lush.

Rasher sparks up a fag while we're giving it loads on the floor, he looks like the right hard fucker with the fag hanging out of the side of his gob. Just over from us are some fine looking girls. Well, two of them are rides and the other two are madras altogether. How come you never see a group full of good looking girls? There's always a couple of rough friends in the mix. Still, the Townhall has a good rep for pulling women.

--Will you shift my friend?

Sometimes it might take a little finagling to seal the deal.

--She'll shift you if I do the friend.

Mostly it's the lad who asks the girl. Girls can ask lads, though it doesn't happen very often, except out in the N17 which is another disco out Kiltwomey way. Apparently girls ask a lot of fellas out there and sometimes play a game called beat the slapper. The aim is to try and shift as many lads as possible. Here in the Townhall you might ask any amount of girls depending on the night that's in it, some nights you mightn't shift any women at all at all, other times you might shift two or three birds if things were going your way. Girls are somewhere on a scale of loose and frigid. A loose girl means that she's up for doing more than just shifting. She might let you go up tops or if you're really lucky, let you go for the finger. If a bird's frigid, she has a rep of being a bit too tight and sure that's no craic so it's not. Though, you

37

don't want a girl who's too loose and just goes around shifting every lad that asks her. If she's at that type of carry-on then you're dealing with a bit of a slapper.

"Where's Rasher?"

Clueless, Chris shakes his head. I scan the crowd in search of himself.

"There," says Chris.

I turn and see Rasher, the divil, chatting away to a lovely looking bird. Myself and Chris give it a minute till Rasher's finished charming.

"Who's that young wan?"

"That's Niamh, shifted her before during the summer."

"Nice one."

Fair play to Rasher, your one Niamh is a fine bit of stuff.

"So are you going to do her again?" Chris asks.

"Yeah, I have to, she let me go up tops last time."

"Well, get over there before someone else lobs the gob."

"I can't just go over there."

"Rasher, if you shifted her before then I'm sure she must know you'll try it on again."

"Will one of ye ask her for me?"

"In Canada, we just walk over and make-out with the girl," says Chris, pulling the piss.

"We're not in Canada for fuck's sake... Go on Seanie, ask her for me, to fuck with it."

"You're sure, Rasher?"

"Do it, man."

Niamh gabs away to one of her gal-pals. Her friend notices me and whispers in Niamh's little lug.

"How's it going, I'm Seanie."

"Nice to meet you, I'm Niamh."

"Come-here-to-me, what do you think of our dear friend Rasher?"

Bashful, she smiles and turns her head.

"I think a lot of our dear friend."

"Well, do you think you might shift him?"

She knew that was coming. Niamh looks to the friend and consults

38

her for a few secs. They giggle a little. Chris and Rasher do the: look-cool-and-pretend-to-talk-about-something-profound act. That's what you do when you send someone to ask a woman for you.

"I will, if, you or your friend shift Erin?"

"Who's Erin?"

She cranes her head towards a big lump of a girl. Erin Basquille. She has short shit coloured hair and a face on her like a bulldog licking piss off a nettle. The Lord save us from this monstrosity of a yoke. She rotates her fat head in my direction. The horror. Her soggy mid-section hangs out over her massive waste, she's sporting a green boob tube that's too short for her body. Looks like someone could do with cutting back on the oul breakfast rolls. Whenever someone is atrocious looking like this wan, people always say,

--She mightn't be the best on the outside, but she's beautiful on the inside.

I've heard stories about herself, and Erin's not one of those girls. She's mouldy outside and in. Back in primary school she terrorised girls in her class and tried to steal their lunches every day, the fat oul bitch.

"What did she say?" asks Rasher, nervous as fuck.

"Doesn't look good."

"Why?"

"She said she will, if me or Chris shift Erin Basquille."

Rasher knows what that means. No fucking way, José. I fill Chris in on the craic.

"I've to take a slash," says Rasher.

After weaving and twisting through the crowd, the three of us make it to the jacks. I'm dying for a piss myself. We wait for urinals to free up to pass some Buckie and Bulmers. The slashing starts after a sec.

"Lads, I know this is asking a lot, but one of ye has to do the friend."

"Come on, Rasher, you know if it were most other girls that we would do it, but Erin Basquille, forget about it."

"Please lads. If I do Niamh again I can say we're shifting and

39

eventually I might be going with her."

"Rasher, what you're asking is way too much," says Chris.

Myself and Rasher are back on the dance floor, we wound up losing Chris though, he met a cousin of his and the two of them disappeared into the crowd. In the corner of my eye I notice Rasher's Niamh bopping away. Rasher catches a glimpse and immediately dances over in Niamh's direction. Look at Rasher go. He starts bumping and grinding up against her, God above, he's like a dog riding a leg. Erin dances her gargantuan arse over in our direction and interrupts the groove between Rasher and Niamh. Rasher's fit to kill with Erin taking his Niamh away. Why is there always that girl friend who has to ruin the craic? If she's not shifting then no one is. The music changes. It's a shite girly song, me and Rasher step off the floor to the side. Rasher glares at me.

"What?"

"Seanie, please. No one will ever know."

"Rasher, no, I'm not shifting her."

"Even if ya just shifted her for a few minutes, a minute even."

"Look it, I'm not doing it."

Where the fuck is Chris when I need him? Rasher has me driven soft in the head with the fucking nagging.

"Come on, if it wasn't for me you wouldn't have got lush or anything tonight."

Jesus fucking Christ, did he just break out the fucking you-owe-me shite?

"You said you'd get me back for tonight."

Yes, he fucking well did.

"Yeah, but Rasher, this is a bit fucking harsh."

"No, Seanie, you said you'd sort me out. Here's your chance and now your reneging on me."

"Because I thought sorting you out would be getting you lush sometime or giving you a hand with something, not fucking doing your wan."

I can't believe he's pulling this shit. I'm fucking beholden to him now till he's happy that we're even Stevens. The state of him there sulking on a Friday night.

"Rasher, why don't I ask some other bird for you?"

"It's too late in the night now. Niamh or nothing."

Why the fuck can't Chris be here to deflect some of the scorn? That fucking Yank is probably getting wanked by some young one. Fuck it anyways.

"Seanie?"

"What?"

He's a right prick for doing this, the night was going great till this fuckacting, now he doesn't want to do anything. I'm fit to go bananas. Fuck this.

"Sound, Rasher, be a prick, you win. I'll be over in that corner. Tell that fat cunt to meet me over there."

"Seanie, you're a ledge, man."

"Just fucking do it, Rasher, and I swear to fuck if you tell anyone, I'll beat the head off ya."

"Not a word. I swear."

The night has flown so it has. I feel like I don't have enough time to do anything. We should've come in earlier instead of fannying about. I'm livid at Rasher for holding this over my head, it's a low road that bollocks has taken. Tis the last time I'll ask him for anything, that's for certain. Two poorly defined pork sausages stomp towards me. I can't tell where the ankle begins and the leg ends.

--She'd kick points with those legs.

Erin steps into the dark corner and gawks up at me with a swollen pudgy smile.

"How's she cutting?" says she, in her thick bogger accent.

I look into her googly eyes, there's a smattering of glitter under each one.

"Come-here-to-me, ya fat bitch ya."

I pull her close. We lock lips. She wraps her arms around tight, squeezing the life out of me. Oh My God. Ooohhhaaahhh. Her fat wet tongue slobbers in my gob. Aaahhh, it's like a fucking slug... This must

41

be a minute. This must be enough. For fuck's sake. I have to break free. The beginning of the National Anthem starts. Yes. The night is over. Yippee!!! I tear away and escape into the crowd a free man. Over at the coats I see Chris looking happy as Larry.

"There you are."

"There I am? Where the fuck were you?"

"Shifted this bird from Balla. A second year."

"Fair fucks to ya."

"How about you?"

"Wait till you hear the craic."

Chapter 4

I'm a nice ginger puss with a pretty pair of white paws, front and back. My bright white breast and striped ginger and white tail are well kept in sound times and sad. My whiskers are impeccably straight. I always make sure they're nice and neat after din-dins or after lapping up a saucer of creamy bainne. I'm a fairly young puss, no longer a kitten, but still not a full grown feline. My eyes are as curious as could be. I saunter around greeting and flirting with those whose pawpaths I cross.

--Meow, mews myself.

Up against my new friends' legs I graze my ginger striped cheek and chin.

--Well look at the cateen, they say.

--Meow, meow.

I beam up at them.

--Howya, puss? Hasn't he a lovely faceen on him?

They fawn all over me.

--Meow.

I roll onto my back in the form for play-acting.

PURR. PURR. PURR. PURR...

--What's the craic with ya at all at all?

PURR...

--Meow.

Was it Shitler or the Jesuits who said?

--Give me a child until seven years of age and I'll give you the man.

If there's any truth to that, I reckon I'll be a grand-master in the field of boredom endurance by the time my arse starts sprouting hair. Why in the name of God Almighty do they have me sitting here listening to teachers ramble on about the hardship and the poverty and the misery of the rural island people?

--Blasket anyways.

If things were so bad why didn't they stop sucking their mam's tits and feck off to America like half the country? Tis mind numbing beyond belief. Why not give us something of interest? Something we can relate to? Tis no wonder I have to imagine myself as a fecken puss while they blather on about stuff I've no use for at all at all. Irish is the best time for day-dreaming, not because of the lingo itself, but the forceful boredom we're subjected to every other day. I actually don't mind the language, at times it's fairly interesting, when they aren't on about verbs and tenses and people on fecking islands. I remember when I was learning to spell my name in English agus as Gaeilge. The English is handy enough, but if the version as Gaeilge was any longer it'd be late. What is it again?

--Ó C.E.A.R.B.H.A.L.L.Á.I.N.

Sure t'was no wonder the Brits made us anglicise all our surnames. My cousins have neighbours and their last name is Mc'Kittrick, unfortunately for the Mc'Kittricks, Mc'Kittrick as Gaeilge is Mac'Shitrig.

--Howya, I'm Seamus Mac'Shitrig from Ballinashite.

The Brits must have taken pity on them when they were changing the Mac'Shitrigs' name.

--Bloody hell, I say, that's a rafher unfortunate name.

--Let's help poor Paddy out, change it to somefhing else.

--How about a K in there?

--Sounds jolly good, governor.

Who was it I wonder that got to make up the words as Gaeilge?

--Wanking.

--Feintruailliu.

--Self-pollution.

Whatever eejet invented that word was clearly inexperienced in the act of self-pollution. You're not really polluting yourself, more so the designated rag or sock. Really it should have been something like rag-pollution or sock-pollution. They seem to have been always trying to one-up each other as well.

--Dia duit.

--Dia is Muire duit.

It's like a fecking gang bang.

--God to you.

--God and Mary to you.

--God and Mary and Jesus to you.

--God and Mary and Jesus and Joseph to you.

--Everyone to you, times infinity. Now, put that in your pipe and smoke it.

Look at Costello there, out of it so he is. It's amazing how some of us can go into a sort of half daze, we nod when we should and stare at the floor for the rest of the class like spuds. Some days I get restless something shocking. What to do on those days? Well, either I can act the maggot and risk getting a sceal or dream a dream till the bell dingalingalings. Sometimes I take a rubber and with blue biro draw a nice big cock on it, I keep going over it till there's plenty of ink on the outline. Depending on who's around me I might stamp the back of their necks gifting them with a little prick. I try to make sure I don't hit their shirt collars though. I don't want their oul ladies coming in to biff the head off me for getting ink on sonny Jim's school shirt. Especially ink in the shape of a willy. Look at Dwyer there, he has a bit of a bird in him for sure, like one of those tall birds with the long legs that strut about the marshes. Everyone has some likeness to some sort of cratureen or other. Dwyer's a bird, and I'm a wee cat.

Paddy is the daddy of all the other laddys.

Chris doesn't have to do Irish, there's some rule or loophole that if you weren't in Ireland for the first couple of years of school then you don't have to study Irish. He has a handy time of it sitting near the back and doing his other homework. The two of us used to sit together, but we're not allowed anymore. We were always talking and messing. I miss sitting beside him, it was savage oul craic, way less boring than sitting all by my lonesome. You know what? I shall write a little ditty in honour of my dear oul pal Chris...

45

Chris sucks floppy donkey cock.

I'll send it around the class before himself gets a gurch. I tear the ditty from the top of the copy page and hand it to Dec Gallagher.

"Pass it on, Decker," whispers I.

Dec has a look and a laugh before handing it off. The critics give it a thumps up. A few of the boys in class always have a gander at my musings and give me a thumbs up or thumbs down. They know well my style and have come to appreciate it throughout the arse deadening days.

-- Courtesy of the bally bard.

Our Irish teacher is new to the profession. A rookie teacher can be smelled a mile away, they haven't yet learned how to crack the whip and keep the class in line. Her name is Miss Ní Naughton. We have yet to find out her first name, but I bet she's a Gaeltacht gal if she goes by Ní Naughton. Since she started we've done nothing but play puc like there's no tomorrow. Luckily her classroom is in the prefab beside the main building so other classes can't hear us acting up. Although, I think they might be getting a biteen suspicious, there's a big fuck-off hole in one of the walls. I'm not a hundred percent positive how it came into existence, some of the lads were saying that someone stabbed it with a compass and that the prick from that started the whole thing. It has become progressively bigger as the year has gone on from all the poking and prodding. The wall is flimsy enough to begin with, it's made of some sort of hard cardboard. Plus, the hole's not too bad, I mean, it could be way worse, it's not like you can gawk into the car-park, only the interior wall. The caretaker is supposed to drop in some day and board up the whole hole good and proper. This is just one of the things that's been driving Miss Ní Naughton,

--Up the wall.

The breaking point came about two weeks ago. We were all acting the pleb at the start of class, after a couple of minutes she managed to calm things down to an alright level of jigacting. Then came Charlie Ward's comment. Charlie is the one and only tinker in Saint Pat's, he's

46

in our class even though he shouldn't be because his surname begins with W. Usually when a tinker finishes primary school they don't bother much with secondary school. They generally go into various enterprises that the tinkers excel at like selling horses or sprucing up cars and caravans. Charlie's a bit different from most tinkers though. Instead of travelling from place to place, he lives in a proper house, his parents were offered a house up in Rock Rose estate and the oul pair chose to take it and stop living in caravans. Charlie doesn't get along awful well with some of the other tinkers around the town, probably because his crew have settled. Back in primary school he got in a massive scrap outside the swimming pool with another tinker.

--Fuck you pig's eye.

--Go way from me ya townie bastard ya.

Charlie was rightly pissed off so he was. The two scrapped away beating lumps out of each other till Charlie eventually got the other fella in a headlock and started piling on the punches.

--Jab it up, Charlie.

One time in the Townhall it was gas altogether, Una Ward, a first cousin of Charlie's, had this leopard print coat with her. Everything seemed grand till some girl sitting next to her put a fag burn in the coat by accident. Well, Una went stone mad. She fucked the girl out of it and made her lick the ashes from the burn on the coat. It was mental altogether. Charlie's whole family are a tough crowd, they stick tight together. Anyways, the day Charlie sent Ní Naughton over the edge, we were engaged in a bitter war of throw the tuna sandwich. The sambo barely missed Charlie's head. He picked it up with the intention of returning to sender and as he was about to launch the sandwich, Miss Ní Naughton turned from the blackboard and caught a glimpse of him firing it across the room.

--Charlie Ward, any more and I'm going to tell Brother Leary about you.

Charlie looked her up and down with a tinker's usual disdain for authority. Then in his husky tinker accent said,

--Tell Brother Leary, he can bite my shite.

Miss Ní Naughton stood in silence. People in the class didn't know what to say. After a few seconds a couple of the lads giggled. There's not really much of a come-back for Charlie's,

--He can bite my shite.

She didn't bother telling Brother Leary, but she's been in foul form ever since.

The ditty has made the rounds. It lands on Rasher's desk, right in front of Chris. Just as he's about to turn and give it to Chris, Miss Ní Naughton sees him shifting in his seat.

"Mr. Corrigan, what were you about to hand to Mr. Conway?"

"Nothing, Miss."

She heads down to Rasher's desk.

"Hand it over."

"Miss, I have nothing."

She puts her hand on Rasher's closed right fist. Oh shite. Everyone in the class, except Chris, knows what's scribbled on that piece of paper.

"Come on. Hand it over"

Rasher slowly opens up his palm. She takes the note from him with a sense of delight on her face from catching him out. Christ. Rasher's fucked. On the way back to the blackboard she reads the note. Immediately, she stops in her tracks and blushes rouge as fuck. Miss Ní Naughton begins to breath quite heavily. In and out. Out and in. She turns to face Rasher.

"Mr. Corrigan and Mr. Conway wait behind after class," says she, fuming with her brow knit and her jaw locked.

Rasher sits, frozen in his seat.

"What?" Chris asks. "Miss, why do I have to wait behind?"

"Because I said so, that's why."

"But Miss-"

"-Ciúnas."

They're going to get fucked out of it over this.

"Mr. Corrigan, do you understand me?"

"Yes, Miss."

Chris looks over to me and mouths,
"What the fuck?"

The bell sounds. Should I stay or should I go? Everyone but Chris and Rasher leave the room. Maybe I should bail out. After all, it's their own fault if they get caught with something... Ah, Fuck it. I better stay. I did write the flipping thing. Chris, Rasher and myself stand before Miss Ní Naughton's desk. She's raging altogether. We do the: I'm-guilty-so-I'll-stare-at-the-floor routine.

"Seanie Carolan, why are you here?"

"I wrote it, Miss," mutters me.

"What do you think this is, hah? You're in here to learn, not peddle this filth."

"I know, Miss."

"Ye all should be ashamed of yourselves. Wait till Brother Leary hears about this."

"Miss, come on," pleads Chris.

"No. If this was the first time ye misbehaved it might be different, but ye come in here day after day and disrupt the class."

"Miss, I didn't do anything, may I be excused?"

"No Chris. You don't even do Irish, yet, you're constantly mixed up with the messers of the class."

"Ah, come on."

"No. Now out of my sight!"

Jesus, she must be on the rag. The three of us head for the door and on to the next class. What is it? I check my crumpled up timetable. Here we are. Science is next.

"Seanie, son of a bitch."

"Don't blame me, Rasher's the one who got nabbed. What type of turn were you at, at all? You looked like you were stretching out before the match."

"You wrote the fucking thing."

"Jesus Christ."

"Do you think she'll lick?'

"I doubt it, I'd say she's only bullshitting."

49

"My mom will flip if she does."

"What's she going to say to Leary? *'Chris sucks floppy donkey cock?'* I don't think so."

"She better not."

Outside the prefab, some of the lads wait wondering what's going to happen over the bastarden note. I play everything down to make the two boyos feel better.

"It'll just be some lines or something, wait and ye'll see."

"Do you reckon?"

"Worst comes to worst she might say something to Miss Keogh, but no way will she go further than that."

"Yeah, you're probably right," says Rasher.

"I hope so," says Chris.

"I'm telling ya, it'll be nothing."

To be honest though, I'm talking out my hole. Ní Naughton might very well rat on us. She was seriously ripping in class. Madder than I ever seen her before. Worse than Charlie. Way worse. It would be a good way for her to lay down the law and make a name for herself.

--Down to face the wrath of Brother Leary she sent them.

Into science class we go. Mr. Mulroy stands at the door in good spirits as usual. Will Leary come down for us or won't he? Rasher and Chris have the same faces on them as myself. Shitting bricks. Everyone sits down and relaxes the cacks. God above, Miss Ní Naughton. She won't lick. She will not. Still, you wouldn't know. She might. The only first hand account I know of Leary's office is from Mc'Hugh, when he got caught cheating during the Christmas exams in Irish. On the day of the test he was seated beside Gerard Maguire. Now Maguire went to Scoil Rafteri, so naturally he's brilliant at Irish from speaking it every day of school for the first eight years. Mc'Hugh hadn't done a tap of work for the test, he thought to himself, fuck it, may as well copy off of Maguire. Tis better to have something written down than just your name and class at the top of the page. And that's exactly what he did. He wrote his name at the top of the page, then proceeded to copy Maguire focal for focal. The only thing was, Mc'Hugh, the gombeen, was so faithful to Maguire's writings that he unknowingly wrote Maguire's name down as Gaeilge a rake of times. When Miss Ní Naughton was correcting Mc'Hugh's exam, the source of his inspiration was fairly obvious. Mc'Hugh had to go to Leary's office and his parents were brought in for a sit-down, he said Leary chewed the bollocks off of him and scolded his oul pair for raising such a,

--Dishonest, no good pup.

He suspended him for a week and said,

--If you're ever caught cogging again you'll be immediately expelled.

I'm fond of Mr. Mulroy's class, he goes about teaching science in a grand enough way, even with the maths he's fairly good. Most maths teachers make you feel like an eejet if you don't cop something the first time round. Mulroy's always sound about it though, and does plenty of examples on the board so we can copy them down and try and figure them out at home. My head is wrecked with this note business. I can't keep up with him at all at all. Our parents will kill the three of us. It's always worse if you get in trouble with other people because then there might be a few sets of oul pairs trying to decide how to straighten out the young ones. Mulroy squiggles something on the board, he must be doing some formula. I'll have to learn it later so I will.

"So, if $pV=k$ where k is a constant value representative of-"

-Knock, knock.

"Come in," says Mr. Mulroy.

Bollocks. The door opens. Fuck. It's himself.

"Can the gentlemen who stayed back in Miss Nì Naughton's class please come with me," says Brother Leary.

The three of us pick up our bag and baggage and head for the door. The class feels funny. They know the amount of shit we're in now that Leary's involved.

"Thank you."

Wading in it so we are. Rasher, Chris and myself follow Leary down the hall, there's not a peep out of us as we plod. He takes us to his office and leaves us be with the door wide open.

"I'll be back in a minute," says he.

The three of us take a seat across from his cluttered desk. The office is filled with reams of paperwork and stacks of files, he has to keep tabs some way I suppose. Still, you'd think he'd have a computer.

"Jesus, why the fuck did you have to pass that note?" asks Chris.

"I was bored shitless."

"Sure I'm just the messenger and I'm going to get leathered for this," says Rasher.

"I don't know what Naughton got so offended about anyways, it's not like it said she was blowing the head off a donkey."

"Seanie, this is your fucking fault, you're taking the blame."

"Come on, what is it the three musketeers say? All for one and one for all."

"Try telling that to my parents."

"Musketeers my blue arse," says Rasher.

"Well, Rasher, you did try and pass the note on so technically you're considered an accomplice."

"Arra, shite on it."

"If anyone here is the wronged party, it's Chris. You're the one it says is doing a Nelson's Pillar."

"My mom is going to go bat-shit over this."

"Mine too," says Rasher.

For fuck's sake. They're right. We could be in serious bother over this, three gurriers abusing a young female teacher. It doesn't look good so it doesn't. I bet she'll play it up like she's the big victim to really fuck us. Leary hates when people mess on young girl teachers, which is really every new teacher that comes into Saint Pat's.

"Lads, whatever he says just deny, deny, deny."

"I didn't even see it," says Chris.

"That's it, he won't be as harsh if we seem less involved. Don't crack no matter what and we might get away with it."

Enter Leary. Boiling so he is. He slams the door behind him and takes half the air out of the room. The office seems way smaller with the door closed.

"Stand up! Ye don't deserve to sit down."

We hop from the chairs to our feet in a snap. My legs are trembling like fuck. Leary lines us up against the wall ready for interrogation.

"Names?"

"Sean Carolan."

He takes down our names in his book of messers.

"Ruaidhri Corrigan."

"Christopher Conway."

He shuts the book closed and pings the pen off the desk.

"Who do ye think ye are? Hah?"

"We're sorry, sir," says Rasher.

"Sorry? Sorry my backside."

He looks all of us in the eye, marching back and forth. He stalls at Rasher, right up in his face.

"What did it say on the note?"

"I don't know, sir."

"How can you not know?"

"I didn't get to look at it, sir."

God above. She didn't tell him what it said! She must have said it was some rude words or something. Leary takes a step over to Chris.

"What did it say? Tell me!"

"I don't know, I didn't get to read it either, sir."

He steps to me.

"Carolan, you wrote it?"

"Yes, sir."

"Why?"

"I was bored, sir."

"You were bored?"

"Yeah... Yes, sir."

"What did it say?"

I glance over at Rasher and Chris. The two bastards look like they're going to start laughing. I hesitate.

"I can't tell you, sir."

"Why?"

"It's rude, sir."

"Tell me."

"Sir, please."

The laughs are somewhere at the back of my throat. The two buckeens have their heads down. They're dying to let go.

"Carolan, tell me!"

I stare at the floor and hold in the guffaws.

"Look at me when I'm speaking to you!"

"Yes, sir."

He can tell we're all dying to laugh, we're skitting our holes off.

"Is there something funny! Carolan, what was on that piece of paper?"

"Sir, I can't tell you."

I'm going to piss my pants.

"Someone better tell me or ye'll be on detention for the next month. Do ye hear me?"

He tries once more to get Rasher and Chris to spill the beans.

"I'm warning ye."

They keep the gobs shut. He comes back and questions me again.

"Carolan, what was it?"

I gaze at him unable to control myself and burst out laughing, Chris and Rasher follow suit and lose it.

"HA, HA, HA, HA, HA, HA, HA..."

He's red in the face, I think his head might blow off his fecking shoulders.

"Get out, get out of my sight! Ye pups ye!"

We bout it out of the office in tears with laughter. Up at the lockers, we stall to gather ourselves. The three of us can't stop laughing. My lungs hurt from the belly-laughs.

"Stop the lights, it's fucking gas."

"It would've been savage if you said it to him," says Rasher.

"Oh Lord above," says Chris.

"It's none of his business what it said sure."

"For a second I thought you were going to say it right to his face."

"Who, me? Always coolaboola under pressure."

Chapter 5

I must never misbehave or disrupt the class during Irish.
I must never misbehave or disrupt the class during Irish.
I must never misbehave or disrupt the class during Irish.
I must never misbehave or disrupt the class during Irish.
I must never misbehave or disrupt the class during Irish.
I must never misbehave or disrupt the class during Irish.
I must never misbehave or disrupt the class during Irish.
I must never misbehave or disrupt the class during Irish.
I must never misbehave or disrupt the class during Irish.
I must never misbehave or disrupt the class during Irish.
I must never misbehave or disrupt the class during Irish.
I must never misbehave or disrupt the class during Irish.
I must never misbehave or disrupt the class during Irish.
I must never misbehave or disrupt the class during Irish.
I must never misbehave or disrupt the class during Irish.
I must never misbehave or disrupt the class during Irish.
I must never misbehave or disrupt the class during Irish.
I must never misbehave or disrupt the class during Irish.
I must never misbehave or disrupt the class during Irish.
I must never misbehave or disrupt the class during Irish.
I must never misbehave or disrupt the class during Irish.
I must never misbehave or disrupt the class during Irish.
I must never misbehave or disrupt the class during Irish.
I must never misbehave or disrupt the class during Irish.

There, I'm finished at last thanks be to Christ. As part of our punishment myself, Chris and Rasher received a month of detention, and we have to write,

--I must never misbehave or disrupt the class during Irish, 200 times and present it to Brother Leary every Monday morning. It's such a pain in the hole writing lines: 22 lines a page, 200 times works out at 9 pages and 2 lines. Soul destroying so it is writing them out over and over and over again. After the first week I decided to see if I could make life a little easier for myself. I fastened two pens together with some sellotape, that way I only had to write half as many lines. Leary, being the bell-end he is noticed the pattern of the lines, as every other line was a little slanted because of how the pens were taped together. The big bollocks told the teachers on duty to make sure I'm not doing any funny business with the two biros. Of course they comply and watch me like a hawk. The three of us have probation books now as well, after every class we've to get the teacher to write a remark concerning our behaviour and sign off on it. Such a load of shite. You'd swear we fucken clipped someone with all this bullshit. Detention is from nine am till one in the afternoon, we get a fifteen minute break at half eleven and usually stretch it out a few minutes longer by coming back late so the last hour or so doesn't drag on too much. I always hit the jacks at about half tenish to break up the first two and a half hours.

"Sir, bathroom?"

Mr. Higgins gives me the nod. It's weird walking through the hallways on the weekend, there's not a sinner to be seen, only a few unclaimed coats hang on hooks outside the classrooms. I'd say it must be awful spooky at night. In the main foyer I have a quick gander at the notice board, most of the notices have been taken down, the detention list is still up though. Our names are posted for all to see. Name them and shame them says them. The outside doors shudder, it's Brother Coleman, he treads in through the main entrance. Brother Coleman was the Head Brother when we were back in primary school. The Brothers have a special kind of monastery or rectory, whatever they call it, situated next to the Church car-park

56

and across from the primary school. The gafe itself is a mysterious type of a place, a big dark mansion, nobody's ever returned from to tell the tale. Brother Coleman belts on to Leary's office as I enter the jacks. At least in detention they let us wear our own clothes, I hate the uniform so I do. The shirt always aggravates the acne on my neck. I can't wait for it to be gone, hopefully I will grow out of it sooner rather than later. A good dose of sun always clears it up, for a while anyhow, or till I have to put on the uniform again. Some people have awful acne. It seems to engulf their entire face and neck. One lad in our class, Paul Dunleavy, has a wicked case of it, big angry boils full of festerings, they look like they could explode at any moment.

    KA-BOOM!

Poor Paul would be blown away by them, like land mines on his face and neck that detonate if stepped on. You can tell which of the sixth years had bad spots. They have pockmarks and scars on their faces. I don't have too bad a dose of spots and hopefully it won't get any worse. One thing about the sun though, if you're fair skinned like myself you might be prone to getting freckles, I have a few here and there, but I'm not too bad for a red head. Some fair skinned folk are covered from top to toe in freckles, they end up with a face like a bowl of beans. I wonder if they got enough freckles would they join together and make a grand tan?

    --Hey, former freckle puss, nicey nice tan.

    Still, I'd rather be a freckle puss than a crater face. Freckles lighten or disappear as you get on in the years department, but those craters aren't going anywhere fast. They're there for life. On the border between my neck and where my school shirt chafes me I have a big bastard of a spot. It's looking back at me with an inflamed head, mocking me.

    --Go on. Give me a squeeze. You know you want to. Just one squeeze. Only the wan.

    Tis awful tempting to give it a pinch, I reckon the spot needs another day before it's ready to pop. No need to be too hasty. I hate when you try and burst a spot and it hasn't fully come to a head, it only becomes more aggravated and gets bigger and throbs rhythmically. Best to play it safe and leave it be for now.

--Patience is a virtue have it if you can, always in a woman never in a man.

I better get back to the classroom or Mr. Higgins will think I've done a runner. The caretaker leans casually against the wall at the entrance of the hallway, he looks at me a little confused.

"Where do ya think you're going?"

"Detention."

I try to continue. He stops me.

"What?"

He points up the stairs.

"One way system."

"It's a Saturday, there's nobody in the hallway."

"Doesn't matter, one way system. You have to go round."

"Jesus, what does it matter? It's a Saturday."

"They're the rules so they are."

Most times I'd be extremely annoyed by this act of fucken idiocy, but fuck it, at least it wastes more time and if Higgins says boo about me dossing, I can say,

--Well, the caretaker made me walk round the long way. One way fucken system, didn't you hear?"

In addition to my lines this week I've to write a punishment essay for my history teacher Mr. Langan. He's one of the few non-local teachers in Pat's, during the school year he lives in Ballybar, then goes back to west Cork for the summers. You'd know it too. His accent is fierce strong, even though he has been working up here for yonks. At the moment we're covering the Irish Civil War, there's not an awful lot about it in the history book, maybe three or four pages. On Thursday, after Langer had finished more or less beatifying Michael Collins,

--The man who got the Brits out of Ireland.

He asked in his high pitched People's Republic accent,

--Does anybody have any questions like?

--Didn't Michael Collins have Irish people put to death as well?

--No, Seanie boy.

58

--But the Free Staters executed a load of people.

--Michael Collins didn't do it, Seanie.

--But he was apart of the Free Staters, so sir, he mustn't have had a problem with it.

--Ha, ha, ha, Michael Collins would never do that, like.

--Didn't he give the order to bomb the Four Courts?

--No, Seanie! That was someone else and if you're so smart you can write an essay about it to hand in for Monday, wasting the class's time.

The bollocks gave me a bad remark in my probation book to boot. I think the only time I've seen him get more vexed was when he asked Keith Friel,

--What was the Ulster Plantation about?

To which Friel confidently replied,

--Sir, the Plantation of Ulster was about a rake of English lads who came over and planted a load of trees up the North.

My granduncle John was big into politics, he had tons and tons of books on Irish history. When I was small he used to mind me when Mam was at work, he'd tell all sorts of stories about the Black and Tans and the Fenians. I loved going to his house out the Turlough Road and watching the telly. Mam didn't get the BBC channels for ages so it was always a treat watching the English programmes down in uncle John's. At lunch time, he'd put on the Irish and British news. While we watched both news reports, he'd point out the differences between the two, most of the changes were small things, but a few of them were blatant enough like when the Brits wouldn't let Gerry Adams talk on air.

"Hey, lower it please," says Mr. Higgins, from the top of the classroom.

Chris has his head buried cosily in his coat with both eyes shut and the volume of his discman going full whack. You can clearly hear the music even though the earphones are in his lugs. Higgins heads down to him and taps him on the shoulder. Chris glances up with one eye shut.

"Turn it down, please."

Chris closes his opened eye and complies. Where was I? The Civil War. Right. I don't know why they don't have more about it in the textbook? My granduncle's book says the Free State executed almost 200 people. That's some serious killing. Bloody awful. Irish people killing other Irish people, they're as bad as the Brits so they are. Why execute them? What if they got the wrong fella? That poor bastard would be killed for committing no crime at all at all. So much for innocent until proven guilty, plus, killing them is fairly harsh, at least give them a chance, put them in prison till they figure something out. Why didn't they do that? Maybe they were all out of space in the prisons, they would march them down the prison road and some fella would pop out of a hole in the gate,

--No more can come in, not nobody, not nohow!

A grand new prison, they should've built. It would have saved them killing all those people. I can see it now,

--Super Mac's Security Prisons.

At least it would've been better than killing the poor whores. And wouldn't it have put plenty of people to work as well, save them from lining up for the dole every Tuesday.

"Alright, be back in here in fifteen minutes," says Mr. Higgins.

Everyone rises, dreary faced, and heads for the yard. There's 17 people on detention this week, around 20 is the average. Chris, Rasher and myself stall outside at our usual spot near the back of the school facing the lake.

"Almost there and we're free."

"I know, I can't wait," says Rasher.

He sparks up a fag and takes a quick drag.

"Such a pain in the ass, thank fuck it's the final week," says Chris.

"Ye finished your lines?" asks Rasher.

"No, I prefer to start them a bit later so I rush more, makes the time go a little faster," says Chris.

Mini-buses and cars fill out the Sports Hall car-park across the yard from us. Ten or so lads, togged out in baggy shorts and basketball vests, stand outside the Hall's main entrance.

"Must be a tournament on with all the cars," says Chris.

"Probably."

"Your sister plays, doesn't she?" asks Rasher.

"Yeah, for the school and in the town league I think," says Chris.

Faintly audible is the noise of two men arguing.

"Shhh, who's that?"

The three of us look around wondering where it's coming from. We creep along the back wall of the building. The arguing becomes louder and more pronounced. We chill near the end of the wall, it's coming from inside Leary's office. The blind is half closed, but there's a view of Brother Coleman and we can hear Leary shouting and roaring.

"Brother Coleman," says Rasher.

"Yeah, I seen him on the way in, when I was in the jacks."

"I wonder why he's here?" says Chris. "Don't they live together?"

"He's probably mad because Leary left before the morning bumming." In my best Leary voice, "My arse needs a rest, it's stinging like fuck." A Coleman impression, "It's time for the Brother Leary bumming. Prepare the arse at once!"

Chris and Rasher chuckle at my Brothers.

"It doesn't matter, you bummed me before bed last night, it's my turn. When I get back to the rectumry, I want you lubed and ready for the bumming of a lifetime. Do you hear me? Up the bum, no harm done."

"How do you know they take turns, maybe one is like the bitch," says Chris.

"I bet you anything, Leary likes to watch," says Rasher.

"I wouldn't be surprised if they have Brother gang bangs back at the rectumry and Leary is like the fecking Hugh Heffner. Banging all the bum chum Brothers like a barn door."

"Sure it's no wonder they bum each other, they're not allowed go near women at all at all," says Rasher.

"Yeah, I mean it must be great for the Brothers who like men, but what about the ones that wouldn't mind a woman every now and again," says Chris.

"Same craic with the nuns. Married to God, so they are," says Rasher.

"Does that mean the Brothers and the Priests are married to God too? I thought God was against gay marriage."

"I'd love to hook up with a nun," says Chris.

"Why? Half them are mouldy," says Rasher.

"There's just something about corrupting somebody that holy."

"Ha, ha, the missionary position is it?"

"Oh yeah, imagine undressing her. Taking the penguin suit off of her, one of those slutty nun outfits though, not the normal ones."

"I still have yet to see a hot nun," says Rasher.

"They're few and far between alright."

Through the half closed blind we can see the bottom halves of Leary and Coleman exiting the office.

"Looks like one of them won."

We walk back to where we were before the Brothers' row.

"What are you up to after this?" asks Chris.

"Going to the astro turf for a kick around," says Rasher.

"Nice, how is it up there, I haven't played on it yet."

"It's cool so it is, the only bitch is if you hit the ball too high, it might go flying off over the fences into Ballybar Celtic or get caught in the nets between the different pitches. Besides that, it's savage enough."

"We must go down some evening and book it."

"Defo," says Chris.

"I was surprised to see Higgins in here again this week," says Rasher.

"I know, yeah."

"Do you reckon teachers get paid for coming into detention?"

"Haven't a clue, but it's usually a different teacher every week so he must be covering for somebody."

"True enough. Someone pulled a sicky," says Chris.

"What are you two up to for the day?" Rasher asks.

"Not sure. Might pop over to the Hall and see if there's any rides shooting hoops."

"Good luck with that," says Rasher.

"Why?"

"Arra..."

"You don't have to be in the Townhall to get women. Tell him Chris."

"He's right, in Canada you can just ask a girl out, or ask for her number."

"Yeah, in Canada you can do that. Could you imagine asking a girl from around here for her phone number? Or to go on a date? You wouldn't be able to leave your house."

"Don't knock it till you try it."

"Lateral thinking."

"That's it Chris, see, Rasher, a bit more thinking like the Canadian would go a long way. And anyways, what's the craic with your one, Niamh?"

"I broke it off."

"How come?"

"Ah, I was bored with her. Same shite all the time, ya know."

"So it wasn't because she shifted some fella in Moore College?"

"Who told you that?"

"A birdy."

"I broke it off before that."

"If you say so."

"I hear she's going with him now."

"Well, fair dos to them. What about ye two? Any women on the go?"

"Not at the moment."

"Wait till later on, when me and Chris head over to the hall on the prowl. You'll be hearing all about it on Monday morning, Rasher."

"Like fuck."

"I bet they're all from different towns, and you know women from other places always look better because you're not used to looking at their faces. We'll be around the back of the Hall shifting them by the dozens so we will."

"I'll believe it when I see it."

"It'll be like a fecken film."

"Well, it won't be one set around here, that's for sure."

"Did you hear about the other day? Apparently someone stuck a tampon to Mr. Horkan's door," says Chris.

"Would you go away."

"It happened, they don't know who did it."

"That's gas."

"My cousin was telling me his class had Mahill once, and anyways, he headed out of the room for something and left his keys on his desk, next thing didn't they lock him out for half the class," says Chris.

"Unreal," says Rasher.

"They played fuck altogether, they were racing the desks and everything."

"Racing the desks?"

"They'd put their desks back to the wall, sit into them and then start hopping them forward. Whoever got to the front of the class won."

"It must have been fierce loud with the desks banging and hopping."

"I'd say so."

"Mr. Neill must have been going ballistic."

"The poor fella probably had a fecking heart attack."

We make our way back to the classroom, dragging our heels to waste as much time as possible, only another hour, give or take, and we're finished our stint of detention. I better get back to this essay, I don't want to be doing it on Sunday evening. The Civil War. What were the causes? The Treaty. A lot of people cross over the Treaty, alright. They lit up your mano George Moore's gafe like a flaming Christmas tree when they heard his brother was pro Treaty. The crew up in the six counties must have been fucking furious. Sure they're still furious. After all the fuckacting the poor bastards weren't part of the deal. Who could blame them. It wasn't the best of deals sure twasn't, but I suppose it was better than no deal at all at all. You have to laugh how de Valera didn't go over and negotiate the Treaty himself, yet he had no problem going mental when the boys came back with it signed. What would he have done differently? Collins was right about calling it a stepping stone. Although, the killing and executing they did after it was bad oul form. By the looks of things it seems it doesn't matter who gets into power, they always end up abusing it. Sure I suppose it's the same in other countries, every nation has its dark times in one way or another. Down here has been in good nick for the last while, pity I can't say the same about the North, they've had an awful time of it. That fecking Treaty. Thankfully the oath of allegiance shite is gone. You wouldn't see me swearing any oaths to foreign kings and queens. They can go and have a good hard shite for themselves. Still, the first main cause of all the hassle was the oul 800 years of domination and persecution. Fuck me, that's a long time when I think about it. 800 yonks. How did it take us so long to fucken straighten things out? It's a good thing the rebels didn't give up. I mean after 800 years there could hardly have been that much optimism.

--It's not the winning or losing, lads, tis the taking part that counts.

One of the things I cannot understand is if there were millions of Irish people, why are there only a small number of fellas mentioned in the history books? Lads like Wolfe Tone and Charles Parnell, before Collins and de Valera, it looks like they were the only lads who said,

--Right lads, tis time to get the fingers out.

I wonder what's written in the English history books?

--And then, the Paddies invited us to come over for an extended staycation.

I'd say there must be a lot of massaging of facts in those history books.

--We decided to leave America because we got homesick.

What are they leaving out of our history books? The only people who seem to have had a problem with this 800 years craic is the Michael Davitt and Padraig Pearse types. What was everyone else doing if they weren't fighting for freedom? What about the people who wanted the Brits out and didn't fight? Were they cowards? Did they have any right to complain if they weren't willing to fight or

65

contribute to the cause? I mean there were far more Irish people on the island of Ireland than British soldiers. Even here in Mayo, they're forever on about the 1798 Rebellion and the Races, when Humbert and the boys kicked the British out of Connaught. Why didn't everyone band together and do what they did? Is it that they were cowards? Or is it that they liked to feel sorry for themselves and shout that Eireann mo chroi shite? If I'd been there, I'd have rounded up a load of fine strapping lumps of lads and said,

--Get your hurls and your pikes because by-jaysus, we're going to open a fucken vat of whoop-arse the size of Belmullet on these shower of shites from across the Irish Sea.

I would have invited people from Ulster, from Munster, from Leinster, and we would have got them out to fuck once and for all. Afterwards, we would march to the Guinness Brewery and have a grand old style piss-up to celebrate the victory. At the party I'd make sure to write a nice letter to King George III, just to let him know there were no hard feelings.

--Hey, anyone have a quill on them?

Dear King George III,

Howya Georgeen, ya mad whore ya? You're looking well ha, ha...
Come-here-to-me, awful sorry about kicking your fellas out. But they
were making a right cunt of themselves here in Ireland. Couldn't
speak the lingo or anything, all over the shop so they were. Listen,
we're going to be busy for the next while, decided to give the place a
bit of a make-over. So don't contact us, we'll contact you, okay?
Anyways, hope there's no hard feelings and best of luck against the
French... not.

Slán go fóill
Poblacht na hÉireann

Chapter 6

We're flying it past the hogies. Sharp left turn at Marrian Row. The two of us free-wheel down by JV TV, then make a quick right through oncoming traffic to the dismay of an oul red Ford Cortina.

BBEEEPPPP!

"FUCK OFF!"

Chris swerves into a lane between two houses. I'm right behind him. Myself and Chris have decided to do a Lord Lucan and disappear, only for a day though. The school bell sounds in the distance. We tear through the pebbly path on our way under the bridge.

"Oh Jeesssuuuusssss, tis too late to go back now!"

On the mitch, something the powers that be at Saint Pat's don't take lightly. If nabbed it's a suspendible offence. We pull up under the bridge and park our bikes against the railing. The reason we decided to take a day of leisure is because the second year GAA team is heading off for an away match against Saint Jarlath's up in Galway. A good few lads in the class play on the team so there'll be a rake of people missing. On a day like today, absences are way less noticeable. Chris and myself had already planned to take off one of the days and prepared fake sick notes by tracing our oul ladies' handwriting.

"Looking good, Mr. Carolan," says Chris.

We change into our normal clothes and stuff our uniforms into our bookless school-bags. I sit back for a minute against the sloped concrete wall opposite the river.

"How many spons did you bring?"

"Fifteen."

"Nice one, me too."

The two of us had a nice little scheme going for a while to earn a couple of extra spons. We printed off fake Mitchels GAA cards at the library and went house to house asking for sponsorship, it was a handy little gig till some eejet down in Chestnut Grove decided to give the same racket a go. One day he went up to a fine looking house out the Station Road. He knocked at the door expecting the usual contribution of a few pound, low and behold didn't the gafe belong to one of the head fellas in the Ballybar Crokes. Naturally, the Mitchels buck went absolutely apeshit, he even went as far as calling the Guards on your mano. There was a big brouhaha about it in the Connaught Post and everything. After that, myself and Chris said we may as well quit while we're ahead, no need to have our names blackened in the Connaught.

A mist begins to fall.

"Damn, I thought it was going to be dry today, it was so nice on the way in," says Chris.

"The weather's like a child's arse so it is, you can never depend on it."

"Yeah, right."

I hate the rain. There's never any sun here at all at all, even during the summer, you get the bare minimum of sunshine and that's it, like it or lump it. I'd love to live somewhere nice and bright, but with a cool breeze for when the sun's cracking the rocks. At least today it's not too windy. The drizzle is annoying though, it's like the world is spitting at you non-stop.

"Do you think oul Willie will drop by?" asks Chris.

"Oul Willie, you never know, I think he sleeps down the lake sometimes."

"Man, that's rough."

"If that's what he wants to do, sure off with him."

Willie Egan is the type of fella who subscribes to the notion that,
--Work is the curse of the drinking classes.

I'm not sure how old oul Willie is but he's no spring chicken that's for sure. He's a gaunt grey haired man with a face that would stop a clock. I'd say Willie has definitely been in a scrap or two throughout the years, he has a permanent lump on his right cheek, and Christ, you'd want to see his nose. God above, that srón is in an awful state altogether. It's big and bulbous with a prominent split down the middle. The colour is somewhere between deep red and purple, it kind of reminds me of a baboon's arse. Willie's been like this for a good long while. He has a wife and daughter or I should say, had a wife and daughter. The story goes that one day Willie decided to give up on them and stick to what he knows best. The Drink. His daughter is a good bit older than me, she went to college in Galway and decided to stay there when she graduated. I don't know what type of scum would do that? Abandon his family the way he did. Whenever you see him roaming round the town if he doesn't have a bottle of whiskey it's a bottle of wine. Along with the bottle, you usually see himself with a hurly on hand in case someone tries a bit of funny business while he's conked out.

"I doubt we'll be graced by his presence today. I think the lake is his summer home, or when the weather's nice."

"I guess, where else could he go? There's not that many places besides here where he could drink in peace."

"True enough. There is that castle, you know when you go to the end of this side and walk on through the fields."

"Never been."

"We'll go down some day when it's dry. It's a bit of a walk through the field."

"Defo. I wonder does oul Willie sleep in the castle?"

"King Willie, I don't know. That castle must get fairly cold as well. Sure it's more in ruins than anything, the roof is gone off it and the windows are gone out of it. But you never know, that might be his summer home."

"What's his winter home?"

"Haven't a clue. St Teresa's maybe."

"Probably."

"Come here, what do you reckon, McDonald's or the bowling alley?"

"I got a hankering for Mickey D's, I haven't had any in a while."

Across from the old graveyard, they opened a brand new McDonald's fast food place. It's the first one in Mayo. They've been building loads of new shops and stuff the last while, there's an Aldi across the way and a Tesco as well so you can shop till you drop.

"The only thing though, if we go to McDonald's and wait too long, we might get spotted on the hop by anyone who gets off for lunch early."

"Right."

"Plus, didn't you say you wanted to stop in to Stauntan's and see if they have them runners?"

"Yeah, you're right, let's go to the bowling alley and take a rain check on Mickey D's."

"Sound as a Pound."

We push the two front tyres together and lock our bikes up to a lamp-post at the back of Boland's Alley. Chris' birthday is coming up and there's a pair of runners he really wants. Stauntan's has everything, you name it they have it: soccer jerseys, GAA jerseys, track-suits, football boots, the whole shebang. The shoe section is near the back of the shop.

"Oh, hold up a sec."

Chris notices a cool looking basketball. He picks it up and spins it in his palms.

"The Chicargo Bulls is it?"

"Yeah, I wish Jordan didn't retire."

Chris likes the Bulls alright, he gets up every Saturday morning to watch NBA Action on TG 4.

"How are they getting on these days?"

"Terrible. They've been trying to rebuild the team since Jordan and Pippin left."

During the summer he brought back this class looking Bulls jersey from Canada. It's embroidered and everything, usually the names and numbers are just printed on, but his one looks like the real Mc'Coy.

"Man, this ball fucken rocks."

"Well, ask the oul pair for both, you never know they might get them. You only turn fourteen the once."

Chris places the ball back on the rack. We stroll down to the far end of the shop, there's a big wall of runners looking back at us, rakes

71

of them so there is, we scan the shelves for a moment. The shoe pops out at me.

"That's it there, isn't it?"

The runner's perched high up on the top shelf. Neither Chris nor myself are tall enough to reach it.

"Hold on."

I grab a boot from a shelf below and reach up, using the toe of the boot, I nudge the runner off the edge into Chris' hands.

"Wow. These are fucken sweet."

"Yeah, class."

"Look, air bubble all the way around."

"Savage."

Nike Air Max 97, they look fucking unreal. They're metallic silver with a white tongue and red Nike tick on the side. The air bubble all the way around is pure class. They must be awful comfortable.

"How much are they?"

Chris checks for the price tag, he tries the sole of the shoe. A sticker:

£110:00

"A hundred and ten squid."

"But they're so worth it."

Surely to fuck, they're a lovely pair of runners. Even the laces are silver.

"Seriously, I have to have these."

"No harm in asking sure. Get on to the oul pair."

"Yeah, it can't hurt."

Chris leaves the shoe on the ground because we can't reach the shelf.

"Ready to go?"

"Let's bounce."

I love the chips they have here, they're so tasty and different than the ones Mam makes at home in the deep-fat-frier, she just chops up the potatoes and fries them. They get them really thin here, the same way they do at Mickey D's. The jumbo sausages are nice too, good and thick so they are. The bowling alley's a sound place to hang out. Besides the bowling, they have pool tables, a games room, and a snooker room, the cinema is right next door as well and there's a bar called the Hogs Heaven, named after the old abattoir that was here yonks upon yonks ago. It's a good spot to spend a rainy day so long as you have a few spons to spare.

BURP...

"Jesus, I'm full up."

Chris and myself are on our second helping of chips and sausages and Coke.

"Right?"

"Let's do it."

We strut over to lane number six with our bowling shoes in hand, still chewing on the last few chips. Chris gives the fella behind the counter a thumbs up to start us off.

"Chris and Sean?" asks the fella.

"Yeah, that's it."

He types in our names on the screen above the lane.

"There ye go."

"Thank you," says Chris.

I'm fond enough of bowling, if anything it's a simple game, just get as many pins as possible.

"Ah, they're cuntish tight on the heels," says me, trying to squeeze on the shoes.

"Yeah, you got to loosen them up more."

I unlace them at the top and try again.

"There we go."

I finally get the bastards on. The shoes are fierce narrow, crushing the little piggies, if they were any tighter the piggies would cry,

--Wee! Wee! Wee!

"Ladies first."

"We'll see who's the lady at the end of the game."

Chris has bowled a good few times before, it's much more popular over there in Canada. This is only my third time so he might be right about the match's outcome. Chris picks up the bowling ball.

73

"Hold on a sec."

He realises his Claddagh ring is still on his right middle finger. Chris has been shifting, well, going with this girl Fiona for about two months now. They both wear Claddagh rings with the hearts facing inwards to show that their hearts are captured. Gay as Christmas if you ask me but what can you do?

"I don't want to lose it or scratch it."

"Here, give me it. I have zip pockets."

He hands it over, I place it in my track-suit bottom's right pocket.

"Now, you're heart is close to my sack."

Chris lets out a laugh, "Just don't lose it."

In the corner of my eye I see the big man himself gabbing away on the mobile phone. Barry Ennis. He owns the place, actually, he owns half the town, Ennis built this bowling alley and the cinema beside it and a big new pub in town. The pub is doing so well that a few of the smaller ones are closing down. He's absolutely loaded. The richest man I've ever seen by miles. He has a big fuck-off mansion out in Moneen, a span new Benze, and more spons than he knows what to do with. What a lucky whore. Ennis must be awful busy to keep everything going though, sure I suppose that's why he has the mobile. He's never off of it, ordering people around, keeping on top of things. One thing he might want to do with all his money is get a fitness trainer or some liposuction, whatever it takes to lose a couple of stone. He's gone as fat. I remember when he was younger, I used to see him at Mass on Saturday evenings. He was way thinner in those days and without the high colour and big bloated face. Chris prepares himself to bowl, he looks back at me and waddles his arse.

"Will ya throw the fucking thing, will ya."

Chris holds the ball in his right hand, he takes four steps then gracefully slides forward on his left foot while kicking back his right leg. The ball leaves his fingers and lands smoothly on the greased lane. It spins on the outskirts near the gutter for a second, then begins to curl towards the centre as if there's some sort of invisible hand guiding it.

CRASH...

A good number of pins are bowled over. A machine descends from above and picks up the two remaining pins, another machine clears away the fallen pins and whips them off to the pin bin or wherever it is they go. A pin on the end and one near the middle are the only two fellas left standing.

"Fair play."

"Just getting warmed up," says the cocky bastard.

Chris' ball pops back up through the hole in the floor, he takes the same approach as before for his second go. The ball spins out then bends back. He hits the one in the middle, it slides across missing the pin at the end of the right hand side gutter.

"Son of a bitch."

"Nothing wrong with knocking over nine of them."

Next, my go. I step up, waggle my arse at Chris, then with a couple of clumsy steps and a high swing let the ball fly off of my left hand. It hangs for a second then drops with a sharp thud. Straight down the middle it goes.

CRASH...

A mess of pins fall, a couple wobble drunkenly, unsure of themselves. The machine does its thing again. I knocked over seven, there's three standing, two on my left-hand side and one on the other side nearer the gutter.

"Seven. Not three bad."

"Wow, that's a tough spare."

"You don't think I can get all of them?"

"I don't know, it'll be a hell of a shot if you do."

"Watch and learn my friend, watch and learn."

I step up for my second chance. With the same routine as before, I bowl the ball. It spins down the middle.

"Come on ya bitch, curl, curl."

I need it to go to the left.

"Curl, curl... Bollocks."

It just flew straight down the middle, doing my score no good at all at all.

Three games later and I'm fecking red raw. Chris beat me in all three, the bastard. I nearly had him in the second one though, I was talking shite to him like there was no tomorrow. In the most exaggerated American accent I can do,

--So, bro, you taking Fiona for cheese burgers and sodie pop on Friday night?

--Whatever.

--Under the thumb, under the thumb.

It must have put him off a biteen, he only beat me by twelve in that game.

"What time is it?"

I check my watch.

"Almost three."

We're low enough in the spons department.

"Do you want to go kick the football around for a bit?"

"Can't, I haven't been able to find it lately, I think some motherfucker stole it," says Chris.

"What else?"

"Why don't we get some eats and go up the hill?"

"It's a bit too close to the four o'clock bell, don't want to be caught up in that."

"True. You know what we could do to waste a bit of time? Check out the Circus."

"It hasn't started yet."

"Yeah, but we could still have a look-see behind the scenes."

"They're not going to let us go gallivanting around while they're setting shit up."

"How do you know?"

"Fuck it, let's do that so."

"I got to take a piss before we leave."

"Grand, same here."

A dirty oul smell stings my srón.

"Jesus, that's rank altogether, what is that?"

The smell's source reveals itself, it's oul Willie and he's marching towards the jacks as well. Oul Willie looks fecking polluted drunk, he

76

swans in ahead of us, unzipping his fly in mid-stagger.

"We'll give it a minute."

"Right."

Baz Ennis stomps over to us, his turkey-neck and jowls quivering with anger.

"Did he go in there?" asks Ennis, out the side of his mouth.

"Yeah," says I with a nod.

Ennis, thick as a bull, heads in after the man himself. The door swings closed and then quickly swings open, Ennis, with his hand clasped around the back of oul Willie's neck, drives him out. Willie didn't even have time to shake and zip up his fly, poor little Willie is hanging out for all to see.

"Didn't I warn you to never come in here!"

"Will ya go easy, will ya," pleads oul Willie.

Willie manages to make himself decent before Ennis sends him flying out the door onto the footpath.

"If you're not spending money you have no business in here, do ya hear me, do ya!"

Ennis slams the glass door closed and returns to where he was before Willie popped up. Poor oul Willie, thrown out on his arse again. You'd think he'd know better at this stage, he's better off in his castle.

"That guy's a fucking mess."

"Sure if that's what he wants to do, let him be."

Willie, confused, picks himself up.

"Look at him, you'd swear he's hard done by."

He takes off in the direction of Mc'Hale Road.

"Sure in his mad mind he probably thinks he is."

"Where's he off to now?"

"Who knows, he's barred from must pubs. I'd say he'll head off and start a fight somewhere."

The Circus has set up show in the Fruit Garden across from Charlie Cuffe's Garage. It'll be their last time around there, apparently they're going to build a big load of houses after the Circus closes up. I don't know why they ever called that field the Fruit Garden. It's really French Park and I don't remember there ever been a fruit tree, there is that one big tree but not an apple to be munched. I'm not that into the Circus, it's better craic when the Carnival comes to town. They have a few good rides like the Skymaster and the Wallsers, they'll shake and spin the shite out of you. Going to the Circus lushed isn't anywhere near as much fun. The Carnival is way more sociable as well, there's birds to be chased and drinking to be done around the back of Vaughan's car-park. Myself and Chris leave and lock our bikes up at the edge of the field. The main tent is a fine size. It must take up half of the land. We stroll around the side till we come to the back of the lot, six massive trailers and a couple of caravans are in a cluster.

"They're a bit like the tinkers by the looks of them."

"They are, yeah."

The faint buzz of an electric fence draws us over.

"I dare you to touch it," says Chris.

"No, I hate that funny smell in the nose after ya get a shock."

"Yeah, you do get a kinda of taste don't you, like metal. Go, you touch and I'll hold your hand, then you won't get shocked and I will."

"Would ya go away, we'll both get shocked."

"I'm telling you we won't, it'll be just me because I'm at the end of it."

"Do you think I came down in the last shower?"

The ground is covered in straw, and the rear of one of the large trailers is half open. We peer inside to see a bunch of dirt bikes with the massive front wheel suspensions.

"They must have some deadly stunts if they have bikes like that."

"I'd say so."

Inside a small makeshift stable, a chubby little pony quenches its thirst in a dusty metallic trough. A tuskless elephant, with a big tarp over it like a coat, waits beside the stable over near the far side of the tent.

"Savage."

"Wow, an elephant in Ballybar."

"Do you reckon it's an African or an Indian one?"

78

"Don't know, let's see if it likes curry chips or not."

Away from the other animals, the saddest looking lion is all on its lonesome, locked in a cage. The cage is tall enough for him to stand, long enough for him to walk back and forth, but the breadth of it is so small, so tight.

"This is awful, man," says Chris.

"I know, this is all wrong."

His mane is all matted and his eyes seem really red around the rims.

"The poor thing probably has conjunctivitis," says Chris.

"Do you think this is legal?"

"Probably not, but what are you going to do?"

"Jesus, this isn't right, man."

Just over from the lion's cage is a barrel of pigs heads. It's a fucking sickening sight.

"They must have gone to the butcher to pick those up."

"I highly doubt rotten pigs heads are in a lion's natural diet."

The poor lion looks like he's in pain, suffering from a lack of freedom. His head bowed, he slowly paces back and forth in his tiny cage. The lion stares out through the bars at us for a moment, then lies down and huffs.

"How do you think they tamed him?"

"I suppose they must have broken his will. If he doesn't do what they tell him they'll crack the whip till he gives in and does what he's told."

The poor crature probably wishes he was back on the savanna with his pride, free to do as he pleases without some cunt cracking a whip off his back. I don't blame lions for attacking people. It's not right to be fucken caging them up and feeding them dirty swine. If I were a lion, I'd eat them all. I'd tear them to shreds and bite off their heads.

Chapter 7

"Chris, don't ye have pumpkins in America?"

"I'm not from America, dumbass. But yes, we do have pumpkins in Canada"

"Do ye have turnips in Canadia?"

"I don't know about Canadia, we have turnips in Canada."

"Mr. Carolan, are you finished carving your turnip yet?" asks Miss Lavelle, our Art teacher.

"No, Miss."

I like Halloween, it's a nice break from school and always a bit of craic with the bangers and the fireworks. Chris and I have arranged a nice deal with a lad we know in fourth year called Jack Smith. Him and his brother go up the North every year and buy a load of fireworks to sell down here come Halloween. I don't know why they don't allow places to sell them here, if they think it's going to stop people getting their mitts on them, they're dead wrong. Someone will drive across the border and sell them down here on the QT whether they like it or not. Every year you hear the same oul story about some young fella losing a thumb to a banger. Anyone who loses a thumb, or a finger to a firework is an amadán plain and simple. It's a small explosive with a fuse on the end of it. If you can't piece two and two together and realise that when you light the fuse and it reaches the end it will explode, then you absolutely deserve to lose a body part. Think about it, whoever lost a thumb, instead of lighting the fuse and throwing it away like a normal person. Lit the fuse, held the banger in their hand till the fuse ran out and watched it blow up. It's not fecking rocket science. If someone doesn't have the general cop-on to know something as simple as this, then I'm sure losing a thumb will be the least of their worries in life. It's like standing on train tracks and thinking that when the train finally arrives it will not flatten you like a penny. For the love of Christ, even birds know not to rest on the tracks. Fucking stupid people have to ruin all the fun for everyone. Chris' turnip is turning out fairly good, the facial features seem very sharp. I've made a haimes of my one. The face is kind of crooked and weak around the eyes. I wonder does the oul lady have a candle at home that'll fit inside of it? She probably won't let me have it lit in the house anyways.

--Amen't I telling you, t'will burn down the house!

I used to love getting dressed up when I was younger and trick-or-treating, we would get loads of lovely chocolate and sweets. Of course, you'll always come to the one house where they think it's a sound idea to give out apples and tooth brushes, they're usually the gafes that get egged, but I suppose they mean well. They don't want toothless obese folk chomping and stomping around the place causing havoc. I hate when fat people blame the world for their big fat arses, actually, they kind of remind me of the crew who lose thumbs and fingers to bangers. If you light the fuse of an explosive it will blow up. If you eat like a fucking hog every day your arse will blow up. It's simple, cause and effect.

A quarter to eleven. The usual bucks congregate at the back yard for small break. I tear the top of my Mars bar wrapper and start chewing away on the chocolate covered nougatie goodness.

"Carolan, leave us arse of that will ya?" Mc'Hugh asks.

"Sound."

"Call arse," says Chris.

"Ah, too late Conway, I beat you to it."

"Bastard."

Chris has some salad sandwiches with him for small lunch.

"Anyone want to swap?" asks Chris.

"What type of sangwich do you have?" asks Tony Collins.

"Salad."

"Is it salad dressing or mayo?"

"Salad dressing."

"Nah."

"What's wrong with salad dressing?"

"It's not worth switching for a chicken and brown sauce

81

sangwich."

"McHugh, are you going out trick-or-treating for Halloween?"

"I am, sure I'm mad for treating so I am."

"What if you knock at a door and they say trick?"

McHugh ponders for a second.

"I'll tell them a joke."

"A joke?"

"...Why did the chicken cross the road?"

"To get to the other side."

"Right, now, why did the dog cross the road?"

"Haven't a clue."

"Because his finger was up the chicken's hole."

"Ha, ha, ha, McHugh you're gone wrong in the head altogether."

"Sure what about it. Were ye doing Art this week yet?"

"We were yeah, carving turnips."

"Same craic as ourselves. I brought my one home. I'll throw it on with the spuds for the dinner on All Souls day."

"Is that right?" Aren't ya a mighty man to be making the dinner."

"Arra, sure why wouldn't I? I'll go to the early Mass so I can take my time getting it good and ready."

"One day you'll make some fine young man very, very happy."

"It'll be love at first taste of my bacon and cabbage."

"Will ya kill the pig yourself?"

"Bejezze I might," says McHugh, half laughing.

"Sure it would be a mighty sacrifice like in olden times."

"T'would. Only sacred pigs in my household."

"Always better to play it safe."

"A bit of breac then maybe for the dessert. That's it, breac, and a mug-a-tae to wash it down.

"Lovely. You'll be farten like fuck after it.

"Better out than in."

"We do get the oul breac with the cloth and yokes."

"Same with ourselves this time of year. Sure isn't it brilliant for fortune telling."

"Oh marvelous. Do you have your heart set on anything?"

"Well not the stick. I have no wife to beat, I'll leave that to the oul fella. Hopefully I'll get the coin."

"What about the ring?"

"Christ no, doesn't that mean I'll be getting married soon. Would ya stop."

"Well if someone else gets the coin ya might be stuck with the ring, or the medallion."

"Mighty choice, get married or join the priesthood, either way I probably won't be getting any gowl."

The high pitched squeals and screams of rockets blowing themselves to smithereens can be heard from the different estates around the town. Chris and myself scale the fence at the Sacred Heart Home. We're on our way to meet Jack Smith and get our order of bangers and rockets from him. A full moon looks down on us, there's no rain promised, perfect for Halloween night so it is. There's three lines of barbed wire at the top of the fence, luckily someone before us has thrown some carpet on it so we can safely climb over it without being bothered by the barbs. We jump down on the other side and make our way through the field. The Sacred Heart Home used to be a Workhouse for starving people back in the Famine, a place for them to waste away and die, now it's a place for old people to waste away and die. I bet there's loads of dead people buried beneath the land, skeletons galore right under our feet. Overhead, the whirring whistle of a rocket flies skyward, it's followed by a massive explosion of red and white.

"Wow," says Chris. "That must be a big ass firework."

"Defo, looks like it came from up Rock Rose way."

Jack lives out the Snugboro Road, not too far away from ourselves. We told him we'd meet him near Ryan's shop, he said he had to make the rounds and sell off the last of his gear beforehand. Jack's a strange type of a lad with a wild streak like few others I know. I remember one time about two years ago, me, Chris and a few other bucks from around had a massive water balloon fight. Jack joined in and got along mighty with everyone. Later on in the day we decided to have a bit more craic and throw a few water balloons at cars as they drove past in the hopes of getting a chase. There was a small wall by the roadside that made for perfect cover. We ducked down and lobbed water balloons as cars and vans and jeeps cruised by. Rarely did anyone even pull over, never mind get out and chase us. After a while of throwing balloons we noticed that Jack had disappeared. A car drove by so we got down on our hunkers and readied ourselves to launch the water balloons. I heard the sound of someone laughing and took a glance up the road. Who was it but Jack, with a look of divilment in his eyes and a carton of eggs in his hand. We fired our balloons, but Jack, like a mad bastard, didn't even bother to hide behind the wall and started pelting the car with eggs.

SPLAT! SPLAT! SPLAT!

He nailed the windshield with three eggs. The driver, enraged, slammed on the brakes.

SCREECH!

We legged it. Jack waited a second and fired the rest of the eggs at the driver as he hopped out of the car. Jack started bouting it. The driver chased after us, ready to bust heads.

--Wait till I get a hold of ye little fuckereens!

Another time the farmer who owns Bane's Hill and the surrounding fields cut all the grass and wrapped the hay in those round, plastic, black bales. There were about fifteen bales at the top of the hill, all were a good height and close together so we were able to climb on top of them and jump from bale to bale. When we got a bit bored with the bales, one of us said,

--Why don't we roll one of them down the hill for the craic?

On one side of the hill were fields, on the other side were houses. Obviously we didn't want the bales to go flying through someone's kitchen window. They were a good size and could do a fair bit of damage. We managed to roll one down the hill and it went flying altogether, burst through the fence and into the other field. Great entertainment. No harm no foul. Jack showed up. He must have been walking by and seen it from the road. We chatted for a bit, had a few laughs, then didn't he come out with,

--Let's roll one down the other side, hey.

--Jack, no way, it could fucken go into someone's house.

--T'will not, sure the fence below will stop it.

--Jack, look at the other fence, it went straight through it.

--It'll be grand, sure this side of the hill isn't as steep.

--Are you serious? It's way steeper than the other side. Jack, I fucken tell ya, don't do this.

We tried to talk him off the ledge, no good. Once he got it into his head that he was pushing a bale down the hill, there was no changing his mind. That's the type of lad Jack is. Christ himself could come off the cross and he'd still pay no heed.

We said,

--Fine, do what you want, but we won't help you push the bale.

It didn't matter, Jack has two years on us and was strong enough to push it himself. He turned the bale on its side and lined it up towards the cinder block wall. Jack looked at us cackling in anticipation, he caught his breath and readied himself to push the big black bale.

--Ha, ha, ha, ha, here we go, hey.

With his back up against the bale, he dug his heels in and started pushing like fuck. At first it seemed glued in place because of its weight, after a couple of secs it slowly began to roll. Once he rolled it in a full rotation he had enough momentum to let gravity take over. It took off down the hill like a fecken rocket.

--HA, HA, HA, HA, HA, laughed Jack.

--Oh, fuck!

A slight sort of hump bulged up in the ground before the wire fence. The bale going full tilt, hit the hump, soared over the fence and crashed through the wall. Cinder blocks flew all over the shop, bouncing off the ground as if they were made out of foam. The bale eventually came to a halt at the back wall of the house. We all legged it and stayed home for the rest of the day. There was no way the shades weren't going to be involved. Fecking Jack, the mad bastard, loved it and shouted as we ran away.

--Let's roll another one, hey!

At Davitt's Terrace, across the road from Ryan's shop we stall for himself to arrive with the goods.

"What do you think?" asks Chris, staring at the shop.

"About what?"

"Eggs, toilet paper?"

"I don't know, do you have your heart set on anybody?"

"Not really, but I could think of a couple of houses I'd pay a visit to."

"You have a packet of them smoke bombs, don't ya?"

"Yeah."

"Just use them, light up a black one near someone's wall, that'll do plenty of damage."

"It's a pity we didn't get a couple of stink bombs."

"They're nasty though, remember the time one broke in my pocket."

"Man, that was rank."

Last year one of the lads in class dared me to break a stink bomb in the front yard. I was all set to follow through and didn't the bastardan glass vial leak in my school pant's pocket. Lord above, it was stink-red-rotten.

"I had to throw out those school pants. The oul lady went spare so she did."

"Yeah, that was funny. You know what would be cool? Getting some of that stuff from Science."

"That phosphorus stuff Mulroy was on about?"

"That would fuck up a lot of shit."

"Did you hear him on about the fella who put some in another fella's bag?"

"Oh yeah, they had to bury the school-bag."

"That's right."

Jack, with a smirk from lug to lug, trots past the Fáilte Inn towards us.

"Finally, himself's coming."

He snaps his head to the right and gives myself and Chris a wink.

"Howye, buckeens? How's tricks?" asks Jack, chewing some

chewing-gum.

He sports a black hoodie, an old pair of denims, and a fucked-up pair of runners.

"What's with the shoes?" Chris asks.

"Sure you couldn't be wearing a good pair out on a night like tonight. They'd be destroyed."

"True enough, so did you get rid of the last of that stuff?"

"I got rid of everything, except the stuff ye wanted."

"Nice one," says Chris.

A satchel hangs on Jack's left shoulder, he swings it around, unzips it and hands us our stuff. Myself and Chris got two packets of Black Cat bangers and three Roman Candles each. The Roman Candles are the best of the lot of them. The ones we have are six-shot-repeaters, that means they will shoot six consecutive shots. They're savage yokes altogether. You're supposed to plant them in the ground and let them shoot up into the sky. I think it's even better to light one up and hold it yourself. It shoots off like a bazooka.

"Hey, can I grab a stick of gum?" asks Chris.

"No can do, I've only got the one left."

"Stingy bastard."

"What do ye want to do?" asks Jack. "Do ye want to go up Arthur's field and shoot off some of these?"

"Yeah. May as well, we'll be close to town in case there's any craic going on in there."

We cross the road, giddy with the prospect of blowing the shite out of things and head up towards Arthur's field. The oul Arthur's gafe is at the bottom end, so we'll head near the top, no need to get oul Arthur vexed. He'd beat lumps out of us if he found us jigacting on his land. The field is a fine size and sloped a bit like Bane's Hill. We hop the stone wall. It's fairly dark, there's just enough orange light from the street lamps allowing us to navigate our way to the top without breaking an ankle. Chris, dying to give the gear a go, lights up a banger and fires it down the field.

... BANG!

"Whoa."

"That was fucken class. Them Black Cat bangers are unreal."

"Wait till you see this," says Jack.

He whips out a Roman Candle, plants it in the ground, lights it up and steps away. The spark works its way up the fuse as the sulphury fart smell from the banger Chris threw wafts its way in our direction.

"Oh, Eggie."

"Lads, who opened the lunch box?"

HISS...

The fuse runs out and the first shell is shot up into the night sky.

...BANG!

The shell explodes into an expansion of green, blue and white. It's followed by the second shell.

...BANG!

This time it's red, yellow and orange.

"They're fucken savage, hey."

Myself, Chris and Jack saunter past Arthur's field happy as Larry after lighting up most of our bangers and rockets. The best was when Chris put a banger in a pile of cow shite. He blew the shit out of the shite so he did. After that we went down the Pontoon Road and did a couple of knick-knocks. Jack wanted to go into Brandywell which is kind of a posh estate, the houses are fairly big and the residents are a bit hoity-toity, making them all the more tempting. The three of us walked in through the main driveway only to see a cop car parked outside one of the gafes. We said we may as well head back to town and see the craic instead of messing around with the rich people. They're well protected so they are.

"Which teacher's gafe would you love to egg the most?" asks Jack.

"That's a tough one, there's so many," says Chris.

"Kenny, definitely. The bollocks gave me a double sceal three for not having my homework done on time last week."

"I think Lydon, just for being so fucking boring."

"Both good choices. I'd have to go after Prendergast," says Jack.

"Never had him."

"We have him for this fucking transition year accounting module

88

and he gives us homework every week. You know fourth year is supposed to be a bit of a doss, but Prendergast, no. He has to give us shite to do."

"Fight!"

Just outside of Universe night club next to the Fáilte Inn, there's a fucken massive scrap happening. With all the young ones knocking about the place at Halloween, both the Townhall and Universe have teenage discos. You always get a few fist fights outside the discos, but this is a fucking epic one. I'd say there's about twenty lads. A mini-bus waits across the road. It must be going to Southport.

"Jesus Christ, this is fucking mental."

Out of nowhere Jack falls to the ground holding the back of his head. I turn and see some cheeky bollocks standing there thinking he's fucken tough, what a hard man that sucker punches someone in the back of the skull. Chris and me leg it over and start dishing out boxes, left, right and centre to the Port-hole cunt's face and torso. One of his mates joins in with a fucking fly kick. Chris ends up with the sucker puncher. I end up with Bruce Lee. One thing about having red hair is that it teaches you how to fight awful fucken quick.

"Come on, ya cunt ya!"

We both swing a couple of times, but miss. He lands a blow to the body. I get him with a jab as he tries to dodge. He goes for a headlock. I hit the fucker with a good upper-cut to the jaw, separating the two of us. Now I have the bollocks. I can tell he's rattled from that last shot so I start throwing boxes to no end at his head. He covers his face with his arms to try and protect himself. Someone grabs me under my oxters.

"Let fucken go of me!"

I try to arch my head and see who. It's some fucken Guard dragging me away.

"Let go of me to fuck, will ya!"

A Paddy Wagon parks right up on the footpath. The fucken Guards are just grabbing people and throwing them in the van.

"Seanie!" shouts Chris.

Next thing the rear door of the Paddy Wagon swings open, the fuckers throw me and about five others in the back. The door slams shut. There's nothing but darkness and the hurly-burly from the street, some of the lads start shouting and banging on the van's side panels.

"LET US OUT!"

I start kicking the door in the hope that the bitch will budge. Christ, I need to get the fuck out. The cop shop may as well be hell if I don't get out of here. Mam will go fucken lula. Pelts and bangs ring inside the van from people throwing stones and shit. The Paddy Wagon starts rocking. People outside must be shaking the van.

...BANG!

What the fuck? The rocking stops.

...BANG!

It sounds like a Roman Candle.

...BOOM!

That one hit the side of the van. Jesus, someone must be shooting at the Paddy Wagon. There's a fidgeting noise. The back door flies open. It's Chris!

"Quick, let's go, let's go, let's go."

We all leap out of the van to freedom. One fella, with a pair of handcuffs on him, legs it off up the street. Chris turns his attention to the side of Universe.

"JACK."

What a crazy bastard, Jack stands there with a Roman Candle in hand, shooting at the Paddy Wagon. After a shot he flings the firework at the Guards, lights another and throws it too. It crosses over the other Roman Candle, rolls and stops at the front left wheel of the van. Both of them are firing away. The Guards, scared shitless, are trapped inside the Paddy Wagon. We start booting it towards Flax Street. Jack catches up to us.

"YEUP!" Screams he.

People scurry away from the Guards. We run into the alley beside Heneghan's Butchers to steady ourselves. My heart is going a million miles an hour.

"That was insane, you firing at the Paddy Wagon."

"We were hardly going to let you go to the Garda Station."

"Lunacy," says Chris.

He's as high as a kite like myself from the adrenaline. We relax the cacks for a few minutes.

"Jack, I can't believe you fucked two Roman Candles at the fucking Paddy Wagon."

"I can't believe you shot the fuckers at them, if they'd seen you, you'd be in awful bother."

"Yeah, could you imagine them bringing ya in for shooting fireworks at themselves. Holy fuck. You'd be finished."

"There's no way they could've seen me, I was hiding near the bushes beside the entrance."

"When the Guard grabbed me, my heart nearly jumped out of my chest. I'd probably have been charged and everything. Could you imagine, they'd tell the oul lady, the school. It'd be the end of me so it would."

Across the road we can hear the trance tunes pumping from the Townhall disco.

"What do ya reckon?"

"Don't know."

"Do ye want to go in?" says Jack.

"Will we get in, is more like it?"

"Do you have any bangers or anything left?"

"All gone."

"Jack, what about your bag?" asks Chris.

"The two rockets were the last of it, plus I hid the bag in the bushes. I'll go down for it tomorrow."

"Good thinking."

"You know what, it mightn't be a bad idea to try the Townhall in case the shades start searching for us."

"Sure there's no harm in trying, who's on the door?"

We gawk across the road and see one of the bouncers.

"I know his face, he lives out near the driving range."

"What's his name again?"

"Haven't a notion," says Jack.

"Chris?"

"I can't think... Peter something is it?"

"To fuck with it, let's try it."

We stroll across the road, calm as could be, acting like we have business to take care of inside. Peter, whatever-his-face, sees us and says without hesitation,

"Sorry boys, not tonight?"

"Why not?"

"There's been a lot of trouble around town and we're not letting anymore in."

"Ah, come on, three more won't matter."

"Can't. I was told by the Guards not to let anyone in."

"Sure they won't know," says Jack.

"I can't lads."

"Alright, come on sure."

The three of us head up towards Main Street.

"It would've been the icing on the cake if he had let us in after all the fucken chaos," says me.

"Fucken, Peter, what's-his-face, you'd swear he's a fucken saint with the going-ons of him."

Chapter 8

Ballintubber Abbey, a fine spot so it is. Sure isn't Agent 007 supposed to be getting hitched here in the height of style come the summer. The penguins decided to take our class on a tour of the grounds after Mass. Sister Nano, a dry shite of the highest order, is in flying form.

"This is the beginning of the Tochar Phadraig, the pilgrimage up Croagh Patrick, we get lots of foreigners every year who want to climb the reek and they start their journey off here."

I have to say, for a place that's nearly eight hundred yonks, it's looking well enough. I wish I could say the same for Sister Nano.

"Although there was a lot of damage throughout the years, it was continually used, even during the times of the Penal Laws. I assume everyone knows what the Penal Laws were?"

--The Penal Laws: Law number one, don't take the penis out in front of nuns.

"They were woeful times, but the Emancipator soon put a stop to that carry-on. Who was the Emancipator?"

"Daniel O'Connell," shouts everyone, except moi.

"Daniel O'Donnell."

Everyone laughs except Sister Nano. By the cut of her I thought she'd be a fan of O'Donnell's whinging. The oul tombs and graves are cool, the Celtic crosses look like they could do with a bit of a scrub though. I don't know if the white speckles spattered across them are from erosion or bird skitter or both. At the top of the upward curving path there's a stone shrine and a cross, below it is a wee little pond.

Chris and myself are back to pay the wee pond another visit on our lunch break.

"See them," says Chris.

"Look at them there, swimming around, not a bother on them."

The pond has a couple of big fuck-off goldfish living in it. I dip in my

93

right index finger to gauge the temperature.

"Bollocks freezing."

I'm surprised it isn't too chilly for goldfishies' delicate sensibilities.

"They're big fuckers so they are."

"I wonder where they come from originally?" says Chris.

"Not here, I'd say."

"Yeah, probably some exotic place like Tenerif."

"Yeah, suppose. I dare you to pick one up."

"I'm not sure if I can, they might be too slippery."

"Go on, if you do I will."

"Alright, I'll give it a shot."

Chris stoops down and rolls up the sleeves of his school jumper. The pond is very natural looking with moss matting the stones and a little lily pad floating on the water for any frogs who might want to chillax. Chris waits with his hands near the surface for a fish to swim by.

"Now!"

He dashes his hands into the gelid water and with a big outward splash wrangles a fish from the pond.

"Gotcha."

"Nice one."

Chris holds the dripping fish up as best he can so we can get a good gurch. It wriggles and writhes like mad. Its gills gasp open and closed and open in a panic.

"There'd be a bit of eating in this one."

The fish continues to writhe. Chris' grasp is waning. As it's about to slip completely, he drops it into the pond with a plop.

"Oh, that fella's got spunk so he has."

"Your go."

I unbutton my sky-blue shirt sleeves and roll up my navy jumper to my elbows. Using the same strategy as Chris, I wait for a fishy to swim within my midst, the pond is fairly murky, it's difficult to see the fishies clearly unless they come near the top.

"See it."

Here we go. I plunge my paws into the pond and snatch another from its watery dwelling.

"Bingo."

I have a good grip of it.

"Is he as big as your one?"

"Bigger."

We glance to our right. Another little pond is down the small slope at the bottom. Mary's Grotto. It's cleaner looking than this one, and has a statue of Herself looking out over it.

"Do ya dare me?"

"No way, you'd never do it."

"Do ya think it wouldn't make it? I have a good aim ya know."

"You don't have the balls to do it."

I take a gander around to see if there's any teachers knocking about. They're all in the Church drinking tea and eating buns with the nuns. Most of the students are around the front, there's only a few of the boys smoking at the wall nearby.

"What if ya miss?"

"Sure we could run down pick it up and throw it in, fish can go a while out of water."

"Don't do it."

"Why?"

"Just don't."

"I'll do it to fuck."

"Don't."

"Why?"

"Just don't."

"I'm doing it."

"I'm not taking any part in this if it hits the ground and dies. I'm not getting blamed."

"It'll be grand."

Chris can hardly watch me as I line our fishy friend up.

"For the love of God..."

I send our golden scaled friend through the air like a fecken Rugby ball. It belly-flops into Mary's Grotto with a loud splatter.

"Bullseye," says Chris, in stitches.

"Now, didn't I tell you, didn't I?"

Ccccaaaccaacrrrrrraaacccccc.

Something mechanical comes to a halt like the grinding of gears below in Mary's.

"What the fuck?"

We make our way down the slope. The water in the Grotto is clouded with pink.

"Oh, bollocks."

"Shite."

The small pond is sullied with the fish's blood. Chris notices something in the corner.

"Look at that."

He moves a branch of a small briar bush to reveal a fecking motor, the goldfish's head is caught up in it.

"For fuck's sake."

No wonder the water in this pond was so clean looking, it had an electric filter. Bloody hell. Some of the lads puffing on fags at the far wall jog over upon noticing the bloody Mary's Grotto.

"What the fuck's going on here?"

The fish is half chopped and half caught in the electric motor.

"Man, this is bad fucken news," says one of the lads with a laugh.

"Hey man, what the fuck are ya going to do hey?" asks Alan Flynn.

The lads are kind of skitting, they don't know what to make of the whole thing.

"Seanie, what do ya reckon?" asks Chris.

"Act innocent. Deny, deny, deny."

Miss Keogh was not one bit fucking pleased when she found out about the fish and decided to hold the whole class back once we returned to school. Sister Sally Rod beyond in Ballintubber went ballistic when she saw the bloody Mary's Grotto, she scolded the class for our disgraceful behaviour. I could care less about what nuns think, they do what they're told by priests and tell young girls they'll get pregnant if they shift a lad open gobbed. They're a waste of a fanny. They do nothing but dress up like penguins and make girls less loose by scaring the bejesus into them.

--Only a shower of nunts!

I must fix the inseams of my pants. I cut a small slit at the end of both pants legs so they'd come down over my runners. The only downer is that the threading is beginning to fray, I'll have to get Mam to stitch them up a bit. The four o'clock bell sounds. I prefer the old fashioned dingalingaling, now they have a new modern bell, it reminds me of a fecking ice cream truck.

"Miss," says one of the lads. "Some of us have to get the bus out the country."

"I don't give two hoots, nobody is going anywhere until someone owns up."

Bollocks. I have to own up now. I can't be holding up the lads that have to get lifts. Fuck. What's she going to do? More detention? Sure I'm used to that. I rise from the desk.

"I did it, Miss."

"Right. Everyone except Mr. Carolan can go."

I wait beside her desk as the classroom empties out. I'd say she must be livid inside, religion teachers always like to keep in the good graces of nunts and clergy. It must kill her that the penguins think of us as little hellions. Keogh turns her scrawny frame towards me.

"Why did you do it?"

"I don't know."

"What do you mean you don't know?"

"Seemed like a bit of craic."

"You killed a goldfish, and ruined Mary's Grotto."

"It's not like I meant to."

"What did you mean to do?"

"I just thought it would fall in the water and then I could bring it back up. I didn't think the fans were going to make chop-suey out of it."

"Well, they did, and you ruined the reputation of the class."

"Ah, but-"

"-No buts. When you wear the uniform you're representing the school, and today you damaged its reputation."

"Miss, it was an accident."

"I don't care what it was, I'm going to bring this up with Brother Leary and see where he wants to take this."

"Jesus, miss."

"Don't Jesus me."

"What can I do? It was an accident, do you want me to replace the fish?"

"No, you can speak to Brother Leary about it."

"But-"

"-End of discussion."

"Miss-"

"-Ah, ah, ah."

The skinny bitch shows me the door without listening to a word I have to say.

Christ, the oul lady has been on the horse all week with me. Ripping mad so she is. After the Ballintubber Abbey incident the school called in Mam and gave her a lugful of how I'm,

--A good for nothing pup.

She has been in foul form of late anyways. She was saying how she's leaving the union at work because they're no good, they only work for the management and couldn't give two shites about a ward-aid like Mam. I'm surprised half of them haven't gone doo-lally working in the nut house all these years. Not to mention they've closed down a good load of wards to make way for the Galway-Mayo IT. Now they'll have a bunch of mental college students hanging around with a rake of normal mental people. Sure they can share all the drugs between them.

--I'll give you two yokes for three Prozac.

All the headers will be off their tits and mad out of it in Universe. I think most schizos aren't really schizos, it's the outside world that drives them soft in the head. I wonder if the voices in their heads are different from their normal voices? It could be like listening to a recording of yourself, you never think the recorded voice sounds like your own voice. That's it. Half the voices in schizophrenic people's

98

skulls are their own voices, they just don't know it. I have a voice in my head, but I know it's my own voice.

--Hence, why I'm not demented.

On the way to PE so we are. I made extra sure to bring fresh socks and jocks with me this week. The last time I forgot them and had to sit and watch everyone playing badminton like a fool.

"How are ya, Seanie?"

"Barry, what's the criac?"

Barry Loftus, he's in fourth year and works at the off-licence in Dunnes Stores. He said he'd be able to sort myself and Chris out with a crate of Dutch Gold on the wink-wink.

"Still on for Wednesday?"

"Should be sound as a bell," says Loftus.

Loftus is a great fix nixer, we're supposed to meet him with two duffle bags in the alley around the back of Dunnes, he's giving us a grand price as well. Twenty spons. We asked him about getting some vodka, he said he could never get spirits. They keep way better tabs on the hard stuff compared to bog water like Dutch Gold. Loftus said even a missing shoulder or naggin would be enough to arouse suspicion. Mam is letting me out this weekend for the disco, I thought she mightn't because of all the shite I've been getting in lately, but she promised me a while ago I could go if I painted the kitchen. I painted the hell out of it. Did a lovely job so I did. Mick Angelo himself would be proud. I'm looking forward to a good session down the lake, I haven't been out for a while now. The last time I was let out was absolutely nuts. A fair few of us were down in Tobin's car-park drinking away and having a laugh, next thing, didn't a Paddy Wagon show up gunning it straight towards us.

CRASH!

The gobshites hit the seven foot barrier full on. The Guards had put it up a while before to stop the tinkers setting up shop in the car-park. It was fucking hilarious, the van there, stood up in the middle of the road. There was a big bend in the barrier and everything. The Guards were raging, they got out and didn't even bother to chase us.

They just started fucking each other out of it.

--Look at the state of it, what were ya thinking?

--Take it easy, will ya.

--I will not, the fucken thing's as bent as a nine pound note.

Good enough for the bastards, you'd think they'd have better things to be doing than chasing after young ones having a few drinks. They were quick enough replacing that barrier though. The last thing the Guards want to be doing is trying to get travellers to shift on out of a car-park. No way. They're more afraid of tinkers than normal people are.

I change into my track-suit bottoms as fast as possible. Our PE teacher, Mr. Campbell, steps in to check the socks and jocks situation.

"Let's have a look," says he, in his hoarse voice.

Campbell potters around nodding and smiling, with the gammy teeth on full view, when he sees the change of jocks and socks. Two of the lads didn't bring gear with them. They wait at the door, sick notes in hand, Campbell hates it when people don't do PE, he takes it very personally for some odd reason. I slip on my runners and tie them up tight, some lads wear the same runners for PE as they wear in class. I never do that. The pong off the shoes becomes dire after a while, then you can't wear the shoes anywhere for fear you'll stink everyone out of it.

"Seanie?" says Chris.

"Yeah."

"You were talking to Loftus on the way in?"

"I was, we should be sound for Wednesday."

"Great."

"I was talking to one of the boys and he said he'd take a couple of those cans off our hands."

"Which boy?"

"You know, Tom Gavin from out Derreenmanus."

"Tom, in third year?"

"Yeah, I was talking to him yesterday."

"Well, do you think we should sell them?"

"I'm not sure. I mean, even if we drank five or six each, which is pushing it, I'm not crazy about the idea of hiding another twelve cans in a field or whatever."

"True, one of the things about selling them though is if Gavin gets plastered and his oul pair catch him, the subject of who he got the drink from will come up. And before you know it, he'll be blaming us for forcing it on him, or whatever peer pressure shite he comes out with to save his arse."

"Gavin's a good guy, I don't think he'd ever lick."

"You never know. Isn't he the same fella who lost an eyebrow when he conked out at Fitzmaurice's house party?"

"Yeah, but still, hiding them would be a pain in the nutsack."

"You're right, I'm just trying to see all the angles, is that the right terminology?"

"Probably."

"What do you reckon?"

"Hiding cans isn't a good move."

"Fuck it, sell them on."

"Okay, let's make sure nobody else knows though."

"Right, don't want to be fucking dealers or whatever."

"Yeah, I'll get on to Gavin and sort it out."

"Nice one. Actually, did you tell him how we got them?"

"No, no, not a word."

"Good, no need to screw Loftus."

Mr. Campbell is in the store room dragging out the chin-up bar, he has had us doing this fitness stuff for the last two weeks.

"Do you think we'll be doing the bleep test?"

"I'd say so, it's supposed to be the last one you take," says Alan Flynn.

The bleep test is a cardio test where you run back and forth and have to get across the line before the beep. Mr. Campbell carries the tape player under his oxter and pulls out a table from the store room.

"Look, he has the player out."

Some of the GAA lads have done it before, for most of us though, this

101

will be our first time giving it a lash.

"Are you getting a drink?"

"I have one in my bag. I may get it now seeing as we're doing the bleep," says Flynn.

I forgot to bring a shagging drink. I should have a squid in my coat pocket. I follow Flynn to the dressing room and grab the pound from my coat. Outside the dressing room is a vending machine. Let me see. What do they have? Coke, Fanta, Lucozade. I think I'll play it safe and just get a bottle of water. Usually, I'd use the fountain in the women's jacks but the yoke hasn't been working for a while. I slide my pound coin into the slot and wait a second to hear it drop. Nothing happens. I hit the button for bottled uisce. Nothing again. I push the bastarden button good and hard. No luck. Alan Flynn notices me and comes over.

"What's the craic?" says Flynn.

"The bitch won't work."

"Well, isn't it a whore."

Flynn gives it a bit of a box while I try shaking the machine hoping it will right its wrong.

"Come on, ya bitch ya."

Mr. Campbell enters the corridor.

"What are ye doing? We have to get the class started."

"Sir, the machine took my money."

Campbell inspects the vending machine.

"How much did you put in?"

"A pound."

"Did it give you any change?"

"No, it just swallowed it."

"I think you've lost it so."

"Shite."

Mr. Campbell reaches around the back of the machine and switches it off.

"Piece of shite machine so it is."

"C'mon," says Mr. Campbell. "We're losing half the class."

102

What time is it? Ten to eleven. Oh God, my head is going to blow. It's throbbing like an infected thumb. I need to close the curtains more. The light'll kill me. I can't face it. My mouth is as dry as a nun's tit. The taste of rotten Dutch Gold is painted to my tongue and gob roof. My clothes are strewn across the bedroom floor.

Sniff. Sniff.

All I smell is the faint remnants of deodorant, stale sweat and beer fart. No sign of puke. I can tell by the coarseness of my throat I must have spewed at some stage last night.

"Ahhhhhh."

I'd say I got away with it. A confrontation with Mam would have sobered me up no matter how steamed I was. I'm so fecking dehydrated. A shower will put some uisce back into me. Oh Lord. I'll wait a minute before I start making any moves. Last night was some craic, as much of it as I remember anyways. Things started getting bleary once I got into the Townhall. I'm not used to downing cans so I'm not. They're awful gassy. The telly is blaring away in the kitchen below. Downstairs I go. Play it cool with Mam and I'll be sucking diesel. Mam sits at the table with a mug of tea flicking through the newspaper.

"You're up, how are ya?"

"Tired."

"How was the disco?"

"Yeah, good. The usual."

"I didn't hear you come in."

"I was quiet enough."

Nice one. Mam got some baguettes, I'll throw a bit of butter on them and they'll reline the stomach nicely.

"Are you not having cereal?"

I can't stand the idea of ingesting anything with milk. I'd spew again in seconds.

"No, no, bread is grand."

"Before you do that, come here and look at this."

What the hell is she on about? Mam opens the back door. A pile of partially dried up yellow puke waits outside for me. Bollocks

103

altogether.

--I'm nabbed.

"Is that yours?"

Christ, what the fuck am I going to say? Caught red handed.

"Yeah," says Mam, as she inhales. "I thought as much. Didn't I warn you before? But you go out and do what you want regardless. You have my heart broke, the school's calling me in because you're playing puc in there. When I let you out, you abuse the freedom I give you. I'm fed up with it now. I've tried everything with ya and I give up. You haven't a bit of thanks of the dogs..."

"Sorry."

"What can I do? You'll only do what you want anyhow, you don't think of anyone but yourself. You live under my roof and pay no heed to me at all at all. Last night was the last straw. It's not like you had a drink, you must have got plastered to be throwing up like that. Do you know how dangerous that is? Do you?"

I nod the noggin.

"Anything could happen to you when you're like that. You could fall and hit your head or end up above in casualty getting pumped... Well, that's it now, I'm sick of trying to control you. Do what you want. You don't care anyways, keep going the way you're going and you know whom you'll end up like."

She walks over to the table and picks up her car keys.

"Where are you going?"

"What do you care?"

"Ah, come on."

"I have a few bits and pieces to get in town. And I want that cleaned up by the time I get back."

"Right."

She closes the kitchen door behind her and heads off. Mother of God, things are bad when she doesn't even bother to get proper angry. What's more, she's right so she is. I have been acting the bollocks a lot lately. I can't believe how upset she seems. She didn't even speak with that high pitched tone like she normally does when she's worried. Christ. I better cop on to myself.

Chapter 9

The fecken wind would cut the srón off you today. And the dampness, Christ above, you only get this type of dampness when the next piece of proper western land is thousands of miles away across the Atlantic Ocean. I can't wait to get home and relax, we just have to get through this hour and we're off for the Christmas holidays, all the exams are finished, no homework, just enjoy the break. We always have a half-day on the last day of term, the only downer is we have to go to the end of term Mass. At least we're nearly there now, the good oul Church of the Holy Rosary. There's zillions of Holy Rosary churches around here. Probably because the Blessed Virgin Herself appeared down the road in Knock.

--Knock, knock.

--Who's there?

--Mary and John-Joe.

It was over a hundred years ago when a few people said they saw Herself outside the church gable. Still though, the Blessed Virgin showing up in a small town in the West of Ireland is a biteen strange. Unfortunately, Mary must have been busy that day in Knock, she didn't have time to sign autographs or take any pictures. Imagine people ambling up to the Blessed Virgin getting their Bibles signed.

--And who should I make it out to? asks the Blessed Virgin.

--Could you make it out to Mossie, thanks... And would you mind signing this picture?

--Not at all.

How come Mary decided to come down that day? What was so special about that day? She mustn't have liked here too much, I don't think she's been back since. The weather was probably shite as usual.

--Too fecken damp, says Mary.

She prefers a warmer climate when she decides to come down on holidays from Heaven.

Up ahead, I can see Brother Coleman leading the primary school boys into the church. Beside them is that oul bitch, Miss Powers, she was my first class teacher in primary school, a nasty oul cow with a nose like a parsnip. She used to always hit me in class just because I didn't know something or got it wrong. Everything was wrong in her class.

--Duck eggs.

That's what she wrote on my homework every day.

--Wrong, wrong, wrong, wrong, that's all she would say.

The Christmas time I had her as a teacher, I asked a question about the nativity picture she had up in the classroom.

--Miss, how could there be baby lambs at baby Jesus' birth if it was in December?

She looked down her long witch-like nose at me and said in her horrible smoker's voice,

--They're the Lambs of God, they can be there any time they want! They can come in September if they feel like it.

That was the last time I ever asked a question in her class. I remember the way the blue ink in my copy would smudge and streak down the lined pages when my tears fell and mixed with the words. I hated her so much, just a rotten oul whore. We march in file through the high arching main entrance. The holy fountain stands between the two large oak doors, everyone dabs their fingers in the holy water and blesses themselves. There's no lack of water in the fountain. I'd say the rainy Mayo weather keeps it full twenty-fecken-four-seven. All the primary school boys are queued up at the confession booths and look like butter wouldn't melt in their mouths. The priests will be put through their paces today, dishing out all sorts of punishment in the name of Our Lord. We advance up the centre aisle and take a seat in a pew not too far from the altar steps. Some genuflect before they sit, others don't bother their backsides. Leary is at the top of the aisle gabbing away with one of the priests, it's funny to see him conversing with someone like they're a normal human being. You don't see that too often so you don't. A couple of more priests appear from behind a curtain near the altar, they march over to the far confessional booths.

"These booths shall be for the secondary school students," announces Leary.

Our class will be one of the first to go to confession. Mc'Hugh, sitting directly behind me, whispers in my lug,

"Anything you want to say before you get the oul soul cleaned?"

"Nah, I'm grand, you?"

"I have one, this is wicked bad though, that's why I'm saying it right before confession, don't want it on my soul too long in case it leaves a permanent mark."

"Good thinking."

"What does a priest and a pint of Guinness both have in common?"

"Ah, haven't a clue, what?"

"If you get a bad one, they'll both rip the hole off ya. Ha, ha, ha."

"God above, Mc'Hugh, you're an awful man so you are."

People start queuing up nearby. I think I'll leave confession for today, I'm not really in the form to go in there and start listing off sins. I forget half of them anyways when I go. I usually make up a few so I have something to say, a little blasphemy here, a little barbarity there. Most of the primary school pupils are finished, half of them are on their knees, paying their penance to God. The priests must love hearing all the gossip. I bet they get all the good stuff, especially from young people. Sure they've all the time in the world for holy boys.

--Bless me, Father, for I have sinned, it's been one month since my last confession and these are my sins.

--Go ahead my child?

--I wasn't loving God when I used the Lord's name in vain at my mother.

--Accidents happen.

--I wasn't loving God when I didn't go to Mass last week.

--Nobody's perfect, sure didn't Jesus himself once commit a sin.

--I wasn't loving God when I was...

--Yes, go on.

--I wasn't loving God when I... had unclean thoughts.

--Did you touch yourself in an unclean way?

107

--Yes, Father.

--Where did you touch yourself?

--On the...

--Where did you touch yourself, my child?"

--On the privates, Father.

--I see.

--Am I going to hell, Father?

--No, no. Worry not, my child, although you have committed a great crime against Our Lord you can still be saved from eternal damnation.

--Whatever it takes, Father, I don't want to go to hell, I'll do anything.

--Anything?

--Yes, Father, anything, so long as I don't have to go to hell.

--Of course, my child, meet me here after school next Tuesday and we'll find a way for you to pay penance for your sins.

--Thank you, Father.

--You're very welcome, my child. Oh, and be prepared to spend a lot of time on your knees, my child.

--Why? From praying is it, Father?

--Yeah. Yeah. From praying. Why else would you be on your knees. Ha, ha. From praying. See you next Tuesday.

I hope this is over soon. I'm dying to get out of here, the parish priest, Father Brady is giving the usual hail Jesus and away in a manger shite. Humble beginnings? The fella can turn water into wine for Christ's sake. He could have set up a nice wine bar in Nazareth and made a bomb, his stepfather Joseph would never have had to work again. That carpentry takes a toll on the body, his knees and back were probably wrecked. I think they do a bad job of teaching Jesus, I'm awful confused by a lot of things he said and did, like when they say Jesus died so we could be forgiven? Who asked him? And anyways, Jesus is the only person who knows for certain God exists, he even has powers with the walking on water and bringing people back from the dead. Why is it a big deal if he died for us? He knows for a fact

108

he's going to Heaven for all eternity. If I were given the choice of living out a bog standard life, or an eternity in Heaven, I think I would probably go the Heaven route. Plus, there are much more efficient ways of getting people to do what God wants. Wouldn't he have been as well off appearing in the sky like it was a big telly screen and saying,

--I am Jesus, Son of God, listen to what I say.

It would have saved him all that walking around and donkey rides through the roasting hot desert. Wouldn't it have been better if he had said when Pontius Pilate declared,

--Jesus, we are going to nail you.

--I'm sorry, I don't think so.

--What do you mean you don't think so?

--Nah. It's just not my cup of wine.

--Well, I said you're going to be crucified, so, you know, we will crucify you.

--Listen, Pontius, do you know who my Oul Lad is? Motherfucking God, that's who. The one and only creator of the shagging universe! I have magic powers for shite's sake, there's a lot of stuff I could be doing instead of being up above on a fecken cross.

--Like what?

--Maybe, cure cancer.

--What else?

--Ah, how about an end to world hunger? Just give me a couple of loaves and fish and I'll sort that one out before lunch.

--Nice, JC, you're not messing around are ya, any other ideas?

--Oh, I have a good one, did you know the world isn't flat?

--Get out of here, you're only codden me.

--Amn't I telling you, the world is round.

--Arra, tis leg pulling you're at.

--I'm deadly serious, round as a spud, you couldn't sail off the edge if you tried.

I wish he'd have done some of those things instead of squandering his powers. God knows, his Oul Fella's as lazy as sin. Whenever you ask about him you just get the,

--He moves in mysterious ways.

When I was small, Mam had one of those pictures of the Sacred Heart of Jesus up on the wall and it used to scare the living shite out of me. I couldn't stand to be left alone with it. The picture had Jesus with a halo around his head, looking upwards, the face on him was of total anguish, I could almost hear the groans of pain forming in his larynx,

--Ohhhhh, God.

In the middle of his chest Jesus' heart had the crown of thorns wrapped around it, then on the tip of a thorn was a drop of blood. Gruesome. It reminds me of the painting in Ghostbusters 2. I still get shivers up and down my spine when I think of that fecken portrait. Why don't they have a nice picture of Jesus smiling and having a laugh instead of him in holy agony? They should have him standing with the Apostles having a cup of wine or eating an oul fish.

Stand up. Sit down. Kneel. Heel. It's funny how everyone does what they're told. What would the priest do if I stood when he said kneel and sat when he said stand? I'd say he'd get fairly vexed. One time these two tinkers were eating popcorn while Mass was going on, eventually, the priest went mental and booted the two gypos out of the church.

--Hooossssannnnnna in the Hiace.

The Lord does not look favourably upon popcorn eating in Mass. It's funny how religious the tinkers are. Although, I think their faith is waning a little nowadays, you never see them out doing the wren on Saint Stephen's day anymore. They used to always come by and knock.

The wren, the wren, the king of all birds,
Saint Stephen's Day was caught in the furze,
Although he was little his honour was great,
Jump up me lads and give us a treat.

I hate when we have to kneel, I usually lean my arse against the edge of the bench so I'm not putting all the pressure on my knees.

--Through Him, with Him, in Him, intheunityofthe Holy Sprit, allgloryandhonouris Yours Al--mighty Father, forever and ever A--men.

That bit always gets a giggle out of me, particularly when the priest kind of half sings it with a bit of a holy hymn. At the beginning they sing on the high side, then descend all the way to the diaphragm for the baritone,

--A--men.

It sounds holier that way. I'm not sure if the priest'll say it or sing it today, these school Masses are a bit different than the usual routine. The most noticeable change is that they don't pass the basket around for spondolies. They know well students don't have any spare spons to be throwing in the money basket. Do the Prods up the North have to pay money at their Masses? I doubt it, otherwise they'd have their own Vatican to show for it. That's a place that looks like it cost a couple of bob. Given it's mostly white, it must cost a fortune just to keep it clean, it's like buying a pair of white runners, no matter how much you clean them and use scuff coat to cover up the marks, they're impossible to keep white. Same craic with the Pope, he's usually dressed top to toe in white. The laundromat bill must be through the roof. At least the priests are dressed in black, it's hard to notice any stains on an all black outfit, but when you're dressing up like Gary Glitter every day, you're bound to ruin a few costumes. Also, they're in fecken Rome, nothing but wall to wall Italian food, marinara stains all over the Pope's dresses.

--Signor Pope, have you a-tried the lobster ravioli?

--No, no thank you, I'm full up.

--Signor Pope, you must a-try it, it's a-truly fantastico.

--No, I couldn't possibly have another bite.

--Per favore, Signor Pope, for a-me?

--Very well, I will try a sliver of lobster ravioli for my favourite cardinal... yum, yum.

--You a-like it Signor Pope?

--Yes, very good.

111

--Oh dear, Signor Pope! Some has a-fallen on your a-holy robe.

Those big hats he wears as well, I'd say he probably gets those dry cleaned, no way they'd fit in the washing machine. And how could I forget the fecken Pope-mobile, the only other mobile I know of is the Bat-mobile. Instead of Robin in the passenger seat, he has a cardinal.

--Na na na na na Popeman! Popeman, Popeman!

--Holy mineral water, Popeman!

That's it, that's what the church should do if they want to make a couple of squid to throw into the oul Vatican bank account. They should start bottling holy water and selling it to drink. I don't know why they haven't thought of it, look at Ballygowan, making a mint for just selling uisce. Sure this is Ireland, there's more water here than you can fecken shake a bottle at. I guarantee if the church started selling blessed bottled mineral water they would outdo their competitors easily. Think about the average person, if they're given the choice to buy Irish mineral water or holy Irish mineral water, at the same price, which one are they going to go for? The holy mineral water without a doubt, sure who wouldn't?

--Tisn't it better to be safe than sorry.

I can see the telly ads already.

--Now in three delicious new flavours: Jesus Fruit, Sparkling Mary, and Diet Joseph.

"This is the Lamb of God who takes away the sins of the world. Happy are those who are called to His Supper."

"Lord, I am not worthy to receive You, but only say the word and I shall be healed."

Communion's another puzzler, I always have a hard time swallowing it. Is it actually supposed to turn into the Body and Blood of Christ? If it is I don't want the fecken wafer getting stuck to the roof of my gob while Dracula above on the altar is washing his down with a chalice of O negative. There they go, the Eucharistic ministers, proud as punch to be distributing our Lord piece by piece. Out with the tongues, up with the palms, and swallie it holy. I always show my palms. It must be dreadful placing the wafer on someone's tongue, them standing there with their gullet open and a big slimy licker. The four of them disperse to the different Communion areas, Father Brady is rooted in the centre aisle. The long lines immediately form. Everyone queues silently with that pious Mass face of spiritual seriousness. If you have to fart, now's the time for it, let it out nice and slow and you can crop dust up the aisle while you wait. We'll be quick enough in line because we're near the front of the church. Today we have the pleasure of Father Brady for Communion, he has his nice little gold bowl in hand while we do a Hannibal Lecter on the Lord's only Son. Well, do you know something, I might bow out of the swallowing for today and settle this body and blood craic once and for all.

"Body of Christ?"

"Amen."

Father Brady carefully places the Communion wafer in my paw. While walking away, I mime putting it in my mouth, then hide it underneath the face of my watch. Now by Jesus, we'll soon see what you're made of ha, ha. I return to where I was, kneel down and pretend to pray like everyone else. It feels so long since I made my Holy Communion, I cannot remember the prayer for the life of me. Sometimes, when Mam and I go to Mass, she likes to leave after she receives Communion to get a head start on the traffic around town. The priests and ministers are flying through the queues, dishing out Communion left, right and center, tongue and palm, it's all the same. I think I've been kneeling long enough to give the impression I've engaged in some sort of a dialogue with Our Lord. I perch my arse back on the pew. Father Brady finishes with the Communion, the ministers return to their seats. Come on, Father, get this over with, I can see him shifting down to friendly priest mode.

"I'd like to thank you all for coming today, it's always a pleasure to have you here. I'd also like to thank your teachers and of course, Brothers Leary and Coleman," says the good Father with a grin. "Don't forget, Christmas is a time of giving, and being thankful for the birth of Our Lord, Jesus Christ."

He shifts back into to holy priest mode.

113

"I now ask you all to please stand."

Everyone rises.

"The Lord be with you."

"And also with you."

"May Almighty God bless you, the Father, and the Son, and the Holy Spirit."

"Amen."

"Go in peace to love and serve The Lord."

"Thanks be to God," says everyone, except me.

"Thanks bit of God."

I'll say my Christmas fair-thee-wells to the class-mates I'm not going to be seeing hammered drunk in the Townhall. After, I'll do the: I-need-to-take-a-shite walk, and briskly make my way up Monument Hill. I'll wait till there's no one around who might witness my desecration of Jesus' body. Then I can have a good gander under my watch and see if it's a wafer of yeast and flower or one of flesh and blood.

Chapter 10

"**S**EANIE?" shouts Mam from the hallway.

"Yeah?"

"Phone, it's for you."

The receiver lies upturned next to the phone book. Mam has the sitting room door securely shut to keep out any drafts that might be looking to give her a crick in the neck.

"Hello."

"Hi, Seanie?"

"Yeah."

"It's me, Fiona."

"Oh right, what's the craic?"

"I need you to come down and get Chris, he's absolutely pissed."

The line crackles away, I can hear incoherent babble with a slight Canadian accent in the background.

"I assume that was himself."

"Yeah, Seanie, he's in an awful state, can you come down and get him soon?"

"Where are ye?"

"We're at the Credit Union, we'll wait here at the pay phone."

"Okay, that's sound, I'll leave now, should be there in about ten or so minutes."

"Great."

"Okay, bye."

I pop my head into the sitting room, Mam's curled up beside the briquette fueled fire watching the mid-week movie.

"Are my shoes there?"

I see them beside the couch and step inside to slip them on.

"Where are ya off to?"

"Just heading out to meet Chris."

"Oh right, how is he?"

"Grand."

"He won't feel it now till he's off."

"I know, yeah."

I tie up my brogues and set off towards Market Square to bring my drunken best friend home safe and sound. It's still nice and bright out. That's the good thing about the summers, it's bright till ten or eleven at night. I'd say Chris is probably ossified at this stage. I don't blame him, tonight is the last night he's going to see Fiona for a while. A few months ago Chris' parents thought it would be a good idea to move back to Canada. I'm not sure what their reasons are, if it's work or family or whatever, I suppose it must be hard on his mam being away from her family in Toronto. Chris visits there most summers, they have a cottage by a lake and everything. It's like something out of a film with boats and lovely weather. He says the water is never cold in the summer, it's like jumping in a big bowl of lukewarm soup. Unlike here, if you stay in the water too long your balls might go up and never come down, that's if you're lucky and can get a clear day to even think about going near a lake or beach. In the winters he was saying they get big doses of snow and ice, hence why ice hockey is a big hit over there. Chris used to play a good bit when he was younger but had a few too many bad spills, his mam thought it might be better if he hung up the skates for good. They're flying out of Shannon on Friday morning at like eight o'clock. Flights to America or Canada always go early in the morning, he says because of the time difference. It must be tough on himself and Fiona, they've been going together for a good while now. I'd say she must be fairly sad. There aren't many like Chris, he's about as exotic as it gets around Ballybar, being from a different continent and all that jazz. Chris was on about giving the long distance thing a go. Although, you know what they say,

--Absence makes the heart go wander.

She'll be back to bog standard Mayo men if they decide to throw in the towel. Chris said the girls beyond in Canada are fucken savage. It's not like here, where everyone's the same, over there they're all mixed with every type of nationality: Irish, African, Mexican, Chinese. You name it. They have it. I suppose by that token the food must be a

116

bit better as well. They won't be saying,

--Are you a savage for bacon and cabbage?

More like,

--Are you a poodle for chicken and noodles?

His sister is fairly upset, she finished her first year in the Convent in May. Sure they're both as well off over there, living it up in the big smoke. They're even letting him skip a year of school, our Junior Cert must be highly acclaimed compared to the dog and pony show they have over there. The Junior Cert isn't much use unless you want to do a trade, in that case it's the bare minimum for bucks like Rasher. He's doing a plumbing apprenticeship with his uncle. Rasher's mighty with his hands, and with all the building that's going on these days there'll be plenty of work for him in the future. I don't think I'd be much good at a trade, even though I did do Woodwork for the Junior Cert, I have to wait to see my results but I'm confident enough I did grand. My project was a toy truck with LEDs and a little buzzer, it turned out fairly good. There's a couple of lads in the class that are unreal at trade type of things, they could craft anything out of anything. Like Rasher, they have a knack for working with their hands. Rasher is terrible at most subjects. He can't spell. If he lost a finger he wouldn't get past ten. Yet, when it comes to something like woodwork he's an artist, miles ahead of everyone. The results night in September will be mad craic. Everyone will be out, even the people who never go out will be out. Chris won't be here for the results, he might do shite for all they know beyond in Toronto.

On my way through Tobin's car-park I can already hear Chris' shrieks of daft drunkenness. As I get to the corner, what do I see before me? Chris hanging on to a sign post with poor Fiona trying to get him to let go.

"I'mna gooin."

Christ on a bike, she was right when she said he was hammered, there's more blood in his eyes than white.

"Well?"

"Seanie, will you look at the cut of him."

I can tell Fiona has lost her patience with him, she has a big frowny face on her.

"How did he get so lushed?"

"Me and the girls were drinking during the day down at St Teresa's track, then one of the girls didn't want to finish her naggin, so he downed it."

"What was he drinking?"

"He had six cans of Dutch Gold, then we went up the Square for a look and he met one of his cousins who went in and bought him a bottle of Buckfast as a going away present."

"Jesus, no wonder. His hair looks like it's drenched?"

"He decided to dip his head in the dirty fountain up the Square to cool off."

Blessing himself in oul Manannán mac Lir's uisce, he wouldn't be the first.

"We headed up Tower Street on the way here, you know what he did? He tried getting into Stalkie's."

"What they do?"

"What do you think, threw him out."

"Christ."

"He went for Ray's then, but I stopped him."

"Fi."

"My name's Fiona, Chris."

"Sheeaann."

Chris is in a fucking serious state, you know things are bad when he just says words for the sake of saying words.

"I'mmm cooolll."

"Quiet, will ya."

"Yes, Chris, you are cool. You'd be even cooler if you would let go of the bloody pole."

"No!"

Chris, drunk is the biggest child ever, he even speaks more like a child when he's hammered. The drink must work like some sort of elixir which unleashes the child and cages the Chris with cop-on.

"He loves that oul pole, hah."

118

"FIIII."

"That's it, I can't stand him anymore. I'll see you later, Seanie."

Chris groans and whines as he notices her walking away.

"Stall the digger, you're not going to say good-bye?"

"I'm going to meet up with him tomorrow when he's able to talk instead of acting like he's handicapped."

"Okay, safe home."

I tell ya, she's in foul fettle if ever I seen her. I better get this fella home and brief him on the apologising he's going to have to do come the morning.

"Alright, Chris, Fiona's gone. Time to go home."

"Noooo whyyy fi goo?"

"It's late Chris, you'll see her tomorrow, c'mon we have to go."

He's holding on to that pole for dear life. I try to drag him off, he just sits down on the ground with his hands clasped around it.

"Chris, you're acting like an eejet, now let go of the fucken pole."

"Noooo," says he, in his childlike manner.

I'm getting a bit worried now, if a Guard comes by and sees Chris doing a Willie Egan he'll be getting chauffeured home by the boys in blue, and that's the last thing he or his oul pair need before they take off. I'm sure they're stressed enough with all the moving craic.

"C'mon Chris."

I hate to have to do this, but I'm going to have to use a bit of force to get my lushed pal off the pole. To make him relinquish his locked drunk grip I start pushing my house key into his left hand. I push harder and harder. I'm nearly drawing blood at this point, the disobedient bastard won't let go of the shagging thing.

"Oouuucccchhhhh," hollers he.

At last, his left hand grip breaks, I forcefully drag him away, his right hand alone is not strong enough to hold on to the pole. He whines like a child who has just had his favourite toy taken away.

"Alright, Chris, let's get up now."

I put my shoulder under his right arm and try to help him to his feet. Already, Chris seems more lushed than when I arrived a few moments ago. He's awful bad in the walk.

119

"We're going home."

"Wherrrrre Fi?"

"She had to go."

He halts, stands rigidly straight for a second, but can't tense himself for long as his neck swivels over his left shoulder to see where Fiona took off.

"C'mon to fuck with ya."

I nudge him forward and regain his fluttered attention, he stumbles along the footpath with myself supporting half of his weight.

"Are ya right, Chris?"

"I'm coooo."

There's a melancholy tone to his reply this time, it's that type of drunken incoherent sadness that some girls get when they're in the Townhall. Chris has the lad version of it. When girls get it they tend to cry a little and when you ask,

--What's wrong?

You're always met with the,

--I don't know, I just can't stop crying.

The lad version is a kind of drunken introspectiveness, Chris has it in spades. We stagger a little farther through the car-park. He's silent now and has stopped moaning and whinging like before. There's not too many cars, only a few, the owners have probably gone for a good feed of pints in Bramley's. I glance at Chris, his silence is deafening, his eyes are wired with red.

"Chris... Chris?"

"Yeaeaeaah."

I don't like the stifled eaeaea escaping from his oesophagus.

"Chris, are you alright?"

He glares at me, white as a sheet so he is. He heaves then unleashes a violent waterfall of dark brown vomit at the tarmac.

"That's it, Chris, get it all up."

I encourage him and rub the centre of his back in a circular motion. That bottle of Buckie must have put him over the limit, half of it is coming back up the same way it went down.

"Cough it up, it'll do the hens."

It comes in spurts of gassy darkness from within, the obligatory pieces of carrots make a cameo in the tar-like liquid.

"Good man, better out than in."

Another belch escapes, hopefully he's finished for the time being.

"Howya now?"

He's still hunched over, probably getting that calm peaceful sensation you get after emptying out the oul belly. Chris glances up at me, his face drained of blush, his sad expression compounded by the spewing.

"I nee to-to-to ress."

"Alright, okay, we'll take a seat on the benches, but not for long."

The benches overlook the trolly and plastic bag filled town river. Chris hunches on the bench, his head hung, his face long.

"We'll rest a minute, then we have to go, okay?"

The reason we have to go is that a hundred yards away rests another man: Debo Maughan, in his caravan with his wife and batter of offspring. Debo has been in and out of the town for many years and is one tough cookie, apparently he fights in the tinker puck which decides who's the king of the tinkers. He's a bull of a man, built like a brick shithouse and known not to suffer fools lightly. He hates, I mean, fucking hates settled people with a fiery passion. He parked his caravan in the car-park about two weeks ago, the town council has been trying to get him to clear off since. Just across from us is the Maughan's clothes line. Oul Debo couldn't give two shites if the whole town sees his dirty jocks.

"Howya feeling now?"

I'm met with nothing except the rattling hum of Debo's electric motor powering the telly inside.

"Hey, Conway?"

SPEW!

Looks like Chris was only getting started before, he continues to evict the contents of his belly. At least the dark brown Buckfast colour isn't as prominent this time around. I do the usual routine of consoling and encouraging. The poor bastard, one of his last days in

121

Ireland is spent plastering the pavement with his insides. This is probably not how he envisioned the day going, I'd say he thought he'd have one of those good drinking sessions, where you're all loosie goosie but still have some sort of control over the stomach muscles. Chris leans his head to the side, his eyes tear even more, his face takes on a Galway coloured maroon.

"Ahhhhhhhhh!"

The vomit hits the ground with a wet smack, he breathes for the first time in half a minute and sits up slightly. Chris spits twice to cleanse the pallet then wipes his lips with his jumper. The poor gossure lets out a loud sigh of relief. I hope to God his parents aren't awake at home, between the look of utter despair on his puss and the malodorous smell of half digested Buckfast, among others, he'll be nabbed for sure.

"How ya feeling now? Better?"

"Mooooveeeee."

Christ above, I've never seen him so bad, I mean Chris has been totally fucken buckled before, but never like this.

"Maaaa ttuuu aaaaa!"

"Chris, be quiet will ya."

The bollocks must be getting some sort of inebriated second wind. He needs to shut the fuck up, way too loud so he is.

"C'mon."

I put my arm under his shoulder and try to get him up onto his feet. His legs are awful limp, tis a wheelchair this buck needs.

"Ooohhhhhhhhhhhh ffuuucccckkkk."

"Chris, be quiet, Debo'll come out and beat the head off ya."

"Fuuucccckkkkk Decccco."

I cover his mouth to quieten him. He hums his drunken melodies, "Aaaahhhhh raaaa daaaat."

I try to get him to focus by looking him right in the eye. Every time I catch his attention he turns away.

"Chris, look at me, look at me."

I grab him by the temples and force him to take notice.

"We need to go home, alright?"

Chris stops his raving, looks me right in the eye and starts laughing his arse off.

"Ha, ha, ha, ha, ha."

I'm glad someone thinks it's funny.

"Aaaahhhhh, fuuccck iittt!"

Chris springs off the bench in an apparent attempt to get back to walking on two feet.

"Feecccck."

He's face down on the path, thankfully not on, but next to the pile of puke.

"Ouccchhh!"

"Chris, stop it!"

"Mmmmyyyy fffacccee."

I begin to drag him up off the ground. Shite, there's a rumbling coming from Debo's. The plastic door slaps off the side of his caravan. I perch Chris back on the bench. Debo Maughan, belly bouncing, marches in our direction.

"Wa da fuck ye at heire?"

"My friend is awful sick, he's just resting for a minute."

Debo's the hit first ask questions later type of fella, not exactly a deep tinker.

"Ye nee ta shift outta heire, d'ya heiar me?"

Chris is muttering something at Debo, his volume is too low and his diction, like Debo's, is impossible to make out. Debo bends down a little and looks Chris in the eye.

"Ya dirdy oul clown ya, I'll trow ya in dat rivaa if ya dun't muv outta heire, d'ya heiar me?"

Chris, in his own world, can't see two feet in front of him never mind comprehend what surly Debo's saying. If he only knew what he's being threatened with.

"Yeah, he hears you fine, I'll get him out of here pronto."

"Ya betta."

Debo struts back to the caravan, thank fuck.

"Alright, like it or not we're going home."

Chris must have definitely felt Debo's presence on some level, he

123

has quietened down a fair bit. I get him up again, his legs are still like jelly.

"C'mon, straighten up to fuck, will ya."

Chris hangs on to me good and tight.

"That's it, that's the job."

We take a few steps towards the short green bridge, which takes us across to the Church car-park. If we need to take a break we could stall the ball here. One way or another I'll get him back safe and sound... Well, maybe not sound but hopefully safe.

It's his last night tonight for a while. I eventually got him home after a pit stop to empty the stomach at the stream along the Rathbawn Road. And once more for luck outside his gafe. He gave me a bell this morning, he said his mam caught him trying to clean the side of his face with his tooth brush. Chris' mam is fairly conservative when it comes to the drink, he always says they're more cautious when it comes to the lush over in Canada. I suppose if ever there was a time to get nabbed drinking, last night was the night. I'm really going to miss the bastard when he goes, but we're going to stay in touch every week. My Mam said she's going to get a computer next month and I'm going to go to the library tomorrow and set up an email account. I'm no good at typing, but sure fuck it, I'll learn. Chris met up with Fiona today and said his goodbyes. He said she was awful upset. I asked him if they're going to try the long distance thing, he said they'd give it a shot and a see how it fares. It must be really sad leaving someone you care about. He might never see her again. It's going to be hard to say goodbye, though I'm not going to cry, I'm too old to be acting like a woman, no crying, just a firm handshake and a pat on the back. Chris is my best friend. He'll always be my best friend. I can see the prickly green hedges that surround his back garden. I don't want to go in. I'd prefer to pretend this isn't happening.

"Oh, Christ..."

Chapter 11

Time to clock in. SuperValu is strict on the clocking in and out on time. I'm getting paid in euros now, no more punts, it's a pain in the bollocks though, during the change-over we have to put the prices up in punts and euros. At least once an hour someone comes back thinking they got done on the exchange rate.

--You're a bunch of cowboys, that can't be the right friggin change ye gave me.

I usually work from five to nine on school days, then one to eight on the weekends. That's the good thing about being in transition year, plenty of free time. The pay is a bit shite though, minimum wage, sure what can you do? If you want to make a bit of dosh there aren't many other places you could be working at except a supermarket. Deliveries come every Monday, Wednesday and Friday morning. Whenever we have to restock, we bring the older stuff from the back to the front and face off the shelves so the display looks good and symmetrical. Each of us have our very own aisle we must attend to and maintain, I've the cereal aisle, not too bad so it's not. I feel like a man working on the big guns, building big walls of Weatabix, Cornflakes, Coco Pops and the trillion other types of cereal. Start from the bottom, finish at the top. It's better than having an aisle where there might be jars of jam or marmalade. Those are the worst aisles to work on, some customer always knocks or drops a jar of something or other and then you have to mop up the whole mess. The best job would be delivering shopping to people's gafes, at least you'd be out and about cruising around in the van. It wouldn't feel as much like work. And who knows, you could be delivering to some ride's gafe and get invited in for a bit of hanky-panky.

--Easy.

--Down boy.

Tis impossible to hide a horn in work pants, it's the same craic with school ones, push it over near the pocket and hope it subsides before anyone notices. If you have to, put the claw in the pocket, hold it still, close to the quad. If you were in a bad way you could always head to the jacks for a quickie. Be careful not to get any spunk on the pants though, especially the work ones. They're darker, it'd be more noticeable.

--What's that?

--Just a bit of yogurt, a bitch to get out so it is.

The best spot to indulge Palm and her five sisters during work would be the car-park booth, you could watch the tottie strutting about all day and nobody would be able to see a thing. You'd be sound as a bell so long as you weren't pulling mad faces and the wind changed, then you'd be in a bit of bother, a fucked face from hand fuckery. The work is fairly stupefying, luckily school has taught me well how to deal with boredom and monotony. Actually, it's not an awful lot different from school. We have to wear uniforms: maroon polo shirt and jumper, black slacks and shoes. Instead of teachers and Brothers telling us what to do we have bosses and managers. The branch manager is called Ricky Taylor. Pricky's a total fucken knobend, he's constantly bossing people around and he speaks to the staff like they're fucking kids. Talk about power tripping, he thinks he's the man because he wears a suit. It must be all glitz and glam for the manager of a supermarket, sex, drugs and rock and bread rolls. It's funny how everyone hates him, yet nobody would dare say a thing to his face. That must be a great perk of being the boss, nobody questions what you do, the employees can do what they're told or fuck off somewhere else. A couple of the workers in the stock room were on about striking for better wages, they didn't bother in the end. We're not allowed have a union so it's hard for the workers to do anything. I asked some of the older lads, who've been working here for like ten years, why they don't quit or strike? Their answers are always the same.

--It's all fine and good to talk about it, but I have bills and loans to pay off. If we did strike they would probably just fire us and bring in new fellas to do the work.

After a while it's the little things that really get to you: the

126

clattering of the trolleys, the scrunching of the plastic bags, the repetitive questions from the customers, or even just listening to their fiddle-faddle.

Beep. Beep.

God, sometimes I think I will jump out the window if I hear the beep of another check-out till. Only the girls are allowed to work on the tills, they must go daft listening to the beep of barcodes day in day out. The music as well would drive you to drink, always the same jingles on the radio. I'd eat an arse if they'd just change up the music a biteen. Put on 2fm or Midwest Radio. Christ, I'd take CRCfm if they propositioned it. A mam with her child close behind rolls her half filled trolly past my aisle, the child seems to be behaving himself. I like kids, but they drive me mental when they're shouting and roaring.

--Mammy, I want Coco Pops!

--No, you can't have them.

--Why not?

--Because we're getting Cornflakes.

--But I want Coco Pops.

--I told you already, no.

--I want Coco Pops now!

--Shut up or you won't get anything!

--Give me Coco Pops!

--I'm warning ya now, I'll leather ya if you're not quiet.

Sure the kids are wired out of their minds on all the sugar and fizzy drinks they're getting, you can't blame them for being hyper-active. Then the parents are annoyed all day with the incessant nagging, it's a recipe for insanity so it is. I hate when the parents are pushed to the stage where they smack the kids across the arse. The young ones cry and scream even worse than before. It's awful to be around, no matter how good of a mood you might be in that will wreck the buzz. I don't know why they can't leave the kids with their friends? Or why the mammies don't get together, have one parent look after the kids, then have the other parents do all the shopping. They could take turns every week, it would be a nice break for the parents, meanwhile the kids could play together and have the craic while the

127

mammies are buying the fecking Coco Pops. Think of all the hassle and stress it would relieve. No more young ones going ballistic in the supermarket. No more prams on the footpath around the town holding up the whole show. No more reddening of arses. Less stressed customers. Less stressed staff.

SuperValu has a lot more competition these days with Tesco and Aldi in town. Tesco is a powerhouse of a place, they sell everything: sleeping bags, pots and pans, DVDs, they even sell their own Tesco brand beer and vodka. It's awful stuff though, basically just chemicals mixed together. Willie Egan would think twice before necking any of it, and oul Willie's not accustomed to thinking twice about the bottle. I'm trying to think of stuff Tesco doesn't sell... Abortions, that's about it. They sell condoms, but I wouldn't be crazy about purchasing johnnys on the cheap. I'd say they'll get into abortions yet, they're in about every other thing.
   --Need an abortion? Come on down to Tesco and sign up for our Tesco super saver abortions, buy one get the second half price.
   --Knocked up?
   --We'll send you from Knock to London on Cryan Air with our low, low prices.
   That will be their next racket.
   --Step aboard to abort.
   People might abort their flight once Cryan Air rapes them with the overweight luggage charges.
   --Fuck it, we'll have the bastarden child, it'll be cheaper than paying these extra charges.
   There's people stuck abroad who have to take out loans to pay for their overweight luggage. It could all be part of their scam, faulty condoms, some young one ends up preggers. What choice is she left with? Have the child, or head to London and get rid of it.
   --With Tesco's low, low prices who can resist. Tesco, helping you clean up a mess.

I hate queueing up. What takes people so long? Are they transferring money from a fecking Ansbacher account? I'm here in the AIB bank, last in line. The folks at the counters must be telling the tellers their life stories with the speed of them.

A tap on the shoulder.

"Howya, Seanie?"

"Oh Jays, Cormac, long time no see, how are ya getting on?"

Cormac Nolan's a funny fella. He lives out my way and used to always come over and play football with us in the evenings. A mighty man for a chin wag so he is.

"Not too bad. Down for the day to do a few jobs."

"That's right, you're up in Galway these days."

"I am, yeah, doing Arts."

"How's that going?"

"Sure it's handy enough, we've only one set of exams in May and then we're finished for the year. Cram like fuck for them and I should be sound."

"Good stuff."

"What are ya up to yourself?

"Transition year, working in SuperValu."

"Not too bad, I worked in Dunnes for fourth year, it's a handy bit of coin."

"Arra, sure it's not too bad. So what else is going on with ya?"

"I'm doing a J1 visa this summer."

"Nice one, brilliant."

"We're off to San Diego. There's a rake of us going."

"That's an odd oul spot is it?"

"A load of J1ers head out there now."

"Really?"

"Yeah, that's why I'm down, I have to transfer the dosh to pay for the tickets. They've a deal on a student credit card here as well. I said I'd get the lot done in the one day."

"You might as well."

"I tell ya, the bus up was a pain in the ring."

"Was there no student bus?"

"Not on a Wednesday. I had to take the normal one and I swear to

God, it must have taken over two hours."

"Bollocks."

"Stuck in Tuam for ages."

--Tuuuuuaaaaaaaam! The fastest town in Ireland.

"That's a whore."

"They'd want to get some sort of commuter train or something instead of all these buses," says Cormac.

"You'd wonder why they don't? There must be no money in it."

"That shouldn't matter though, think of all the cars off the roads they could have, and the amount of crashes they'd stop. Them roads are like a bottle in the winter, plus the state some of them are in, potholes the size of fecken Lough Neagh."

"You're dead right."

"What goes up the road, down the road, but never touches the road?"

"What?"

"The County Council."

"Good one ha, ha. The train to Dublin isn't too bad though."

"Yeah, but did you ever try getting down to Kerry or Cork? It's like an eight hour bus, you'd be jet lagged after all the traveling."

"Donegal is the same story."

"What they'd want to do is have some sort of rapid transit system like the TGV all along the West from Donegal to Cork."

"True enough, especially with the price of petrol."

"Sure it's no use telling them, hah."

"We'd be as well off beyond in San Diego."

"We would, it's nice and close to Tijuana as well."

"Aw, class, man. What's the story with ID over there? Do you not have to be twenty one?"

"In the States, yeah, but in Tijuana they couldn't give two shites. I'm getting a fake driver's license anyways to be safe."

"An Irish one?"

"Yeah. My mate's brother got one before and he said it worked the charm, once they find out you're Irish over there they're not too bothered."

"I'd say so, alright."

"Here ya go."

I'm at the front of the queue, a teller's finally free.

"Well, that was quick enough."

"Nice one."

"Here, I'll talk to you later, Cormac."

"Drive her handy, hey."

The money's in the bank safe and sound. What to do now? This is one of the vexing things. When I have no money I can think of a million things to do, when I have cash I can't think of anything. I might rent a video from Xtra-vision or buy one in Manhattan Records. What to get? I don't know. I wish it was a Friday, I could have a couple of pints. I'd have some entertainment as well with the usual chipper fights that erupt. The worst is the bouncer, Alfred at Abrakebabra on the weekends, the chippers are always thronged after the pubs, in for the Taco Fries and Chip Butties, whatever it takes to satisfy the false appetite. It gets so bad they need to have someone man the door to let the drunkards in and out.

--Alfredkebabra, I wanna reach out and grab ya.

I've never seen him around the town before so I'm not sure where he hails from originally. Either way, they taunt the poor bastard for hours on end some nights. He'll kick some lushed lunatics out then they'll spend the rest of the night trying to get back inside every time he opens the door. They'll moon him like crazy, arse cheeks to the window. They'll shout, scream, and throw the occasional box at him as well. There used to be more chippers around the town, Chipadora and Casey Jones both kicked the bucket, Blue Thunder's still tipping away though. Maybe I'll head down to Brant Rock and get a new top to impress the ladies come Friday night. I do have a fair few already. Sure fuck it. One more won't hurt.

Same shit different day. Time to stack the shelves.

--Big fish, small fish, cardboard box, stacking shelves, stacking shelves.

131

Look at the state of this Rice Crispies box, some bollocks opened it and stole the free toy that comes along with it. What is it? A reflector for bike spokes or something? You always see the same customers at the same time every week. On Thursdays I usually see George at the cereal aisle buying All Bran. He's a gas ticket, an old fuck, but he'd have you in stitches nonetheless.

--I'm boweled up, Seanie boy, clogged up like fuck.

--The All Bran will sort ya out grand, Georgie.

--I hope so, they have me sickened with shit.

--All Bran and black coffee, that'll clean ya out.

People generally don't work that hard, only when the bosses are watching. Sure why would we? The work is so mindless you can't take pride in it. A fucken handicapped dugong could do it. We get paid the same wage per hour whether we slave hard or not, the thing is to work just hard enough to not get fired, it doesn't make a blind bit of difference to us whether SuperValu makes a bomb or barely stays open. Here comes Pricky Taylor. Better act like I'm as busy as a bastard.

"Carolan?"

"Yeah, what's the craic?"

"I walked down here yesterday and the cut of this aisle was disgraceful."

"I wasn't working yesterday."

"Who was?"

"Haven't a clue. Check the schedule."

"Well, make sure this aisle is in good nick, cereal is a big seller."

"Yeah, yeah."

He marches off like a pair of fucken clown shoes. What a pain in the hole that fella is, he probably knows well I wasn't working yesterday, but he gets to feel like the big man telling people what to do. He'll go off now annoying everyone and their oul lady about something or other. He'll tell the butchers they're not slicing the bacon properly. He'll tell the bakers the bread is too bready. I think he makes the place worse, things go way smoother when that amadán isn't fucking running around the place crying and whinging over spilt milk, literally. I'd say he must have kissed plenty of arse to become a manager. That's usually the way to get ahead in here, plenty of lip service and ring kissing. I can't stand it myself, arsehole must be an acquired taste.

"You see these bananas? These. Fucking. Bananas. Are too fucking green to be put out there with the other bananas!"

"Some people like to buy their bananas a little green so they'll last a bit longer," says Steve.

"Did someone tell you that was acceptable?"

"...No."

"No, they didn't because I didn't tell you."

"I assumed."

"Do me a favour, don't assume. Do-not-fucking-assume. If there's no bog-roll in the bog and you assume that you should get some because if you don't, people will have to endure dirty arses. Don't. Unless I tell you, don't do a fucking thing."

Look at this fucking Pricky eating poor oul Steve Fallon out of it for putting a little thought into his mindless, soul destroying job. It makes my blood boil to see Prick treat people like this. What's worse is that Steve takes the bollocking for doing nothing wrong at all at all. Pricky storms out of the store room, fuming, because his life is full of green bananas. Steve stands there with his gob hanging, he puts his hands in his pockets and steps away embarrassed. Fucking disgraceful so it is. Oh, here he is again. As quick as he left, Pricky flies back through the swinging doors. What the fuck does he want now?

"Carolan, is your aisle tip-top?"

"I told you before it was sound."

"Oh yeah? Well, follow me now and we'll see how sound it is, Seanie boy."

I follow him over to the cereal aisle. A bottle of Milk of Magnesia has leaked all over the floor.

"I thought you said it was sound, hah?"

"It was two seconds ago, someone must have just dropped it."

"Yeah, well, if you were paying attention-"

133

"-Listen, I don't have x-ray vision. If someone drops a bottle of whatever, I have to be told."

"Don't interrupt me-"

"I'll interrupt you whenever I feel like it."

"Listen, I'm your boss, you'll do as I say or else."

"Or else? Who the fuck do you think you are threatening me? Go fuck yourself. I quit."

"You can't just quit."

"What the fuck does it look like I'm doing, ya fucking prick ya."

I strut off to the store room, I'm just going to get changed and get the fuck out of this shithole. If you ask me, everyone who works here should do the same. Sweet Jesus, I hate this fucking place so I do. I grab a box of SuperValu's own brand Weatabix. The staff bathroom is vacant. I step in and lock the door. I'm going to leave a nice going away present for that prick Taylor. There's two rows of Weatabix biscuits wrapped in grey plastic, I pull them out and leave the box on the ground. I drop the cacks and togs and squat down over the box.

--It's coming.

Fittttlllllleeeettttt.

--Push says I, push.

There'll be no pebble shits here.

"Go on ya good thing ya."

Oh, here it goes, it's coming.

--Push says I, push.

"Ahhhhhh."

With my arse hovering, I manoeuvre the load straight into the Weatabix box. Nice and neat, brown like peat. Instead of the usual splash of bog water, I'm met with the unsatisfying tap of crap off the inside of the grey cardboard box. I glance down. There it is looking back at me. I've given birth to a beautiful brown baby shite. It's moist, of regular consistency and unbroken, tis true what they say, a good dump is truly therapeutic.

I head for the exit with the Weatabix box in hand. Given its freshness, I place the shite on the shelf near the back so it can fester with its fellow SuperValu's own brand Weatabix boxes. Whoever buys this one will literally be buying shite, ha, ha, ha.

--The product seems to be defecative.

I'm not going to even bother clocking out, Pricky can do it. Who does anybody think they are speaking to another human being like he does? Boss or not, it's a fucken attack on human dignity. People shouldn't stand for it. Steve Fallon waves me over with a curious smirk.

"What's going on?"

"Quitting."

"No way."

"Yip."

"Cause he shouted at ya?"

"Cause he's a prick, his fuckacting is ridiculous. Why don't you quit yourself? Fuck him talking to you like he does."

"I don't know."

"You're a smart fella, why don't you tell him go fuck himself and leave, you'll find something else."

"Ah, no I'm grand."

"Steve?"

"Sure it's handy work, better than digging ditches."

"Who says you have to dig ditches? We're in a boom. What would you like to do with yourself?"

"Ah, it's easy for a young buck like you to pick up and leave. Different story for me."

"Steve, you're in your twenties, you're not that old."

"Arra sure, I'm grand."

"Alright, come-here, it was good working with you, and sure I'll see you round the town."

"Definitely. Good luck, Seanie."

Fuck the lot of them. If Steve wants to waste his time in SuperValu to hell with him. I make my way out by the tills, I can tell the girls have heard the gossip, they all give me a queer look as I pass them. The automatic doors are only a few steps away. Beside them is the gobshite himself with his clipboard in hand.

135

"Best of luck working for anyone with your attitude," says Prick.

He begins to potter behind the inquiries counter to the right of the automatic doors.

"What the fuck did you say to me?"

One of the new Polish girls notices me glaring at him. I can't read her name tag, too many consonants.

"I don't work here anymore, you can't talk to me like that."

"What are you going to do?"

I lunge at him instantly. He leans back behind the counter, just out of reach.

"I'll crack your skull open that's what I'll fucken do! Do ya hear me?"

Scared shitless so he is. The security guard dashes over to restrain me.

"I'll fucking kill you!"

The security guard tries to drag me away. He's having a hard time with it. I'm fucking bulling altogether. Co-workers and customers gawk on. Pricky stands behind the counter visibly shaken.

"The hard man, I see," says Prick.

"One more word and I'll take that fucking clipboard and bury it in your fucken face!" roars me.

The security guard eventually gets me out of the store, but not without a struggle, as soon as I'm outside I begin to calm down and cooperate with him. I barely turn my head and see a herd of shoppers enjoying the show. I'm glad. It's good for them. Now they'll have something to yap about besides the shite weather and changing over to the euro. To be honest, I couldn't give two fucks. I'll never fucking bow down to anyone. I'd rather fucking die than slave away for some piece of shite supermarket chain or some prick manager at minimum wage, or any other wage for that matter.

Chapter 12

After my abrupt departure from SuperValu's employment, I thought that'd be the end of my working days. However, my Uncle Tommy got sick and tired of Mam giving out stink about me and found me a job in William Thompson's Pub. It's a small oul maneen bar with a modest but steady following. I work on the weekends as a porter, sorting things out and keeping the place tip-top, on a busy day I might do a shift behind the bar, or if I'm stuck for a few extra euro, Liam will throw a shift my way. Liam's an older fella. I knew him well to see around the town for years, normally with his flat tweed cap in and out of the bookies like a mad yoke.

--Moscow Flyer, what a beaut.

Liam's a funny fucker and probably the most sociable person I've ever met. Ages ago Liam was married and had a daughter. Unfortunately, he got dealt a bad oul hand when the wife and daughter died in a car accident out the Southport road. His wife was visiting the sister who lives out in Islandeady, on the way back to town, with the daughter in the passenger seat, didn't some drunk driver plough into the side of them. Both were killed instantly, which when you think about it is probably the best way to go when you go. The drunk driver survived, but was in an awful state altogether, he ended up in some home in Kiltwomey. Liam finished school when he was about twelve, but you'd never think it. He's without a shadow of a doubt one of the most intellectual people you could ever meet. We do have great oul chats, usually about books and history. In his spare time, he reads a lot and watches the odd film if he hears it's fairly good. He doesn't watch hardly any telly.

--It dumbs people down. Makes them as thick as a plank, says he.

Mayo are playing a league game today in Mc'Hale park against Sligo. Liam probably has a couple of euro on the match, he never bets against Mayo. I'm just working the bar till the barman Diarmuid arrives, he was over in Roscommon for the weekend and is running a biteen late. There should be a good crowd here today. It'll be full of oul fellas solving Ireland's problems while necking nothing but pints of stout and baby whiskies.

"Well?"

"The sky is below on the ground," says Liam, as he shakes the beads of rain from his brolly.

"How was the match?"

He stands the brolly in the snook.

"Christ, Seanie boy, they were fucken dire, were ya listening to it?"

"No, the reception was cat so I had to turn it off."

"Lost by four, couldn't put anything over the bar."

"Bollocks anyways."

"I-tell-ya, if al Qaeda were from Mayo, those poor souls beyond in the Twin Towers would've been sound."

Liam lifts the front legs of a stool over the low brass rail and takes a seat at the bar.

"Powers, Liam?"

"Please."

I pour the whiskey and leave it before him.

"Thank you."

In comes Mickey Boyle. He more or less lives in here so he does, the type of fella who stays in the pub till injury time.

"Howya, Mickey?" asks Liam.

"Ya know yourself, only middling," says Mickey.

"I do indeed."

"Jays, they were bad today,"

"They were, it's the forwards, we don't have the forwards, they haven't that killer eye on them."

"That's it, they beat themselves today, I don't know in the fuck."

I leave Mickey's pint of Guinness before him, he lets it settle as he settles in the corner of the bar. He always goes to the corner so people won't be bumping into him. Mickey usually drinks a pint in four gulpings, he takes the first...

"Another pint over the bar," says Mickey, he pretends to kick a football. "Gaahh."

"I finished Portrait of the Artist, by the way."

"What do ya make of it?" says Liam.

"Class."

"It's a good wan alright."

"Young Stephen's off into exile, hah."

"Sure Joyce could never have shtayed in Ireland, he knew it too, that's why he shtayed well clear."

"Ya think so?"

"He would've had a lot of enemies. A hard core sceptic like himself wouldn't have gone down well in a lot of people's camps."

"I suppose it must have been hard writing about Ireland and been away from it."

"Yeah, shtill, there were plenty of boyos knocking about the place. Sure Samuel Beckett was his assistant while he was working on Finnegans Wake."

"I have to read Beckett yet."

"Ya'll get more kicks than pricks without a doubt."

"Have you read Ulysses?"

"Do you know something, I could never get through it."

"Really?"

"Arra, I got a bit into it but I put it down. It's a hard oul read so it is. I prefer Dubliners or Portrait."

"Is that right? Well Portrait is a great one anyways."

"Tis."

Mickey diminishes the pint to half, he licks the tash of head from his top lip.

"Oh, I have a good video for you."

"Do ya? What is it?"

"It's called The Matrix, it came out a few years ago, a mind bender altogether. You'll see shades of Huxley and Orwell."

"Remind me about it again and I might drop down to Xtra-vision some evening during the week."

Here comes the men, John-Joe Moran, originally from Achill Island, followed by his cronies, Frank Gahan and Noel Jennings, both

139

Ballybar men, born, bred and buttered.

"Oh bejeeze, the men have landed," says Liam.

I throw on the pints for them while they go on about the Mayo match. When the three glasses are three quarters of the way there, I rest them on the bar to allow the light-brown suspension to settle somewhat.

"Till they get that killer instinct they'll carry on the way they're going," says John-Joe.

Sometimes I think the boys like losing more than winning. When they lose it's clear enough cut. When they win all they go on about is how they're going to bottle it in the next game. I top off the pints and hand them out to the men.

"Here ye go, lads."

"Don't be afraid to charge them, Seanie. That euro conversion is codology altogether," says Liam.

"Do ya hear himself?" says Frank. "William Thompson, ladies and gents, he pinches every penny till it fecken squeals."

Frank and Noel spark up some Majors. Mickey unveils a little pipe and a tobacco pouch, he starts prepping the pipe for puffing. I'm not too fond of the stench of cigarettes, but there's something nice about the oul dudeen so there is.

"I heard someone say the other day they're talking about banning the fags altogether," says John-Joe.

"T'will never happen," says Noel.

"It wouldn't surprise me with the goin-on-of-them. If they don't ban them, they'll hike up the tax so no one can afford them like they're doing with the drink," says Frank.

"They'll be telling us what hand to wipe our arses with next," says Liam.

"Arra, they're wicked bad for ya anyways. Red rotten oul things. Tis better off without them carcinogenics ye are," says John-Joe.

Mickey fiddles with his pipe in the corner.

"Sure everything gives ya cancer these days," says Noel.

"My grandfather lived to be ninety two and he shmoked and drank every day. Not only that, he ate red meat for breakfast, lunch and tae. And didn't he have fry-ups galore, rashers, sausages, pudding, black and white, eggs, the whole shebang, and he was as fit as a fiddle," says Frank.

"But he was bad in the walk towards the end," says John-Joe.

"Ah, he was ya, sure he was working on the farm all his life, the legs were bound to renege on him sooner or later," says Frank.

"He had gout as well, didn't he?" Noel asks.

"He was never right after the bastarden gout," says Frank.

"He could drink though," says Liam.

"Oh, he could drink with the best of them. Sure that's what kept him tipping away for so long, he loved the oul Paddy. But do ya know something, he would give up the drink every November. He reckoned that the liver could heal itself if ya gave it half a chance at all at all," says Frank.

"Like a lizard's tail," says Liam.

"Never trust a man that doesn't drink," says Noel.

"My uncle used to do that as well for Lent, he couldn't get on the wagon during the winter months. 'The blackness, oh sweet suffering Jesus, the blackness,' he used to say," says John-Joe.

"I don't blame him, sure, dark at four, ya need something to take the edge off it," says Liam.

"Give me a bag of Tayto there, Seaneen, will ya?" Frank asks.

I throw him a bag of cheese and onion Tayto. Those and the Bacon Bites sell the best out of the bunch.

"Ga-man yourself," says Frank.

"Ah, ya need a bit of comfort alright," says Noel.

"I reckon the fags are good for ya, whenever I get a bad oul dose or anything I go down and get a box of twenty Major and shmoke it out of me," says Frank, munching on the cheese and onion crisps.

"God be with the days ya had a biteen of freedom, I remember when ya could drink and drive," says John-Joe.

"John-Joe, you could never drink and drive, they just weren't pulling as much," says Noel.

"Shtill, now they're gone mad pulling altogether. Ya can't even go in for a jar without the fear of getting bagged," says John-Joe.

141

The three buckos take a gulp of their drink.

"Sure nobody gives a shite about freedom these days. They're just out for themselves, that's all they care about," says Liam.

"You're dead right, it has the place ruined so it has. The community is gone," says Noel.

"It'll lead to disaster, wait an-ye'll-see, they'll be bunched yet," says Frank.

"That shower behind in Dublin will have a lot to answer for. They'd fuck up a mug-a-tae so they would," says Liam.

Frank washes down the crisps with a swig of stout.

"Ah, ya had some good people back in the oul days," says John-Joe.

"Whom?" asks Liam.

"De Valera was good," says John-Joe.

"Oh Chrisht, here we go," says Frank.

"I feel sorry for the way they showed him in that film so I do," says John-Joe.

"Tis the poor cratures up the North I feel sorry for with the likes of Eamon de Valera selling them out," says Liam.

"Ah, he did not," says John-Joe.

Mickey turns to his right a bit and takes a few puffs of his pipe, he's keeping the gob shut on this one.

"Didn't Chamberlain and Churchill offer him the North back in World War II, if he let them use the ports. He didn't want the North because it's full of Prods. Some patriot that buck was," says Liam.

"But Liam, the country was in an awful state at the time," says Noel.

"Does that mean he's entitled to sell the people out? Keep in mind this is the fellow who went to the German embassy to give his condolences when the fecken Fuhrer heiled for the final time. And weren't the Germans blitzing the North, it's some gall they have to call that bucko patriotic. Psychopathic tis more like it," says Liam.

"It's easy to say them things now," says Frank.

"Gobshites like Eamon de Valera make me ashamed to be called Irish in the same breath, I'm not codding ya," says Liam.

142

"Ah, he did a lot of good too," says John-Joe.

"Hitler did plenty a good things, didn't he help build the Autobahn and the Volkswagen. You're supposed to do good things. People like him just want to run the show, same as the crowd in Rome," says Liam.

"Go-way with ya," says Noel.

"Who supported fascism more than the shaggin Vatican? If there's wan good thing going on these days tis that the fecken church is losing power, people are copping on to their rackets," says Liam.

"Ah, that's not fair," says Noel.

"Weren't the Vatican and Mussolini great oul pals and look at Franco in Spain. They were egging him on from the beginning. Tisn't a wonder that Dev and the church were thick as thieves," says Liam.

"If it's not the crows it's the jackdaws," says Frank.

"But they themselves didn't do anything," says John-Joe.

"Tis a pity they didn't do anything, weren't half the Nazis Catholics? They could've said shtall the fecken ball on the final solution," says Liam.

"Liam, since you know everything, why don't ya run for the Dáil," says Noel.

"Would ya go-way, I wouldn't lower myself to their level. They're nothing but a shower of gangshters," says Liam.

"Well, who do you want in charge? Miriam Flannery?" asks Noel.

"I can't stand any of them Flannerys, like father like daughter," says Liam.

"It's not what ya know, it's who your father knows," says Mickey, rejoining the conversation.

"In fairness, P Flannery did a lot of good too, he was the only one looking out for the Wesht, it's better than nothing," says John-Joe.

"True enough. But he made an awful show of himself when he was on the Late Late," says Noel.

"The most conniving of the lot of them was Haughey," says Frank.

"Charlie's arse must have Charvet nickers, 'there'll be no Dunnes in my house while I'm the Taoiseach,'" says Liam. "'Except maybe Ben Dunne.'"

143

"If he's paying that is," says Frank.

"Another Ansbacher man," says Noel.

"He got Dunne alright," says John-Joe.

"Dunce Stores is it?" says Liam.

"It's great work if you can get it till the Moriarty Tribunal come marching in," says Frank.

"Shtill, didn't he get the best of everything while half the country hadn't a penny to their names," says Mickey.

"A mé féiner of the highest order," says Liam.

"So no to Fianna Fáil?" asks Frank.

"Take away that fada and it'll tell ya what they'll do in office," says Liam.

"What do ya make of the Sinn Féiners?" asks Noel.

"We'll see if they decommission or not," says Liam.

"I tell ya, Enda Kenny is all talk altogether," says Frank.

"A good Fine Gael man always rises again, sure wasn't Lazarus a Fine Gael man," says John-Joe.

"You'd think they'd be shagged with all the foot and mouth. Whoa hoa," says Noel.

"Did ya see the second referendum on Nice is on in October?" says Frank.

"Half the people don't even know what the Treaty's about, they're too busy watching Big Brother and the likes," says Liam.

"Reality TV, Chrisht above, isn't life real enough," says Noel.

"Reality TV is to reality as prostitution is to love-making," says Liam.

"And there's a price to be paid for both," says Mickey.

"Do ya think someone in 1920 wouldn't have known that Treaty like the back of their hand? Backwards the people are going," says Liam.

"You're right, they take it all for granted so they do," says Mickey.

"Did ye hear the craic with this Corrib gas line?" Noel says.

"The latest shenanigans," says Liam.

"Ah, c'mon, sure t'will create a load of jobs above in Rossport," says Frank.

"But they're forcing that pipeline down the people's throats, going across their land. It's a feckin travesty so it is," says Liam.

"He's right, I'd say Michael Davitt is rolling over in his grave with this fuckacting," says Mickey.

--He'd hardly be clapping.

"The High Court just overturned a challenge to halt that pipeline," says Noel.

"It's dangerous as fuck, they even brought in some professor from Trinity to take a look at the scheme and he said it was awful bad so he did," says Mickey.

"The only ones entitled to the gas is the people. Not Shell fucking Oil. Even if they are employing people, they're only paying them pittance compared to what they're going to make. The people should have the right to decide what happens on their own land," says Liam.

"What if they want the gas?" says Frank.

"That's sound, then nationalise it and let the people reap the fruits of their land and labour," says Liam.

"With the shower of fools behind in Dublin taking brown envelopes from the likes of Shell Oil, that won't happen," says Mickey.

"Sure Shell can just buy planning permission if they want. Make a few donations and a side of bacon here and there. There'll be murder over this yet. The people won't stand for it, wait an-ye'll-see," says Liam.

"True enough," says John-Joe.

"Ya know what'll happen then, they'll send the Guards down to keep the farmers in line. 'That'll soften their cough' says Shell," says Liam.

"They'd never do that," says Noel.

"Why wouldn't they?" says Liam.

"Arra..." says John-Joe.

"Fucken Guards," says Mickey.

"The Guards are just doing their jobs, if they didn't do it they might get let go. What do you expect?" says Liam.

"Ya never know, there might be a blue flu instead, ha, ha," says Frank.

"Yeah, but ya need someone to keep law and order, otherwise everyone would go daft," says Noel.

"Maybe, but where do ya draw the line? I mean, I should be allowed to do what I want so long as I'm hurting no other whore but meself," says Liam.

"At the same time, it's hard to gauge what hurting someone else is, you mightn't hurt them physically, but ya could hurt them in other ways," says John-Joe.

"You hurt me half the time by just looking at me ha, ha," says Liam.

"Whoa-ho ya bollocks ya," says John-Joe.

"But sure can't I close me eyes if I can't stand the sight of ya," says Liam.

"Ya can alright, bejeeze, and can't I give ya a good jab to the jaw if ya won't stop talking skitter," says John-Joe.

"Ya don't need Garda Síochána for that," says Mickey.

"You don't, indeed," says Frank.

"Seriously though, what's the difference between Shell Oil or the Brits taking all the good out of the place? Or what's the difference between orders coming from London or Dublin?" says Liam.

"There's not an awful difference I suppose," says John-Joe.

"We hardly ever need that shower in Dublin telling us what to do. Tis the likes of Shell Oil who need the crew in Dublin, not us," says Liam.

"True enough," says Mickey.

Christ above, Liam is mad late this morning. It's almost ten. He must have gone on an awful session last night altogether, I've to go up now to his gafe on Staball Hill ringing his doorbell like an eejit to wake him up. I'd say he's midered within in the cot. Liam's gafe is a nice two storey about half-way up the hill. Those older houses are funny, the ceilings are always fierce low.

What the fuck is this?

A note:

Please don't go inside just call the Guards.

146

What the fuck is this about? The front door is off the latch. I poke my head inside to see the craic.

"Liam, you here? It's Seanie."

No reply. I wander into the kitchen and sitting room, there's nobody. I better check the bedroom. I open the door at the landing and ascend the stairs. Liam's bedroom is on the left at the top. The door is closed. Should I go in? Or call the Guards? Fuck it. Go. I open the door slowly.

"Liam?"

The drapes are drawn. The room is dark. I hit the light switch just inside the door. In the bed, under the duvet, Liam faces the wall. Oh, Christ above!

"Liam?"

Nudge him. Try and wake him. Nothing. Touch his face. Freezing cold. No. Turn him towards me. He's limp.

"Liam?"

Shake him. He's dead. Going to spew. Turn. Throw up breakfast. Can't be real. Blood leaves head. Face gets cold. Might faint. My God. He's dead. Face is so cold. He's dead. There's no pulse. No nothing. He's dead. Leg it downstairs. Where's phone? Fuck. Where is it? Look in the sitting room. No sign. Fuck. Beside the door. Beside the door. On a little stand beside the door it is. Dial 999...

"Hello, Emergency Services."

"I need an ambulance!"

The ambulance came. Didn't matter though. The Guards came soon after them. They had a sit down with me and took a statement. I told them everything. It looked like him but not. They took the bottle of whiskey and the empty pill bottle. The toxicology report will take a few weeks, I think it's safe to say it wasn't accidental, his family asked me not to mention anything about the pills or whiskey bottle. They want to save face so they can have a Mass for him and all that. They'll probably just say it was the heart or something. There'll be conspiracy theories abound around the town. They'll all be saying,

--He was never right after that.

They're the same people who'd tell you to take two extra pain killers,

--To be safe.

Mugs of tea and custard creams will be drank and munched over this.

--After the crash he was never the same.

They'll say the same thing about me in a few years.

--He was never right after he found Thompson. He was fierce shook looking.

Everyone will be trying to connect themselves to Liam in some way.

--He was mine.

--He was one of us.

--Didn't I see him the other day, not a bother on him.

--We were great oul pals. Didn't I sit beside him in national school, forty years ago.

Then there's always that older woman who makes out that he was a life changing chap. The good deed story.

--Wasn't I stranded in Tesco with no change for the car-park. I was finished, and do you know who came to the rescue? Liam Thompson.

--He was a saint I tell ya. A saint.

They'll all forget him just as quick though.

He's in Kilcoyne's Funeral Home down the hill on Thomas Street only a few hundred yards from the gafe. Thomas Street has changed, I remember the cattle mart on a Saturday morning beside Michael Curtin's Pub. There's none of that these days. No money in farming. There used to be a little shop beside Martin Lynch Motors where my Mam would take me sometimes to get a bottleen of Club Orange after play-school in the Townhall. Hughes' I think. There's a hostel in its stead now. There should be a big crowd at the funeral, there always is when someone like a publican passes. They'll go in to see him, sign the book, shake hands with the bereaved, gawk at his lifeless formaldehyde filled corpse, bless themselves and pretend to pray.

--He looks very peaceful, doesn't he?

Then when they get out to the car-park,

--You'd hardly recognise him, he's so different.

Mam is worried sick about me. She gave me the week off school and everything.

--It's a hard thing finding someone you know.

--I know.

--It's not good to bottle these things up.

--I'm not. I told you he ODed, they told me not to talk about it so I won't.

--You don't know he ODed.

--Mam, I told you the state of his room when I went in there.

--We'll see.

--And the note... It's not the first time someone topped themselves in this town.

--It's a hard thing so it is.

--And it'll go on happening because everyone's afraid to open their mouths about it.

--It's awful for the families. There's nothing they can do.

--I know.

--If you need anything you'll tell me, won't ya?

--I will.

Mam is very shaken. She's right about it being awful for the families. At least Liam's parents are dead and buried, they didn't have to see this. I don't know why he did it though. I would never do it. For the sake of Mam alone I wouldn't do it. It would destroy her, that's the worst thing that could happen to a parent. There's lots of suicides here. I don't know how many people mysteriously fall into the lake. We all know you can't really fall in the lake. Drowning must be a guaranteed way to go. You don't have to do anything, just let the water take you over and fill your lungs till you choke away to unconsciousness. That's probably why the Town Council filled in the outdoor pool by the hoggies at Marian Row, to stop lads drowning themselves. They even filled in the fountain up the Square. It was a lovely looking little fountain with a fine statue of Manannán mac Lir and wasn't it donated by Ernie O'Malley and all. It would be hard to drown yourself with the puny amount of water in it, not to mention the mythical mariner and Enbhar soaring over it. Everyone is embarrassed by suicide. They don't want to draw attention to it.

--Bury it, bury it, bury it.

A mortal sin. It's usually men who do it. I wonder why men are more inclined than women? Why didn't he ask for help? Did he really think he was better off dead?

Chapter 13

iam's personal debt caused his personal death. The fucking Bank of Ireland kept lending him money even though he was gambling like fuck. What type of sick bastards keep giving money to an ill man? They knew well he had a gambling problem and took advantage until he was fucking skinned. There are sharks who wouldn't do what them cunts did to him. He had more or less lost everything to the BoI, the house, the pub, fucking everything. The bar's boarded up with a big fuck-off For Sale sign nailed to the front door. They'll probably turn it into a fast-food spot or some other piece of shite place. How do them pricks sleep at night? They're worse than any fucking gangster or criminal or swindler, and they have the law on their side. Of course no one says boo about the bank,

--Ah, sure ya know, poor oul Liam liked to roll the dice.

Why the fuck were they letting him roll the dice with money he didn't have? The poor fucker was sick in the head when it came to the gambling. He needed help. He didn't need more fucking debt on top of the fact that the pub hadn't been doing great for a while with the big super pubs and the fucking ridiculous pub opening hours. He should be allowed to keep his pub open or closed as long as he wants without the Guards bursting in and fining him. I don't blame Liam. He had it hard enough, I suppose he was tired of this shite life. I don't fault him a bit. The poor buck had his wife and daughter taken from him, it's surprising he didn't go demented ages ago. And the gambling was probably the only thing he got any joy out of at all at all. He should've known better than to trust a bank, he wasn't right in the head so he wasn't. He needed help. Nobody had a notion how far in the hole he actually was. We all knew he liked to bet, but not everything he had built. The only fuckers who knew were the bank and they kept giving and giving till he ruined himself, till he'd lost everything. Something has to be done. I'm sure he's not the only one the banks are fucking up the hole. How many more people will top themselves because of them cunting banks? They should all be destroyed, every last one of them, and I'm going to start right here. I'm going to scorch the fucking earth they're built on.

I have my balaclava so their cameras won't recognise my mug. I have two whiskey bottles stuffed with paraffin soaked rags and filled with petrol. I have all my homework done on the psychopathic fucking bank. Around the back of the building the windows have small cages covering them, all except for two on the second floor. I stalk, stealthy as could be, through the Square and hop down from the wall beside the Boxing Club. It's pitch dark, not a light in sight. The ground is fierce humpy. I tread carefully so I don't trip up with the petrol in my bag. Right, here we are, time to see if these windows will smash or not, there's plenty of rocks back here, big and small, but not much else. Let's give it a lash.

BANG...

Fuck. That was loud. I can tell by the echoie clack that it's a single pane window though. Let me give it another go, I'll peg the rock harder this time round.

SMASH...

Bingo. The rock goes straight though the centre and the weakened window collapses in on itself. I better be quick. The bank alarm dingalingalings like mad, like the old school bell.

--This is for you, Liam.

A couple of sparks with the lighter and the first rag's lit. I fling the flaming bottle in the window, the fire making its way down the fuse as it flies. I hear the bottle break inside. Perfect. Now for number two. Same again, it catches aflame with relative ease. I fire the final bomb inside the bank. The faint whish of flames is audible. I zip up my bag and peer upwards, the orange-yellow light from the fire dances and raves near the window sill. Oh, it won't be long till the whole fucking thing's ablaze. The bell is ringing like fuck. I have my bike stashed for a quick get-away. The Garda Station is right across the Square from me, the fools will probably take ages. I bet the Fire Brigade haven't even been called yet. I peddle as fast as fuck and take a quick look back to see what's flaming. Oh Jesus, the whole second floor's already lit up like a Christmas tree. Lovely hurling. I'm going to cycle the scenic route home, stay off the main roads and I'll be sound as a bell. I'll sneak back into the house, hopefully without Mam hearing me, sure I'm a virtual master at that. The cat burglar doesn't have a peg on me.

We have a free class today, Mr. Coffey is out for the week with the flu.

--Nous ne parlerons pas français cette semaine.

I like free classes, you can usually chit-chat away as long as you're not too loud and even though we don't do any work, the time seems to move faster. Today Mr. Finney is watching the class. He's all limbs, a slender man with a short torso and legs that go on for days.

"Who's out today?"

"Ned Burke has glandular fever. He's going to be out for the next while," says Tony Collins.

--I didn't know you could get that from kissing arses.

"Anyone else?" Finney asks.

Finney's a character, he even has his own catch phrase.

--Christ, man!

He's a great story teller, we used to have him in second year for Geography. Instead of using the book he would go on about all sorts of things, he'd always manage to link it into some story about the time when he lived in Boston, or when he saw some fella getting shot for robbing hub caps off a car. It's a good way to learn something, the story helps you remember the topics. Finney's always on about crows and jackdaws. It's gas when he explains the differences between the two, he beats his long arms like a bird's wings and does his impression of the different calls that crows and jackdaws make. When people laugh he always says,

--Christ, man! I should be laughing at ye for not knowing the difference between a crow and a jackdaw.

People try to wind him up by saying things like,

--There's an animal that's a cross between a fox and a dog, they call it a dox.

--Amen't I telling ya, that's impossible.

153

--Sir, I swear to God, my brother seen it.

They'll keep him going for half the class while he explains that foxes and dogs are too distantly related to cross breed.

I wonder if Jimmy Cohen is Jewish? Jewish fellas in the films or on telly are nearly always called Cohen. Cohen must be like the Jewish Murphy. Cohen's law. Another thing about Jimmy is that he's big into science, half the scientists I can think of have Jewish sounding surnames. Perhaps he's undercover, in hiding, exiled from Israel. Look at him there, sallow enough, he doesn't look that Irish so he doesn't. Still, it's hard to say what Irish looks like. His dad is from Cork and there were a couple of Jews down that neck of the woods some years back, they even have a synagogue down there. I bet the Cohens don't go over to Ballyhaunis, not with the mosque and all the Muslims over there, packed with them so it is.

--Tell the Sunni to go and have a good hard Shiite for themselves.

Although, the name Cohen is a lot like Cohan, it's probable they just misspelled the name somewhere along the way. Or possibly, the Cohen's are undercover. That's it. They're top secret agents from Israel keeping tabs on the crew in Ballyhaunis. If they are, they've fooled everyone, except for yours truly that is. No undercover Jews will cod me.

--In the Plain of the Yews there lives some Jews.

They're good, but they ain't that good. I'm on to you Jimmy, or whatever the Hebrew equivalent is of James. There's no flies on oul Seanie Carolan, and if there are they're paying rent.

"Jimmy, were ya watching BBC 2 last night? There was a good programme on with Stephen Hawking in it."

"Hawking's never off the air is he?"

"Someone has to sell Specsavers."

"My. Eyesight. Means. A. Lot. To. Me."

"Ha, ha, ha."

"I think it might be a repeat, was it the Theory Of Everything one?"

"That's the one. It was good, very interesting. They were on about some serious stuff."

"They're crazy ideas when you think about them."

"That experiment with the electrons through the slit, and it goes through both slits and none of them is a mad one."

"If you like that, you should read Hawking's book, it does a good enough job of explaining all that kind of craic."

"I might do. Jesus, I tell ya, Hawking is some fella isn't he?"

"His mind is perfect but his body is useless. You'd wonder how he does it. He's a good age too, in his sixties so he is."

"I suppose it must help him in some ways, it's not like he's out getting hammered, starting fights outside Abra. He must spend more time thinking about physics than anyone."

"I'd say so. He was doing a thing before about what created the universe and it's really cool, he was saying that it could have created itself, something like it has boundless potential within Einstein's theory and the quantum one."

"That's the theory for the small is it?"

"Yeah, quantum is for really, really small things like subatomic particles. Anyways, he thinks that the universe might have self-created itself and that there could be an infinite number of universes."

"That's mad altogether."

If Durkan isn't gay, the Pope isn't Polish. He has to be gay. He's just hiding like Cohen. Every word out of Durkan's gob sounds queer, in the gay way. The way he walks is very gay, the way he looks at things with that gay,

--Hmmmm.

I was on the computer the other day and I came across gay elephants, they give each other trunk jobs all the time. Who'd have thought? You do see gay dogs around though. I suppose gayness must occur naturally if it's happening in the animal kingdom with such frequency. There must be a gay gene, it's probably like red hair, it can skip a generation or two. Perhaps both parents have to carry the gay gene in order to have gay children. That makes sense. But how would gayness have evolved? How would it be selected? What if

155

there weren't enough of one sex? Or was it a bi-product of something else? It could be like those genes that get switched on and switched off. Either way, Durkan must be gay. Has he ever shifted a woman? Nope. Oh, stall the ball, there was that one I saw him with in the Townhall ages ago. The case could be made though that she was a fairly manish looking bird. There's a lot of gays out and about these days, apparently a lot of men from all over Connaught go down the lake looking for a bit of cock. I'm told they come from as far as Leitrim. They stand around and if they want to be picked up they light up their lighters, then head to the bushes for a session of arse banditry. There's a rumour that some wife was suspicious of her husband and went fucking down and caught the husband at it hammer and tongs. Which would be worse? For her to catch him with a woman, or a fella? She probably asked him,

--Have you ever cheated on me with another woman?

--Cross my heart and hope to die, I have never touched another woman since I met you.

He'd be telling the truth too.

--But darling, I've fucked more Irish fellas than the Black and Tans.

--Come out ye Black and Tans so I can ride ye like a man.

She might think she turned him to the other side. It must be hard on her, she just thought he had a good fashion sense and liked the GAA for the competition instead of watching the men in short shorts. All the same, isn't he as well off to do what he loves instead of putting on a charade his whole life.

"Hey, Durks, did ya hear about Gort?"

"Gort, in Galway?"

"Yeah, half the population are Brazilian."

"No way."

"Swear to God, it was in the Times yesterday. I remember once I was coming down from Galway and we were going through Gort and wasn't there a fecking big Brazilian flag hanging outside a pub."

"Crazy."

"They have a Samba festival and a Carnival, I think they even have Mass in Portuguese."

"What the hell would bring someone from mild sunny Brazil to the miserable West of Ireland?"

"Probably the same as the Polish. Jobs."

"Yeah."

Come to think of it, there's some amount of Polish in Ballybar these days. There must be feck all employment if they're coming over here in droves. The poor bastards probably got an awful doing from the Soviets and their red tyranny. The Polish women are easy on the eyes. They look after themselves and don't fire on the weight as soon as they turn twenty-one like Irish women. They're a bit cold though, they must be north or south Poles. Not that Irish girls are any warmer. If the Polish birds are cold, then the Irish girls are mouldy. Sure the dampness of Mayo is the perfect condition for mould to flourish. The Polish girls know how to clean a house, they Polish everything. My knob could do with a Polishing. Romance isn't high on the agenda for either, you need a romantic girl if you want romance: French, Italian, Spanish. French women are wild, anything goes when the pookies come over on exchange. What about the Romanians? They're romantic, but don't seem to be as romantic as the others. Still, they're often out on a Friday night trying to sell roses to lushed people. Predatory romance. Dracula was Romanian, I think, and he was a romantic sort of chap, always took the girls out for a bite. To be fair to the cailíni there are some nice Irish girls. The girls up the North are fairly hot, they're fiery women and seem better looking too. It must be the more diverse gene pool up there, the Protestant blood mixing with the Catholics over the centuries. Mam doesn't like the Northern crew though,

--They have a chip on their shoulder so they do, be careful of that shower up the North.

In fairness, there are some nice girls in Mayo. They're few and far between, but sure doesn't that make them all the more special? Indeed and it does like a good looking redhead, a diamond in the rouge. If you find a good one hold on for dear life. They're as rare as hens' teeth.

"Mc'Hugh, what do ya make of Asian women?"

--Rice, Paddy?

--Noodles, please.

"Intrigued, man. Intrigued."

"Do tell, what intrigues you so?"

"I heard before that Asian women's fannies are different than other women's."

"How?"

"They say that the slit goes across instead of straight up, so if they were sliding down a banister their fanny would go bubabubabubabuba,"

Mc'Hugh with his right index finger batters his lips up and down repeatedly like a Looney Toons cartoon.

"No way."

"I'm telling ya, them Orientals are a different pedigree altogether."

"They are not. What about Black women? Do you think they're different?"

"I'm not qualified to say, but I'll say this. That Halle Berry is unreal, man."

"No argument there, did you see her in Swordfish?"

"Jabs out, savage."

"If you met her what would be the chat-up line?"

"I'd say to her... Do you know I drank 14 pints in 2 hours?"

"She'd buckle with that one."

"Gets them every time down at Frank Hogan's single night in Castlevary."

"I bet it does."

"Seen a great film last weekend called Last Tango in Paris."

"Haven't heard of it."

"That lad, Marlon Brando's in it. My brother has the French orals coming up so he got a rake of French films to keep the lug sharp for the exam. And I tell ya, it's pure filth."

"Euro Trash bad?"

"Worse."

"Brilliant, I'll check it out so."

"There's a bit in it where he gets your wan to shove her fingers up

158

his hole."

"Oh Jesus, a bit like the time O'Malley went for the barracuda."

"There's some serious stuff in it, the French wan in it is nuts. I dedicated a nice posh wank to her the other day."

"What the fuck is a posh wank?"

"It's when you have a wank with a johnny on."

"Nice one, but I thought you said you didn't like rubbers."

"Not with a woman, they take away all the feeling."

"So you'd rather get some young one up the pole instead?"

"I'd pull out before I blew the load."

"What if you were too late?"

"We'd be off to London then, I suppose."

"That'd be harsh."

"Arra, it'd be grand, we'd make a weekend of it."

"Still, it's bad oul form."

"I was watching Who Wants To Be A Millionaire last night and God help me, your wan was as thick."

"Why? What didn't she get?"

"She didn't know who the manager of Man United is."

"Christ above."

"I don't know how they ever ran the world."

"I bet she'd know when they won the World Cup."

"They need to shut up about that, there's a tribute programme on about it every other week. It'd be like us harping on about Sam Maguire '51."

"Sure, we're as bad as them."

"How?"

"On about 1916 and the Fenians, and all that craic."

"What's wrong with that?"

"People taking pride in things they had nothing to do with."

"Nothing wrong with a bit of pride in where you come from."

"I bet if there was shit going on today half them would be at home hiding."

"I wouldn't."

"It's easy to say that. It's another thing doing it, and besides, you

159

shouldn't be taking pride in other people's achievements. If they raped and pillaged the place you wouldn't take pride in it. In for a penny in for a pound."

They're mad for building things these days, yet loads of spots around the town never get used at all at all. The army barracks never seems to be open for anything and it's a fine size of a building. Likewise with the Protestant church beside the Square. I don't know why they don't do something with these places, they should turn the church into a big nightclub, or a community centre, same with the barracks. It's a shame to put those places to waste.

"Who's your fucking skag daddy, boy?"

Here's an eejet I wish was put to waste.

"Giddy up my wee donkey."

Every stupid word out of Skeff Skeffington's gob is noise pollution that tempts me to cut my lugs off and put them in the post.

"I was fucken yoked out of it, mon, I dropped two speckled mitzis outside Super Mac's then went bertie above in the TF. They were animal, hey."

Look at the eejets listening to the wanker, they actually believe him.

"I was coming up like a cunt and didn't the shades walk by all wirey like."

He thinks he's the man doing laps around town in his Honda Civic done up to look like a shopping trolly. I can't stand wannabe scangers. It's a stupid subculture so they can feel like hard men because they're too insecure to act like themselves. If Skeff was from a poor family or a bad neighbourhood I might be able to understand. He's not. His oul fella is an accountant and they live out the Mac Tíre Road in a lovely house. His brothers and sisters aren't like him at all at all. He's from a well-to-do family yet he insists on acting like a fucken sham. That's all it is. Acting. I know rakes of lads who go out every weekend doing E and they've never once seen him do anything except sniff some poppers. He just looks around the place wide-eyed with his jaw jutted talking about how he's,

--Mad out of it, mon.

Other times he's on about scavenging the golf links out in Moneen for Magic Mushrooms.

--Shrooming, mon.

He's fucken full of it. Now he's here telling everyone how great it is to go buzzing, like he's Raoul fucking Duke himself.

"Skeff, you're full of shite."

"Wow, mon. Carolan, why ya being a wirey feen?"

"Because I heard ya didn't even get in to the TF last Friday."

"Yeah, I was riding your oul lady, ha, ha, ha."

"You have one chance to take that back or God help me, ya better be under the bridge come four o'clock."

"Bring it on, mon."

"I'm not having a laugh."

"Fuck you."

"I'm warning ya."

"Hey, you're waiting for a baiting, Carolan, hey."

He checks around the room for support, sneering.

"Be under that bridge, Skeff, I'm telling ya."

"I'm telling you, mon, you better not be there, cause I'm gonna biff the neuk off ya."

"See you at four."

The arch of the bridge is within my sights. I'm looking forward to cracking this bollocks' head open. Skeff's going to give it waskey in this fight because his rep is on the line. If you're going to walk around acting like a hard man you better be able to back it up. I've got nothing to lose. Even if I fail to win this fight, which won't happen, I'll still have cred because I don't go around rowing with people or pretending to be tough. There's a good crowd already under the bridge waiting for a bit of sport. No ties, no school jumpers and no chicken-shites. Skeff's here, getting warmed up, dancing around the place like a fool. The state of him, he thinks he's fucking Mickey from Snatch. I'm only about an inch taller than Skeff, but I'm twice the width of him. I got a set of weights for my last birthday and like to lift a little, it's good for blowing off steam when you don't have clowns like Skeff to knock the shite out of.

Liam's grave is about seven rows in. He's buried in the same plot as his wife and daughter. It looks well, they have the plot covered in green gravel and his name is freshly engraved into the headstone.
In Loving Memory Of
William Thompson, January 26th 1939 to March 28th 2002
Anne Doyle Wheeler, May 1st 1948 to March 11th 1984
Rosina Doyle Wheeler Thompson, November 4th 1972 to March 12th 1984

--Howya, Liam?
--How's she cutting?
--They've already started to rebuild the Bank of Ireland, it was a waste of time trying to burn it down. If I had been nabbed or connected in any way to that fire I would have been in serious life altering bother. Banks have too much money and power, burning them down does no good. They own the fucking place. They own everyone, people can't do anything without the banks. Beholden so they are. Like you were. You should have seen me after school last week, I beat the fucking unholy shite out of Skeff Skeffington. He put up an alright fight for the first minute, till I got a hold of his skull and caught him with a right loosener to the face. I thought with all the yokes he was dropping that he'd have a stronger jaw. Anyways, in the end it didn't do fuck all good, he still acts bertified, just not around me,
--Deep fried mouse in the house style.
He's one of those ignorant pricks who'll never change, no matter how much of a hiding you give them. The type of person who contributes nothing to the world except fucking tripe... Everything seems like it's an exercise in futility, like pretending you can hear me right now, I'm fairly sure you can't, nor can anyone else for that matter. Once you're tits up that's it. You're rotting away in the ground, done and dusted. The worms and bacteria eat away at you, breaking

162

you down, converting you into something else. Whenever someone dies people say,

--They're in a better place.

Or,

--They're at peace now.

I think there might be some small biteen of truth to statements such as those. What could be more peaceful than an eternity of nothingness? Nothing probably. There would be no pain of any kind in oblivion. As far as I know or anyone else seems to know there wasn't any pain before we existed. Why should there be any after we kick it? All the same it makes you think, why exist at all at all? If there's no grand plan, no design, no be all and end all, why do anything? I don't know. There's billions who never get to exist. There's a lot of people who could have been born that weren't. Are they the lucky ones? Is it better to never be than to be and bear the burden of living? From where they're standing they might think, if they could think, or stand, that we are the lucky ones. At least you and I got the chance to give life a lash.

I'm flicking around and there's nothing on telly as usual. Nothing except fecking ads. Full of ads. There are more ads on telly than actual programming. Sure the programmes are usually pure drivel anyhow. Loads of comedies that aren't comically comical in the slightest. They even tell us when to laugh. Are we that thick that we have to be told when to laugh?

--Ha, ha, ha, he, he, ho, he, ho, ha!

Look at us all, fed on a diet of fast-food, shite telly and fucking Boybands. Jesus, I can't stand Boybands. Most of them don't write the music or the lyrics to their songs. They're glorified karaoke singers. Boyzone only had two bucks who could even sing, for shite's sake, the other three just snapped their fingers and danced. It's all a money racket to get daft people to spend and consume rubbish. Girlbands are the same nonsense. There's a different flavour every month, it's really just the same skitter packaged differently. They're all selling pure mediocrity to the public and we gobble it all up and up and up. Most music and film producers should be put on trial for crimes against humanity. Fuck the lot of it. I don't need it. Any of it. I'm going on a diet, no more dogshit for dinner.

Chapter 14

Your father, who aren't in heaven,
Shallow be thy name,
Thy priesthood cums,
In childrens' bums,
No worth, just like heaven,
Give them this day their daily head,
And forgive them for touching asses,
As you dare not misgive those who trespass against us,
And lead them into temptation,
But deliver them from upheaval,
Ah, Man!

The organised pedophilia congregation is having a sit-down with us today. Father Seamus Ussher, he's the hip trendy priest, I cannot stand the fucking sight of this gobshite. I'm going to go down some Saturday evening to confession when he's in the booth and give him a right shock to system.

--Father?

--Yes, my son?

--I've been wanking again like a mad yoke.

--Oh, good heavens, tell me more.

--I don't like looking up porn on the internet because I'm not sure how to delete the cookies.

--I see.

--Usually I go into the privacy of my own mind, to the wank-bank. Any bit of decent fanny I see trotting about the town or on telly goes straight in the bank for future reference.

--Right.

--But, one day I got bored of the oul wank-bank and I needed something a bit more visually stimulating to get the job done.

--What did you do?

--I used a picture of the only non-related woman in the gafe.

--You didn't.

--I did, Father.

--The Blessed Virgin!

--I gave her a pearl necklace as a present and all.

--Holy Mary Mother of Bog.

That will give new meaning to ejaculations for Father Ussher. The gobshite is late and all, I wonder if he's stuck in limbo? They back peddled on that one fairly lively. Imagine telling a grieving mother her unbaptised child is stuck in some place called limbo. The gall of these sick bastards. Naturally with most things religious, they have no evidence for such crackpot claims. After all the burning at the stakes and inquisitions they needed a make-over, a more affable church, no more strict interpretation of the Bible, they have the people think it's more about,

--What God meant to say.

What a load of shite. Evolution comes around, suddenly the Adam and Eve theory doesn't look so good, now it's all relative, open to interpretation. The more they're shown to be full of shite the more liberal the interpretations become. It's fairly blatant how invented the whole thing is when you look into it, just like any other work of fiction. They interfere in everything. You couldn't even get a johnny in this godforsaken place till a few years ago, never mind a copy of Playboy.

--Fuck Casti Connubii.

That bollocks, de Valera, gave them a special relationship in Bunreacht na hÉireann, we don't even have a secular fucking state. Why should they have any say at all? Why are celibate men telling normal people how to live their lives? If people want to torture themselves by never having a wank, or never trying to pull a woman, or a man, what qualifications do they have to discuss such matters and lobby the government to enforce laws?

In comes the big eejet himself followed by that sycophant, Miss Keogh.

"How is everyone today? You've got awful big since the last time I seen ye. What year are they in now?" asks Father Ussher.

"They're fifth years now, Father."

"Only a year till the Leaving Cert. Ye'll be praying this time next year that's for certain."

"Oh, they will of course."

"But, will they be going to Mass? Who here goes to Mass once a week?"

Almost everyone raises their hand.

"Better than I thought, but I wonder how many of them stand at the side door or outside during Mass, hah?"

"They're all good boys here, Father," says Miss Keogh.

"I don't know, you may as well not even bother to show up if you're standing at that side door."

"I'd say they all sit front and centre, isn't that right?" says Miss Keogh.

A few unenthusiastic "Yes" and "Yeahs," leak out from the lads.

"Well, does anyone have any questions?"

I put my paw up in the air.

"Yes, you there."

"Father, I was just wondering what your thoughts are on the Catholic church's policy of spreading AIDS throughout Africa?"

Everyone in the class tightens up as soon as I open the gob. They know what's coming.

"I don't know what ya mean?"

"The Catholic church helps spread AIDS in Africa, does it not?"

"Well, the church doesn't advocate the spreading of AIDS across Africa. It's very sad though."

"Doesn't the church tell people not to use contraceptives?"

"That doesn't mean it helps to spread AIDS."

"Yes it does. You tell poor impoverished people who don't know any better not to use condoms. So it seems quite obvious to me that the church's backwards policy is helping spread AIDS across the planet. I thought ye were supposed to be pro-life?"

"I can tell you're angry with the church, young man, but I think

167

you're over-simplifying the issues because of your anger."

"It's not complicated. I tend not to like institutions that make it their business to protect child rapists, support fascism, and don't keep their noses out of the affairs of the people."

"Easy, Seanie," says Miss Keogh.

"Ho, ho. It's alright," says Father Ussher. "I can see you've put a bit of thought into this. Everyone should take a lesson from, what's your name again, young man?"

"Seanie Carolan."

"Mr. Carolan here, very good points. All the church does is try to spread the Word of God. That's all. Believe me, it hurts no one more than myself when the Word of God is perverted."

"Right, the Word of God? I would argue now that the Word of God is perverted in and of itself. But where are ya getting the 'Word of God' from? Did He tell you Himself?"

He looks around the room and clears his throat.

"God speaks to each of us in His own way, but the Bible of course is an accurate record of His Word," says Ussher, self-assuredly.

"You do realise that most of the New Testament wasn't written around the time Jesus supposedly existed?"

"Now, that's disputable."

"Not to experts it's not."

"Even if it's off by a year or two it was still inspired by God."

"I could do a finger painting and say it was inspired by God, that doesn't mean it's His finger painting."

"Ah, yes, but ya see that's where faith comes in."

"Fantasy, you mean."

"No, there's a great difference."

"Really, what's the difference?"

"You're a young man, I know, but do you really think there could be a world with such majesty and wonder without God?"

"What's the difference between saying God did it and saying Leprechauns did it?"

A few in the class chuckle.

"There's no proof of either."

168

"The Lord works in mysterious ways."

"Let's try changing the word Lord to, Cabbage. The Cabbage works in mysterious ways. How is that any less valid and daft compared to what you said?"

"That's were faith comes in, young man."

"Yeah, you said that already. Faith? Believing in something without evidence for its existence."

"Not at all, it's obvious when you try and get in touch through prayer, that there's a God and He loves us all very, very much. Oftentimes when people are sick or in trouble they turn to God for guidance and support. They know. They can feel that Our Lord helped them, even if it's only in some small way. Some, very few, have even seen a vision or a miracle."

"That doesn't mean there's a God, it could be a total fluke that they got through the tough time. Has there ever been a scientifically proven miracle or sighting? Of course not. If someone has a vision they should either get the water tested or head up above to St Teresa's and get some psychiatric help. Also, why wouldn't God make it very obvious that he in fact exists?"

They'll be calling me Seán na Sagart when I'm done and dusted.

"He gives us free will."

"Free will? He tells us if we don't believe that we will burn in hell for all eternity. How is that free will? He's coercing our choice from the beginning."

I'm going to leather this fucken Nazi.

"Can you prove that God doesn't exist?"

"Can you prove Leprechauns don't exist? No, because it's impossible to disprove something that doesn't exist."

"Fine. Do you know how everything started?"

"No. But I'm not saying I do. The organised pedophilia congregation does, and they have less evidence that it was God than a cabbage. You can actually see a cabbage at least."

Everyone gapes, slack jawed at my choice of words.

"I'm saying I don't know and that nobody knows, but you're saying you do know."

"How can you know nobody else knows?"

"Because, I'm fairly sure that they don't have any magic fairy powers that I, or any other don't have, and if they do? Then sound as a bell. Let's test them. Scientifically."

"Seanie, a lot of good is done in the name of the church. Just look at Mother Teresa," says Miss Keogh.

"I've looked at that nutjob. She was a sadistic psycho nun, she used to refuse the people dying in her hospital pain medication because she thought pain was Jesus kissing them. Not to mention all the money she took from the Haitian dictator. Mother Teresa is a disgrace. Although her PR people do a savage job of making her look good. Go find out for yourself, it's well documented. You should read her letters where she says she doubts the whole thing."

"Even if there are a few bad eggs, it's not the church's fault if some stray from the righteous path of the Lord."

"First. Let's get this straight. There probably is no Lord. It's a sordid delusion that we're brainwashed with from birth. Second. Yes. It is the church's fault and it's the people who support it too. The church allows them to get into positions of power and for them to abuse those positions."

"I don't know about that now."

I have him on the ropes. He knows I'm too well read to win the argument. Still, it's not like the clown had a coherent case for the existence of the daft delusion anyways. Witless prattle if ever there were.

"If you were part of a social club or a company and thousands upon thousands of its employees were found to be guilty of child rape you would leave or quit it immediately. But when it comes to religion ye do what Jesus said, 'Turn the other cheek!' In fact, has the church not knowingly kept predator priests in their employment and just moved them to another parish to start the fuckacting all over again?"

"Seanie Carolan," says Miss Keogh.

"What?"

"You can't use language like that in class."

"When it comes to a pedophilic apologist, I personally think I'm going fairly easy, don't you?"

"Let me ask you something, do you think everyone in the church is evil?" asks Ussher.

"See, that's too simple a question. Religion is forced down our throats from birth. Passed on from generation to generation, I'm sure you believe everything you're saying. However, what you're saying is a pure and utter lie, poisonous to humanity so it is."

"That's your opinion," says Miss Keogh.

"Is it? Is raping children, supporting fascism, brainwashing people, interfering in the running of countries and people's individual rights bad for humanity?"

The dumb bitch sits there with a frustrated face on her, at least she picked up on the rhetorical intention of the question. Everyone in the class is kind of giggling awkwardly, most of them know my unequivocal stance on the topic. They've heard it out in the yard many a lunch time. Although, I bet they never thought that I would confront a man of the cum cloth to his face.

"Listen, young man, no matter what you say you can't deny that because of the church a lot of good has been done."

"Okay, so we're finished talking about whether or not the magic God is real or not. Because you know that's total idiocy."

I can see he's bulling with that last remark. Keogh sits beside him, silent, like an apple.

"I agree, a lot of good has been done in the name of the church."

"True."

"So let me ask you. Is believing in a made up creator of the universe the only reason good things get done?"

This stumps him totally, he knows if he says yes, everyone will think he has no faith in people at all at all.

"No. Bu, bu, but a lot of good-"

"-Stall for a sec, so good can be done without believing in the church, then why do we need the church? Why not have secular charities to do the good work and stop putting pedophiles in positions so they can abuse children all over the world?"

171

"Seanie, can I speak to you outside for a minute?" asks Miss Keogh.

The whole class goes, "Oooooohhhhhhhhhh."

The taut atmosphere in the classroom is palatable, I step outside with Miss Keogh. She closes the door but doesn't shut it completely.

"Seanie, I'm going to have to ask you not to come back for the rest of the class."

"Why? What's wrong with asking questions?"

"You're monopolising all the class' time."

"With questions about the propaganda he's pushing."

"You have to have respect."

"I was very respectful towards him, believe me, if I wanted to be disrespectful to a priest, I would be."

"Seanie, please, just give it a break till the next class, okay?"

"Jesus Christ. Fine."

"Thank you..."

I traipse off down the hallway with my bag and baggage.

"What's that saying? Those who do not condemn evil, command it to be done. That's it isn't it? That's what goes on around here."

Keogh is ripping altogether, she always scrunches her lips to the right of her mouth when she's cheesed off. She watches me stroll off for a second, paralysed by protocol. I bet she'd love to throw a few jabs at me for showing up her precious priest. Fuck her and that piece of shite in a collar. I make my way to the back stairs near the extension, the steps are cold enough, I rest my arse on them anyways. I'll chill here till the bell goes.

--Oh, so and so has great faith.

Why is that a good thing? Believing in phenomena without sufficient evidence. I'm glad I hushed Ussher, I'm going to keep going after sanctimonious scum like the clergy and those who defend them. People like him, who really believe in such delusions, are away with the fairies. They'll never change their minds. They can't. They've dedicated their entire lives to the babblement, years upon years of fucking babblement. Tis the folks sitting on the fence who are worse again. They say they believe, and obviously there's the occasional cathoholic, but most of them just go with the flow. They don't really believe the bullshit at all at all. If they did, why would they cry when somebody dies? Aren't they supposed to be going to heaven? Actually, why would they do a goddamn fucking thing to prolong earthly existence if they believe they're off to paradise when they go tits up? In their heart of hearts they know it's all made up, but they show up and cooperate with the cunts anyhow.

--I like to pray, it makes me feel better.

It might make someone feel better, though it still doesn't mean it's true.

Or,

--Well, I don't go along with everything they say.

That's like a Nazi saying,

--I don't mind kikes, it's niggers I hate.

If you're part of an organisation that has the track record the church or the Nazis have, it doesn't matter if you believe every little thing. You believe enough to empower them to do what they want. The Catholic church is a totalitarian organisation, orders come from the dictator, or the Pope as he's known, then they're carried out by the minions below. It has retarded the intellectual and moral progress of mankind for two-thousand fucking years! Anyone who supports The Church is a supporter of the tyranny and perversity that goes along with it. They're enemies of freedom and reason. They've tried to dupe us all from the day we were born, tried to make us bow and kowtow to them. It lowers, degrades and demeans everything. Truth is more important than people's feelings. It has to be, or where the fuck are we going to end up? Right where we are now. Enslaved by myths.

There is an Allah, there is a Buddha, there is a Cúchulainn, there is a Dracula, there is an Elf, there is a Fairy, there is a Griffin, there is a Hell, there is an Indiana Jones, there is a Judah, there is a Krishna, there is a Loch Ness Monster, there is a Mohammed, there is a Neo, there is an Osiris, there is a Pooka, there is a Qui-Gon Jinn, there is a Ra, there is a Sauron, there is a Thor, there is a Unicorn, there is a Vishnu, there is a Wizard, there is a Xenu, there is a Yahweh, there is a Zeus...

--My blue bollocks there is!

Chapter 15

<u>Abc</u>
Hey, hey, hey !!! Boo hiss. I gonna b a bit L8 getting ready.

Does !!! Mean shes 3 times as xcited as if she were 2 put in 1? Shes stayin out the wport rd. So its handy cuz were havin din at a nu italian spot in wport. Got the provo recently and im borrowin mams car which is brill. Im v nervous. Ive nev been on a prop date b4. I met her at the end of may. I woz bored at hm so went 4 a walk in2 twn 2 do a lap and c if there woz any craic. Woz walkin up round ell st when I saw her 1st. Shes the prettiest ting I eva did c. Deep brown eyez and a :) that wud lite up the world. I cud tell she wasnt ir by the way she dressed + she woz wearin flip flops on a wet day.

--Excuse me? Twanged Sonny. Hey, if I'm going to the Post Office I walk to the top of this street, right?

--No, actually the Post Office used to be up there, you have to take a right here and walk straight down there towards Tesco.

--Okay, gotcha.

--I'm walking that way, I'll show you sure.

--Great, thanks...

--Where ya from?

--America.

--I'd never have guessed.

--Ha, ha, I'm from Brooklyn, New York.

--I have some cousins in New York.

--Really, where?

--The Bronx. I think it's called Yankers.

--Ha, I think you mean Yonkers.

--One of them, do ya know it?

--Yeah, there's a lot of Irish around that area, you might as well live here if you live in Yonkers.

--Well, they're Irish anyways...

--I'm Sonny by the way.

--Seanie, nice to meet ya.

--You too.

--What are ya up to here?

--Vacation. My dad is from here and I'm staying with my grandparents.

--Cool.

--I'm guessing you're from Ballybar?

--Unfortunately, yeah.

--Why unfortunately?

--It's not exactly a hustling and bustling place like the city that never sleeps.

--No, but I kinda like it. It's pretty, and the fresh air, you don't get that in Brooklyn.

--How long are you visiting for?

--All summer, I go back the last week in August.

--Oh, so you'll have a good while yet.

--Yeah.

--Here we are, An Post.

--Sweet. So do I just get in line?

--What are you posting?

--Just some postcards to my parents and friends at home.

--Do you have them stamped?

--Uh-huh, think so.

--Here, you can just throw them in the post box inside.

--Okay, great.

We step inside and put the pcs in the box. Shes so bful. Evting bout her is pfect.

--So what does somebody do for fun in Ballybar?

--Usually just drink, it rains so much.

--I hear that.

She pushes dark curls away from eyez.

--It would be a great little country if we could only roof it.

--I get ya.

She :)s. Cant let her walk away keep her chattin.

176

--Do you know the town well yet?

Shud I try 4 the #?

--Not really, I've only been here like four days.

She mite lol at me.

--Well, we have a great state of the art bowling alley if that's your type of thing.

Shell lol in the u r weird way.

--Great.

Go 4 it.

--And there's a cinema beside it.

--Is it nearby?

She sounds in2 it just do it man. Shes a yank I bet she gets asked 4 her # all the time.

--Not too far, you could walk it from here.

--Okay, cool.

Shes makin like she gotta go.

--Well, it was nice to meet you, Seanie, right?

--Yeah, very good, Sonny. Usually people never remember names straight away, what's your last name?

--Mc'Cool.

--Really?

She bops her head y.

--That's the coolest name ever.

She lols a luvly lol.

--Mine's Carolan, not as fun as Mc'Cool.

Go 4 it. u will regret it if u dont.

--Seanie Carolan.

He who hesit8s...

--The one and only.

--Okay, Seanie, really nice to meet you, I guess I'll see you around.

--Yeah, yeah, I'm always around the town sure.

--See ya.

--All the best, Sonny Mc'Cool.

Down the st swaggerin she goes wit unshakable confidence and me here like a chicken-sh1t.

177

Thank g I found her. Phew...

She cracks that killer :) again. Shes on2 me. Knows my game. Just play it kool man.

--I don't have any plans, why?

--Oh, ya know, I was just wondering if you'd want to see a film or something?

A film? R u out of your mind? U effing eejet, u r dead in the water.

--Sure. We can do the number thing, I still don't know mine by heart so why don't you give me yours and I'll call your cell so you get mine.

It worked. Thanx b 2 f**k!!!

--Grand.

I take out my 33:10. She unveils an ancient lookin yoke.

--Wow.

--I know. It's a brick, useful for calling people and beating up muggers.

Shes so luvly.

--Where did you get it?

--It's my cousin's old cell from like 2000 or something. So yours is?

--My number is 087-9213-258.

She inputs the # and calls my mob.

Diddle do-do, diddle do-do, diddle do-do-do.

I hit cncl. Missed call comes up.

--Got it.

--Sweet, so have your people call my people.

Look at her wit that little :) she begins 2 strut away.

--I will of course.

1st time I eva asked a girl myself. Wow!

Were here 2 c a gas film altogether. Old school wit will ferrell. Its a rite lol. Shes a huge fan of his since snl. The film has been out here 4 2wks. I seen it last wk wit a few of the lads. Not goin 2 tell her though. Shes so awesome. I just want 2 spend time wit the luvly Sonny McCool. Her hand lies close 2 mine. Shud I go 4 it? I really want 2 hold her hand. Mayb I shudnt. Its a lol movie I shud have asked her 2 a scary 1. Ill grad inch it a little closer 2 hers. She cud be tinking the same. She did give me her # + she took my invite 2 come 2 the flicks. Mayb Sonny tinks im some sort of dreamy po8 from the w-side. Ez stop gettin ahead carolan. Ill move my digits closer.

Its gr8 havin wheels I feel like the man in mams opel astra. Im dressed up 2 the 9s slacks + shirt + pair of black dress shoes eve though they r cuttin the heels off me. Ill giv her a txt 2 let her know im nearly there.
Abc
Howya fixed? Shud b there in 5 mins.

Hope I dont f**k this up. Its been so gud up 2 now. Mayb that means its goin 2 go pshaped. It has been 2 gud 2 b tru. Shes prob well use 2 goin out on dates. Shud I tip the waiter? u r not really suppose 2 tip. Wat if she doesnt know and tinks im a tite ass 4 not tippin. Suppose if it goes well I shud go in 4 the x at the end of the nite. Wat if she doesnt want 2? She doesnt seem like the slutty type of american girl u c in the films. Mayb I shudnt try anytin. That way shell know I respect her or mayb shell tink I dont want 2 x her. G help me I want 2 x her sometin shockin!

"Hey there, Mr. Carolan."

"Buon giorno, principessa, ya all set?"

"Uh-huh, let's do this."

OMG! Looks so hot in her dark red dress + her silver dangly earrins.

"So, you looking forward to our date."

Imagine sayin that 2 an ir girl. G.O.

"Yeah, I can't wait to try the Italian food in Ireland."

"I bet ya it's better than the Irish food in Ireland..."

"What CDs you got?"

She peruses the CD case on the dash.

"A load of different stuff, U2, Oasis, Rory Gallagher, Bob Dylan, The Beatles-"

"-Awesome."

"Who's your fav?"

"I'm a big Paul fan."

"Hold on, you can't like Mc'Cartney more than Lennon?"

"What? Paul is the cute one."

"C'mon, I think Macca is savage, but Lennon is in another league to everyone."

"I don't know, Paul does have some awesome songs too."

"Yeah, but Lennon was a rebel. A Working Class Hero or Imagine, probably the best lyrics ever."

"Ever?"

"Ever."

"You know who I love?"

"Who?"

"The drummer from U2, hottest Irish guy ever."

"Ever?"

"Ever."

"Ha, ha, Larry Mullins Jr. even I can tell he's a good looking fella."

"Oh, like you can't tell when a guy's hot."

"I'm deadly serious, I'm really bad at knowing if another lad is a looker or not. It's easy to tell if a girl is hot, but a fella is tough."

"Bull--shit."

"I'm not messing, I think it's because we're brought up in such a homophobic environment. It was illegal to be gay till, like, the Nineties here."

"Get out."

"Honestly."

"That's crazy, how did they enforce that law?"

"I haven't a notion... By the way you look lovely today."

"Thank you."

She bats her bfull eyez and purses her gorgeous lipz.

"Flattery will get you everywhere."

"Nice one, I'll keep going so."

Here we r giuseppe fanellis. We park the car near and stroll cross the st. All systems r a go. Grá above. She looks incred. The dress fits her 2 a t. Its hard 2 keep my eyez off her as she slinks in2 the rest.

Shes a total K.O I open the door.

"Thank you, kind sir."

"You're very welcome, ma-lady."

I luv her sense of humour tis just like mine.

Ital has gone down gr8. Salmon ravioli. Luvly stuff.

"Go away from me, ya narrow-back ya."

"What the hell's a narrow-back?"

"A 'narrow-back' is like an oul name for an Irish-American. Usually the Yank isn't out digging ditches on the farm, but the Irish person in Ireland is, and they get broad backs from the hard work."

"What does that make you, a broad back? Or maybe a craic baby, ha."

Here comes the cheque time 2 show sum class.

"Go Dutch?" asks Sonny.

"What? Dutch?"

"Like halvesies."

"Oh no, this is my treat."

"You sure?"

"Yeah, of course."

Pfect mr carolan. The pfect gent.

"Thank you."

Look at her pfect :) I can tell shes delighted wit the way tings r goin.

"So what do you want to do?"

"I don't mind."

"If you like, I know a cool little place, it's just off the beach, but I think you'll like it, there's a really nice view."

OMG u sound like a rapist.

"Sure, sounds good."

Gud ting its still sunny out.

Clew bays dotted wit a # of small islands. Its pfect + the day has stayed nice 2 boot. My shoes r effed and Sonnys feet r all mucky from the path 2 the cliffs. Shes not bothered.

"Home is just two thousand miles that way," says Sonny.

"That's it."

"So who was this Clare girl? She must be pretty awesome if they named an island after her?"

"I've never had the pleasure. It used to be the home of a famous pirate queen as well."

"Wow, a pirate queen. That's pretty badass."

"Her castle is still out there, we should go out to see it someday. I think the ferry goes from Roonagh, it's not too far away so it's not."

"Definitely."

"They say there's an island for every day of the year."

"Really?"

"One of them was John Lennon's."

"Get out."

"Yeah, he bought an island years ago, one of them little islands out there. I'd say Yoko probably has it now."

"So a pirate queen and one of the Beatles used to live out there. We should get one of those islands and name it after me. Sonny Island? Or Sonny and Seanie Island. We sound like a music act from the sixties."

Sonny tiptoes a few steps + twirls in her bare feet like a ballerina.

"I got you babe".

"Ha, ha, ha, we do alright. Sonny Mc'Cool and Seanie Carolan, coming to a dance hall near you for one night only."

4 the luv of grá man just hold her hand. Theres no way shes gonna say no. I slowly reach over and touch her fingers. Sonny beams at me and wraps her digits round mine. She turns towards me wit her bright :) her bful :) go on give her a x. I know this is gr8.

After the cliffs + our make-out session we went 4 a spin round wport and out 2 old head. Its nite now. We sit on the bonnet and stare at the billions of ***************

"What's the craziest thing you ever seen?"

"Oh, I don't know, it's probably nothing compared to the things you see in the States."

"Try me."

"Hmm... The craziest thing I can't tell you."

"Oh, c'mon, you can't say that and not tell me."

"I can't, when I know you better, maybe."

"Please?"

"No can do."

She :(+ fake pouts.

"Another time."

"Promise?"

"I promise, but anyways, next to that, the craziest thing I'd say was the time me and Chris broke into the circus."

"Chris is your friend in Canada, right?"

"Yeah, there's a circus that comes to town every year and stays for like a week or two. Anyways we took the day off school, and decided to see what was up behind the scenes."

"Okay."

"It was horrific, I remember all the animals looked miserable, the elephants were chained and it was just awful. The circus had one lion, and he was kept in this tiny cage."

"Oh my God."

"I remember there was a big barrel of pigs heads beside the cage. It was disgusting."

"That's so cruel."

"He had such a look of despair in his poor eyes, it's not right to keep a wild animal like that trapped and feeding him rubbish."

"I agree, that's terrible."

"Well, that's probably the weirdest thing I've ever seen. How about you?"

"I can't top that, I've seen crazies on the subway, but you get used to them. New York is full of weirdos and looneys, you get pretty desensitized to it, but that circus story is terrible."

Theres nowhere else id rather b nothin else id rather do.

"You know what else you see here? Stars. You can't really see a lot of stars in the City, it's too bright."

"I'd say so."

183

"Oh, the Big Dipper."

"You mean the Plough?"

"Potayto, potahto."

"What do you want to do when you go to college?"

"I don't know, I know I want to do something I like doing, that's for sure. How about you?"

"Don't know either. I like books and movies, and I like to write sometimes."

"What type of stuff do you write?"

"Oh, bits and pieces. To be honest, I don't know if I'm any good really."

"I was actually reading some Kafka before I came over, have you read any of his stuff?"

"I have, I love Kafka, pure class so he is. I'd like to write stories someday, but that type of thing's probably not that realistic."

"You never know, in time it might be. And who cares as long as you have something you do that you really like."

"True. Who knows in the future. I just know I don't want to go to college anywhere around here. That means Galway's out."

"How come?"

"Galway's lovely, but it's too close to home, there's too many Ballybar people living there. It's just like a bigger version of home."

"I get ya. That would be like me going to college in Brooklyn or Staten Island. I think I'd prefer to go away to school too."

"Would you ever leave the States?"

"I don't know if I could, everyone hates America now, ha, ha."

"Iraq has done a lot of damage to the rep, alright"

"God, I know, Bush is the worst, he can't even speak without screwing up."

"He's not the most eloquent so he's not."

"Eloquent? The leader of the Free World is retarded."

"I wouldn't misunderestimate him if I were you."

"Sometimes it's embarrassing to be American."

"No it's not, anyone who knows anything knows that most Yanks are nothing like George Bush."

"I hope so."

"They do."

"Since 9/11 people just seem so angry. Especially in Bay Ridge, a bunch of fire fighters from the neighborhood died."

"Where were you when it happened?"

"At school."

"You know, mess with America and you're going to get bombed."

"I know, it just seems like we're not going after the people who did it at all."

"Still, there's loads of great things about America. The Civil Rights Movement, the eight hour day, they were won in the States."

"Yeah, the people are great, the government sucks."

"Sure it's the same everywhere."

"I guess."

"Where would you be if you were at home now?"

"Probably at my parent's house at Breezy Point, or as it's known, wait for it... The Irish Riviera."

"The Irish Riviera?"

"Yip."

"How did it get called that?"

"Because so many Irish people have beach houses there and stuff."

"When I was small, we used to head up to this beach called Enniscrone in Sligo. Me and my cousins used to stay in a caravan, it was mighty oul craic. We should go up some day, I haven't been there in years."

"Cool."

"I remember once, I got an awful burning and it wasn't even a sunny day, it was the wind that did the damage. I don't understand how sometimes you can get a worse burning from the wind than you can from the sun."

"I know. What's the deal with that?"

"It's funny when I think back, it feels like the summers used to be way nicer."

"Maybe it's global warming."

"Maybe."

"Though, wouldn't you guys be in favor of global warming? Less rain, more heat?"

"I'm not sure. They say if the world does heat up and the North Pole melts that Ireland won't get warmer at all at all. The Gulf Stream is what keeps us from freezing, and apparently the melting would mess that up."

"Oh, noooooo."

"I know, there'd be another Ice Age in Ireland."

"Damned if you do, damned if you don't."

"Arra, the snow is better craic anyways, better than the rain. Bring on the global warming, we can go skiing and snow-boarding down Croagh Patrick instead of sprinting out the back to bring in the clothes from the line."

"You'd lose the green if that happened."

"True... I think I just want to be someplace where it's bright out all the time."

Beep, Beep... Beep, Beep...

Abc
Hey babs wats the craic?
Abc
Oh hey babes not up 2 much lookin forward 2 later.
Abc
Wheres my babes?
Abc
Town is jammers ill be there soon my bodacious babs.
Abc
Babs outside yours.
Abc
Comin babes.
Abc
Im bout 2 go ill call in a bit.

Abc

Ttyl xxx.

Abc

Wanna c a film?

Abc

How bout the gud the bab and the snugly?

Abc

I come bearin treats 4 my little babs.

Abc

Oh wat treats?

Abc

Cookies + jaffa cakes.

Abc

Yummy!

Abc

My creds bout 2 go babs. Ive 2 run 2 the shop.

Abc

Txt when u topped up.

Abc

Hey my little banba babs got the tickets.

Abc

Hooray babes! Bring on the saw doctors.

Abc

Home safe babes. Goin 2 sleep now. Had such a blast wish u were here wit me. Sweet dreams xoxoxox.

Abc

I know babs. Nite nite xxxx.

Abc

Hey my babes. Cant sleep. U up?

Abc

Hey babs me 2. U want me 2 pick u up?

Abc

Yeah babes we can do sometin fun.

Abc

Fret not im on the way my bful babs.

<u>Abc</u>

U silly babes.

<u>Abc</u>

Babs don't u know silliness is gud 4 the soul.

<u>Abc</u>

Youll always b my best babs eve if u had leprosy.

<u>Abc</u>

Oh no babes leprosy is contagious I wudnt let u near me id go 2 an island and wait 4 my arms and legs 2 fall off in solitude.

<u>Abc</u>

No babs I wud go wit u and we cud fall apart together.

Sonnys at shannon waitin 4 her flight. I cant stop cryin. I luv her so much. I wud lie kill die 4 Sonny McCool. Y does ev1 always have 2 leave? Always. I wud b perfectly happy 2 spend the rest of my days wit Sonny. I dont want anyting else any1 else. Wat if sometin happens? Wat if I nev c her again?

<u>Abc</u>

Have a safe flight babs txt me when u touch down. Miss ya so much.

LUV U 4 EVA. XXX.

Chapter 16

Meow.

   --Now. Puss, where the sweet skittles are we going a tall a tale?

Seanie and his boisterous young feline friendly make their way on the right-paw side of the pawpath, the kitty Cat, mirthful as could be, leads Seanie a long till they arrive inside out of the oul Pig's Ear Inn, Sullybar, Cunty Mayonnaise.

--Ya want to go on the lock, do ya?

--Meow.

Seanie sighs, vexed with the witty Cat and not especially in the mood to indulge himself in Roolaboola nor Seanfoolery. The cocky Cat leans back on his hind trotters and sits in an upright and proper manner. Restless, he peers up at Seanie with his big green eyerishes and pretty pouting puss, flicking his tail from tick to tock, tick to tock, tick to tock.

--Meow.

After a moment or three of cuckoolation Seanie agrees to tongue liberating thrinks.

--Feckett, camann, but we're only having the wan.

Immediately springing back to all, two, four pawpaws, the iddy Cat gallops towards the porte, his tale straight as a hurley in the air. He circles the door impatiently as he waits for Seanie to opine it for him. Plumes of smoke float around the long, narrow, stool filled pub like gray clouds in the Mayonnaise sky. The titty Cat slinks inside, puss prominent, eager to wet his whitely whiskers.

--Meow.

A number of oul fellas sit at the bar jibberjabbering with rapture about polunatics pan pursing pine pick pints so soppy slack stout.

--Obi wan, Kenobi nil.

--How'd they score?

--PENO. Jesus went up for the cross but got nailed.

--Cheers and tables.

Seanie and the biddy Cat notice two seats before them and plop their bunrocks down at the bar.

--Purrfeck.

While easeing the chair forward, Seanie acknowledges an orderly chap in negotiations with a Barman.

--Please sir, can I have some Moore?

--Bah Humbert.

The sitty Cat settles himself in anticipation of crapulence, his head sits just above the bevel of the bar.

--I'm only going to say this Juance and nonce only, nonly the Juan. Ya tuig?

Plesantly, the giddy Cat bops his head wance, twice, thrice and conkers with the propussal. A Barman leans over and treats them with a grinagringrin and a winkedy wink winkedy, he dons an alabaster shirt and sports a queer pair of spectacles coloured by spumy beer.

--Howye peeping? What can I get yous?

--Can I get a pint-a-porter and a double bainne.

--On the stones?

--If ya could, please.

--No problemo sir.

The Barman evidently produces an ice falled glass tumbler, then proceeds to fill the fall with cooley dreamcreamy milk. Gliding gladly a subpoena ad absurdum before the cushy Cat, he rests his case of crème de la crème on it.

--Úr milk.

Not earlier than finishing construction of Seanie's point, the Barman poors till there's a slight dome of screamcreamy head over the top of the twolipped shaped claen glass.

--Lovely hurtling.

Seanie belts out a tattered tenor note.

--O, haven't seen or heard sight nor light about these in yonks.

--Sure they're all the wan so they are.

--No more Mc'Auley, Joyce, O'Connell, Hyde and...

190

He halts in retrospection, the Barman researches his memebankment for the figaro final.

--Parnell tisn't it?

--That's it. The uncrowned king himself.

Upon heavesdropping the exchange-rate between Seanie and the Barman, a stately Patron with a stout stained grey beard objects.

--Which is a higher rank? an uncrowned king or the third most important man in Europe?

The Barman chortles at the Patron's queery.

--Ho, ho, ho, ho, that's a tough wan, bejeeze.

--Ah, ah, ah, ah, bejeeze an-it-tis, bejeeze an-tit-is. What do ya recoin?

Seanie, unsure of how to manswer, hazily resorts with what he spitspated hitherto.

--Sure they're all the wan so they are.

--You're not rang there.

A compatriot of this loquacious fellow enters the fray, he takes a long pull of his fagette, then juts his jaw like the valve gear of a state train... Wobbly hoops of gray smoke dance and prance from the oval shaped contraction of his sorrowface.

--Whom was it that midered General O'Duffy?

On the farce side of the publick, a figure of many faces curled up in the snook barks,

--Misha, he was only a shambollocks!

--Wisha, they'd froth at the gob if they heard ya.

--Musha, I think he was a gent well meant.

--Moya, in General, I think therefore I amen't.

--Yerra, hibernation he stated.

--Arra, didn't he get killed abroad in Spain?

--Begorra, ya swine ya. Teach poblacht de mucanna.

Raiseing his rite arm in a Roman salute the Barman marches down the bar, his alabastard shirt murpheen to a light blue hue. The multifaceted character in the corner who was rambling before starts gobbing again.

--Duffy's coup, his shirt is blue,

--What'll he do for Sunday?

--Go to bed, cover his head,

--And don't get up till Monday!

The huffy Cat watches, he's not in the least bit amewsed.

--O. The National Guard's marching on Rome.

Seanie pricks up his settled point and salutes the nitty Cat with honour.

--Sláinte, Puss.

--Meow.

At that excat tempo Seanie takes a gulping mootful of port, the lippy Cat lippidylaps up grand tongues of his delicious drencrommy milkoko. Seanie relaxes the cax and leaves the pint be. The silky Cat is still lippidylapping away to his ticker's consent, he feasibly has more than half of it lappedylicked up.

--Now, Puss, go handy on the bilk, I don't want to be hauling ya home in waste, when you're all over the gafe from lappedylicklapping in haste.

He, the surly Cat not fond of being addressed in a bossjoss manner, ayeballs Seanie with a rather cross wee puss, then snakes an extra big lickedylap in undetermined deviance. As soon as he swallies it down the gullet, it comes to his cattention cat there's a few delicat droplets of dreammeme on his whimsical kisskers, he lickedylickz his front pawpaws to clean the dreamcrom from them till they're Daz white. Behind him, a well messed missing minded man with a white pisstache punctually potters into the pub.

--When all beside are shepherd's sheep. The West's asleep! The West's asleep!

He's stink red rotten drunk and carries an argybargy bulbous beer belly.

--If it tisn't the Doctor himself or tis it Mr. Hyde that's in it this evening?

--Tis the Doctor I proclaim.

--What's up Doc?

Every figure in the pub is delighted to see this elderly Dock of debauchery, beneath his messy white mustachio he has a smile comprised of piss yellow teeth on exhibition.

--Faust, I must go make sweet chamber music, he slurs and spits his feckylls.

(The devil era's first precedent.)

--In Doctor, urination, right after gesticulation as it was in the beginning.

The Dyke meanders his way through the hebeen to the magmatory, rolling and jouncing off lows he bumps into while twirling his moustache.

--To the piss pot I shall go, to let the urine flow, whoa ho, and up the long fellow!

Seanie, feeling the urge to purge, fellows not too far behind the pissed Duck. In side, in toxicated, in urination, the Doctrine notices Seanie as he unzips his fly and makes a wewe in the arsenal instead of the urinal.

--Cad is ainm bitch? The pissing Duke in choirs, his voice bouncing and echoing off the tight tiled jills boundaries. Bashful and imbareassed by the slobbering remarks, Seanie tries not to pay hay of the drunken Doctory.

--Are you seán Séan?

--Who nós, seans.

--Old or óg or?

Seanie finishes the job at hand and zips up his cailpíss in a rush to flee the imbroglio.

--O. He go for the door like a just paid whore. He go he-go-hego-h'ego-ego-e'go-go-g'o, keens the drunken dochtúir.

He quackly reruns to whence he was, on the way he notices the drinky Cat, alonia, with his snow-white front pawpaws on the bar.

--Moy O Moy, what are ya at Puss?

Seanie shifts down and spots that the copy Cat has the index pawclaw of his front south pawpaw flicked out and about.

--Away with that, away with it to fulka.

He has crudely scraped something into the bar with his solo pawclaw:

Felis demulcta mitis.

--Holy Mac Ríuil. What the flip are ya at, at rest, at play in May?

--Menow, meow.

--What?

--Menow.

--What war ya on about Puss? You're bamboozled and mewewing nunsense. I medb ya alone for quatre-vingt-un winks and you start scandalising the place like a feckless scallywag.

--Meah.

Your mano is going to go demented when he ogles at your scrabbldehobble.

--Meawe, meawe.

--Helter scaoilte.

(A cat state, they're in, they are?)

--You're warped aren't ya, you'll go back in your box with the goings on of ya. Then you won't know if you're diving or lying.

--Meawe.

Hither and thither the pity Cat careens, Seanie, concerned about the swaying, glances at the empty class tumbler.

--Is it sower Puss?

The doubly Cat is still woefully wabbly.

--You must have the spins.

Burp, bap, burp, burp, bap.

Bloated, the gassy Cat belches a loud little burpburp.

--Pardon your Fraincis.

--Moiow.

Seanie puts his handeens on the side of the fetty Cat's furry white and ginger tumtum to hold him steady and stop him from keeling over like a sack of spuds.

--You'd swear someone cropotkined your whitely whiskers with the pigacting of ya.

(Two full of the milk of human mindless.)

Coouuugggghhhhh.

--Be quiet, man.

The wheezy Cat starts to gasp and whimper as if he might regurgitate a furball or perhaps even some of that cooley

194

creamdreamy milkocow he lickidylapped up so speedily. He glimpses up at Seanie, popeless, the nooks of his wee mewer downward bound.

--We better skedaddle before your mano sees your scrawling and fuckadoodledoodling.

The pretty Cat starts to sob from Seanie's beetrooting, small globes of cries leak down his furry cheekcreeks.

--Ya poor oul Puss. You're on the hind tit Puss, you're on the hind tit.

--Woem...

Seanie picks up the wavering sicky Cat, holding him near to his breast, he treads to the front door, caressing him. After resting his front pawpaws on Seanie's shoulder, the teary Cat kneads and watches the stool filled pub vanish from bibulous perception.

Óró, sé do bheatha abhaile,
Óró, sé do bheatha abhaile,
Óró, sé do bheatha abhaile,
Anois ar theacht an tsamhraidh.
Tá Gráinne Mhaol ag teacht thar sáile,

(Songie Seanie continues his Loose Carrollan.)
--Kellooh kellay! Ar Aghaidh, Puss, almost at the ticktop so are we.
--Mewow.
--Mind yourself.

Up the mountain slumbers them in the best of fettle, negotiating stone and moss barefoot and barepaw. To the west an infinity of westerin waves continually lick and preen the shore in perpetual commotion. Seanie lifts his gaze and peers out on Clue Bay. He admires the superfluity of gemstones as they twinkle and sparkle throughout the Hellman's Mayonnaise.

--A stone for every day of the year. I'd say Grainne has the pupils peeled beyond on Clare's.

Diddle do-do diddle do-do diddle do-do-do.

Seanie answers his diddle-do-doing phone pooka.

195

--Hell-o.

He shakes the phone pooka, but he's not well received being up the rock.

--O-hell.

Without signal the phone pooka returns to his pants puca.

--Tis is it Puss, nearly near.

Seanie and the ditty Cat must surmount un mór hill. On the trot, the clanking of hammered stealing is ireable.

--Rolling, rolling, rolling, keep that turnip rolling.

A denizen turnip of semi-perfect rotundity rolypolies over to the rowdy Cat.

--Ye who enter, believe every dope!

A melodic line of harping trad vibrates in their inner heardrums. The branches rustle and lilt, as the U tree gates riverdance open in grand time altogether, their roots move as if independent from their funktrunks. Seanie and the kitt.ie Cat groove to the yewsic and pass the treeshold, but as they do, a bout of congestion befalls the spazy Cat.

--Ah, mew!

The Fitzy Cat is in a fit of strong sneezes.

--Ah, mew! Ah, mew!

--Oh, Puss, you must be aclergic to something.

--AH, MEW!

--Goodness, we'll have to get you some anti-pisstomeans.

Seanie pulls out a winkled hanky, he bends down to help the snotty Cat blow his nose.

--Blow, Puss.

Pppuuueeeerrrrrpppp.

--There we go.

Seanie dabs around the runny Cat's nose to make sure there's no mewcous on his hisskers or puss.

--Meow.

--We'll get you some verbal remedies and you night be day okay.

The two travellers make their way furward to the panicle of the mountpain till they arrive at an utterly unsightly site.

--In the name of Gob Alshitey.

(The most whoreable sight in all Ourland.)

--A chaphelle they are instituting.

Waves of slaves stand before Seanie and the grotty Cat. The sparespangle and the clinkedyclankclang of their chains barely masks their moans and groans of holy suffering shites.

(He must have counted them earlier.)

Batters of them are inked together from pons to puns and pens to pins, others have the shackhails secured around their scrawny necks and cheques slowly finagling the life out of them with interest. Some carry rocks and locks, others hammer and flatten steal to craft into stocks and bonds.

(A consecration camp, to subjugate the Yewish people.)

--No. No. No. It can't be squeal. Y? Y? Y? Cén faith?

Seanie and the fiery Cat wander around the sight looking for cause and afecked.

--Luke at me! Luke at me! Who hath done such a thing?

The slave ain't got the phuckalls to chinwag and gab, he peers at the chapel in a blue funk. Stonemasons without a ball betweyen them chisel a figure out of slimestone, tis all drafted except for the head, below the belt, and the clayfully crafted feet, on the base of the statue are a couple of fuckhells:

Naomh Padraig.

--In nomine Patris, et Filii, et Spiritus Santie Claus.

On Erin the blessing, both Seanie and the fussy Cat change their locus to inside the Church. An oul man kneels, he possesses striking whitish grey hair and a woolly beard, with a queera oul gimp to him, your oul mano rises, he stands there with a stealy gaze, dressed in a long blowing cloak, taylored of the finest silks and dreads. In right hoof is his golden sceptre of sour.

(Can it be the Patron Saint?)

--Is it ewe?

--I am the hatrick and the mostard for your bread.

--You should know better than this!

--Are you a Protestant?

197

--No, but I doth protest.

(It never dawned on Seanie that befour this, Faketrick exercised the trouser snakes and they haven't popped up since.)

--It's what must be done in the name of our horde, have you not read The Book of Smells?

--I have, Butt.

--This is the Reek I do deeklare, and I am Patreek...

--You antidisestablishmentarianismologist.

--You floccinaucinihilipilificationisimologist.

--Sapere aude.

--The dear knows.

--It Kunt, it Kan't.

The Slaves clamour around Pat, Seanie and the yeedy Cat gawk at the slaves with repulsion in their submission to himself.

--Tis all a pigment of an imagined nation.

Some of the slaves cover their lugs with their shagged hands and yelp in pain from Seanie's focal points.

--Listen not, listen not, it's just propagandhi.

--You're nothing but a hornswoggler.

--Chain'em and pain'rem at once.

A number of serfs follow Podgerick's wholly orders and pin it over to Seanie and the sassy Cat with the intention of indeathedness. Juan grabs Seanie's arm and tries to attach a bond to it. Two slaves nick the knacky Cat and try to collar his furry neck.

--Higgldy diggledy let go of the Puss, or he'll marx ya with his claws O.

The testy Cat with his lugeens flat against his skulleen, struggles and hisses. Seanie flings the paper thin slaves away and timely fends off those who seek to shackle the pesky Cat. Freed from their fiendish grip, none else being by, he shakes himself off in the kitty corner.

--You and your big house.

--What else can you do with the Waste of Arraland.

Padrerick fixes his pocus on the duo with contempt, he scowls at the sideways puffy Cat and hocks a loogy.

--The cat may look at a king.

198

--Otay ellhay roay otay aughtconnay.

Seanie grabs his ash sword from his broadback.

--Ni Dieu Ni Maitre.

--I will smite thee down you naughty buachailli.

--Pat Rí!

--Ainrialaí!

Patrice steps in Seanie's direction, his golden sceptre ready for prostration.

--An Cnoc in the head for you my boy.

The werther changes and the sky starts to heil rain and stones. Great Scot's! 1.21 gigawatts. The sonic shock frightens the flock of slaves. Seanie and Paraic, both ready to mill, wren towards each other and swiftly pick up gait. Both close in on pun another as they take a fairly middling swing of their wepensons.

PHUCK!

Each strikes the other's wepense with squeakqual and apposite force. Seanie lunges at Phadraig and thrusts his ash sword.

PHISH!

He's deflected by Rick's sourful sceptre. Patnick turns his right shoulder as straight as a die, chopping down the angle of strike possibility.

--If you're all sourful, can you create a sucky sweet so sour, even you can't suck it?

--Eyerish bull.

--This scoilbuggery is all part of your seething plot.

--Ha, says a sulken Thomas.

Ratpick goes for Seanie's legeens with his long sceptre.

--You missed sourly.

Both exchange a number of weeping blows before Pucktrick wallops Seanie pang in the puss, cnocing him to earth. Looks like Seanie's in bad oul bother.

--Would you ever shut up.

What did I do?

--Not a fecking tap as usual, you're all tick, talk, tock.

Listen, this is your own fault, so don't be directing your ire at I.

--You're only a cod.

Patricius seizes upon the opportuneity, he presses down on Seanie's trachea and begins to choke him with all his sour.

--Give in!

--Ni... Dieu... Ni... Maitre.

Seanie's face is turning blue from the massphyxiation. Frederick grinds his teeth and chokes even harder to drain the life from him like an oil will. But then, the kitty Cathelpa with the bollocks and bravery of an uncaged Leo flies through the air, his laughing blades and rapier like pawclaws ready to tear and maim.

--AAAAHHHHH, SUGAR TITS!

He catchy Cat-ches onto Poderick's puss fiercely as both become commingled.

(That ain't no scaredy-cat, that's for sure.)

The oedi Cat rips and shreds with his teeheeheeth and nihils, there's skin and hair flying, Phatrick tries to shake him off, but the spiky Cat's clutch is far too tighty. Queerby, Seanie steadying himself, finds the golden sceptre of sour, tis a weighty weapon and crafted to purefiction, he examines it curiously.

--A sceptre the price of duds.

Bedazzled by its divilish charm, Seanie sour hungrily decides to keep it for his eoin and dashes toward Patdrake and the bitchy Cat. After a few bounds, he halts and looks at it once moral in contemplation.

--Ni Dieu, Ni Monstrum, says he to himself.

Seanie fires the sceptre of sour off into the mayonnaise waters of Clue Lay, where none shall ever wield it again. Meanwhile Shamrick, his face now gashed and bloody well bluebloody, finnally grabs a hold of the furry Cat by the scruff of the neck, forcing him to declench and lewison his gripe. He throws the kithy Cat away like a brisfree.

--Meouch!

He lands on all fours and skids along the gravel without major damnation. 1.21 gigawatts! strikes with fury and illuminates the darkened reek, Seanie stands, the rain and hail downpoors even harder than tearlier.

--If you should win the battle and hurl me to the waves, you'll never ever win the war, the sheeple are born as slaves.

The antsy Cat gets his backup and hisses and threatens the diaolcical Patpick with his clawed southern lapaw. Seanie and the odious Phucarick then waltz up to one another.

--Your sin tactics are contradictatorial.

--Fear control to fear using.

--Drab as a divil livid as a bard...

Patsy   who in turn, bobs and
    throws
Two   a right   Seanie,
              a left loosner
      banters with   his
                                              kidney beans.
              stands concentric
Perk,   in the   center while
                          circles   times waiting
Seanie,   nine   to denounce.
                  eccentrically
          trout   breaks his grip,
He goes   the
      for   Patrickal   but while
Seanie
              clocks him
      distracted
                          with a   /   rocker
      tottering and
  righty   him   rickety. lefty
                          leaving
          swings heavy handeadly,   the two crash
Patmick   gravely. Seanie
          to the gravelly ground   dives at him,

...Seanie picks up an Achill sized stone that lies by Patreich's Achilles and begins beating lumps out of Patapatapat.

SMASH. SMASH. SMASH.

--Eamonn.

At last the heil begins to lighten. A mighty ocean gael blows round the bend, bubbling from below, the bearded figure of Manannán mac Lir rises slowly from Clue Basin sporting a fine pair of bladderwrack knickerbockers. He squints upon the reekpeek while eels and elvers swirlpool all around him.

--You da Manannán!

Manannán points his index finger at the half constructed church like a pisstol and shoots.

KABLOOIE!

He blows it to smidiríní.

(Leveled so it is.)

--You're some Manannán for one Manannán.

A fecking massive wave rears from the oshawn, equal, but not greater in size to the mounteen, the clewless slaves scamper in the other direction just as the wave collapses. Whe wave wakes wits way wo whe wock, it licks up Lactrick and with a milk curdling whale, takes him with id to the depths of the murky aigéan, patrically purging the place of his sociopathillogical pretence. In a mass historia, the slaves fall to their knees and weep at their antedevilian loss.

--Fatherick no more, no más, no més, nach mó.

Atop o'reek is barse bare now, just the rock that was always theirs.

--Meow?

--Time to bounce, Puss, time to bounce.

--Mewkay.

The peppy Cat glances over at some of the Hewish people, they wail bewildered with their patholic church a sunder. In a sudden flash, their chains begin to drip from their limbs to earth like mourning dew. Seanie finds his prattle tested ash sword and dusts it off, he takes solas from the am.

--When Ourish ayes are smiling, there'll be sunlight in May Oh.

With Pork's kingdumb done, and nights of running amuc well and truebluely over, the smithy Cat and himself scuttle off on their long trek down the reck. Over hills, through dales and with stealth and help and jokes they might just make it even-keeled.

A corncrake croaghs on the branch of a solitary u3 amidst a flat Céide Field ringed by drumlins, while the pithy Cat stretches and sharpens his pawclaws on the tree trunk. Nearby rests a humangous pile of long flattish stones. Seanie plucks a perfectly average sized one from the heap and with much precision and libertarianess reunites it with its fellows.

(He likes to recreate in his recreational time.)

--Oh, aren't you mighty? Amn't my mighty' mews yous. Are you not going to give me a big bualadh Puss?

--Meow.

--A round of apaws, go raibh maith agat, go raibh míle maith acat.

He arches his back to a taut bow, yawns, then pussyfoots over to Seanie.

--T'will be something else when it's begun.

The mythy Cat I's the top of the wall, he jogs his pawpaws on the spot in preparation for his upward spring. He lands with minimal energy expended and looks up, down and around and around and around. In his gregarious manner he rubs his white striped cheek up against Seanie in a welcoming way.

--T'will take ages to get it proper though.

Tucking his front pawpaws under himself the shiny cat begins to Puuurrrrr...

Seanie strokes him behind the clues, they sit there, elucidated, illuminated and enlightened.

--Do ya Éire that, Puss?

Z sleepy Cat blinkedyblinx his big drowzee iyes.

--Do ya not, Puss?... Listen... What is that? I wonder.

They stall, nay in a mighty, neither great, but in a super position altogether.

Chapter 17

At long, at last, sixth year. The Leaving Cert. The be all and end all. The big kahuna. Come June we will begin a set of exams that decide where we shall or shan't go to college. There's a lot of pressure on this year, the teachers generally agree that if you fuck up the Leaving Cert your life is over. It's amazing how someone's intellectual worth can be quantified by a set of timed state exams. With these motherfuckers looming over the year, we're supposed to keep only one extra-curricular activity. Mine's the school newspaper. Myself, Toland and Collins, after six years, are now at the top of the ladder. Well, not really. We worked fierce hard on the paper during the summer getting it ready for the year and came to a few conclusions, after the shite way we were treated throughout the years, we thought it best to change the whole set-up. We think that the best thing for the newspaper and the students is to run it democratically. Anyone who wants to participate in the paper is welcome to do so despite their class or year. Before, all the onerous work was delegated to the students in the years below, now the burden is shared with all the participating students. Most years there's nobody under fourth year involved, already we have a few third and second years. To be honest, the more the merrier, it means less labour for everyone, especially for us sixth years. In relation to writing, no one or two students are allowed to monopolise all the interesting topics like sports or movies. The writing assignments work on a rotating basis so we all have to cover different subjects. At first some of the lads were a little hesitant, they didn't think everyone could carry out the different tasks, we said we'd give it a go and if it didn't work we'd go back to the old way. After a month, it's now apparent that we can do it. Everyone's catching on fairly quick and sure it's not rocket science, it also forces us all to improve our writing skills now that we have to cover a range of different topics as opposed to being proficient in only one area. In previous years the newspaper was printed twice a month, now we print a paper three times a month, if we wanted to, we could easily print a paper a week. Every Wednesday, regardless of what's going on, we meet at lunch time and discuss any matters pertaining to the paper. We have one person adjudicate and that's also rotated weekly.

This week I'm writing a review of a documentary about this famous professor from MIT in the States called Chomsky. Toland came across the documentary during the summer and we were blown away by it. Essentially, it's about how Big Business and Government use the Mass Media to manipulate and guide public opinion. Modern propaganda. It makes a fair bit more sense than most of the shite being spouted by the likes of churches, schools, or football managers. It's quite evident that the media frames issues in certain ways at certain times in order to serve power structures. After doing a little research of our own, we decided that our newspaper should seek to challenge such power. Along with the local news stories, we dedicate words and pages to taboo topics, social and political, that are purposely ignored by the mainstream media. We do not enforce any censorship at the paper. If we believe in freedom of expression then we must believe in it for the things we hate most, otherwise it's a limited form of expression. Not free. If people don't like a word or article then they are perfectly free not to read the paper. Brother Leary has already threatened to shut us down, but he knows it would probably be a waste of time since a load of the lads have printers at home.

Toland is covering the class elections this week. I didn't really know John Toland until last year. We're great oul pals now though. It's the same story with Tony Collins, even though Collins was in my class I didn't know him awful well. He was a bashful sort of lad until around fifth year. Anyways, last year the three of us were trying to get stuff we wrote into the paper, but of course we usually got bumped in favour of the sixth years. Toland's delighted he got to write up the election this week. Everyone here at the paper has decided to boycott the elections and not vote for anybody. The reasons being, it's always the same people who run to get elected, and, Brother Leary has to agree on all the elected students. It's a joke. A Mickey Mouse election. Ned Burke will probably be made head of the Student Council, all the arse kissing will come to fruition this year for the sycophantic bollocks. He'll be over the moon when he's top of the heap. Burke will get to act like a grown up for the year, walk in and out of the teachers lounge as he pleases, call the staff by their first names.

--He's a responsible mature young man.

--A future leader.

I bet the people over at Young Fianna Fáil will have a big knees-up for the gobshite. Toland and Collins can't tolerate him either. Especially Toland, he nearly got into a fight with him in fourth year during a football match at lunch time. For a minute I thought there was going to be an all out scrap, but didn't the bell go before the jumpers came off. It just ended up being one of those awkward shoving matches. You push me, I push you, we both walk away. They've fucking hated each other ever since. Burke has been in my class for the last five years, he's one of those people you learn to detest over time. He's always working an angle, a mé féiner to the core. If you were to meet him in person he would make a great first impression, cheerfully charming, seemingly sincere, but it's all motivated by self-interest and aggrandisement. Burke reminds me of that type of girl you see at a get-together in someone else's gafe, always helping to clean up and asking everyone if they want another drink. It's not your house, sit down, have a West Coast Cooler, and let the hosts of the party be the hosts of the party.

--Does anyone want another piece of cake?

--Ya alright, peteen?

Burke will win the election handily, he has virtually no competition, plus he knows all the ins and outs from been on the Student Council for the past couple of years. Anyone who wasn't on the Council like Burke hasn't a chance in hell of winning.

This week we're writing an article on Shannon Airport and the use of it by the U.S. military for the War on Terror. I have part one, which deals with Afghanistan, Collins has Iraq. For the last two weeks I've been researching it, and maybe I'm missing something, but the argument for invading Afghanistan after 9/11 seems weak at best. The U.S. more or less said to the Afghan government,

--We suspect certain people in Afghanistan were involved in 9/11. Hand them over or we'll invade.

They wouldn't even present evidence against the suspects. Hand them over without a word? If a terrorist organisation commits an act of terror in a state, does that state have the right to have their military invade the foreign land where the terrorists are supposedly stationed? Also, what exactly is a terrorist? The Brits identified the IRA as a terrorist group. Does that mean the IRA are terrorists? If they are does that give the British government the right to invade New York or Boston because the IRA were funded and armed by people in those cities? Or do the Brits have the right to invade anywhere in the United States because the U.S. government wouldn't deport IRA suspects back to England? And the Brits provided evidence in many cases. Perhaps the first question we should be asking is what is the Irish government doing? They're supposed to be neutral in all of this. The media ignores most of these things, there's no debate about the innocent men, women and children in Afghanistan, or Iraq for that matter, whose blood will be spilled by the thousands, maybe millions. The media puts more attention on the next big reality TV show,

--Celebrity Farm.

Is there no better way to get Bin Laden than invading and occupying the country? Would police work not be better than all out bombardment? Either way, it appears Ireland is nothing but a lap dog, an aircraft carrier for the U.S. military. Do what we are told or else. Imagine if we said,

--No. You cannot use our supposed-neutral country in relation to your Middle Eastern wars.

They'd probably have all the big corporations pull out of the place. Unemployment would go back to Eighties' levels, the Tuesday Boys would be back lining up outside the Post Offices. Pubs and chippers would be filled with restless children and drunken men. Southport would have to export the anti-aging properties of dillisk, instead of making the world's supply of botox. It's disgusting how dependant we are on foreign companies to give us jobs. Corporations have more rights than humans for fuck's sake. They don't have to worry about immigration, they pay hardly any tax, they put home grown talent out of work, they can't be thrown in jail. People go crazy about gays wanting rights, don't corporations fuck people up the hole every day and nobody pays a blind bit of notice. Look at Shell Oil up the road in Rossport. They just rape the land and tell the people to fuck off with the government's backing. Should any problems arise, a few brown envelopes here and there to the people with pull and Big Business will be on the pig's back.

Traditionally, the Debs are held in the Fáilte Inn and the tickets cost around sixty euro. Collins is after texting me. He said he heard that the newly elected head of Student Council, Ned Burke, is planning on having them out in Mac Tíre House. Usually on a school night I wouldn't be taking off from the study, but sure Collins is only a ten minute walk from my gafe. A break will be good to clear the head. That's what I always tell myself while indulging in shilly-shally. The Collins residence has no doorbell to push, I give the letter-box on the front door a bit of a rattle. The smell of fresh turf from the neighbour's gafe curls around the driveway and up the path, you don't smell as much turf these days, everyone gets the oil heating now to warm up the house. Through the diamond shaped window a blurred figure approaches the door.

"Howya, horse," says Collins.

"What's the craic?"

Collins steps outside and gently closes the door behind him.

"C'mon, we'll head to the shed for a bit of privacy, the oul lady hates when I take breaks from the study."

We stroll around the side of the gafe on the narrow concrete path to the galvanize shed.

"What's the story with Mac Tíre?"

"Burke was saying to someone last week in the Convent that we're supposed to be having the Debs there."

"They did it up recently, didn't they?"

"Yeah, it's under new ownership, and I think they're Burke's relations."

"What do you mean?"

"Like his cousins."

"They couldn't be. I doubt they're Burke's cousins, he's not that thick."

"Didn't Toland work out there during transition year?"

"I'm not sure."

"I think he did, he was a porter or something."

"It's not the right spot for the Debs, it's a pain in the balls getting out there. Think of all the taxis we'll need for what, a hundred students, plus another hundred dates?" says Collins.

"Yeah, that is a bit stupid."

"When ya think about renting a tux, buying flowers, bringing a date, the price of drink at the bar. It's a pricey last night."

"You're right so you are. Why pay an extra forty euro to be farther away from town and probably stuck for ages waiting for a lift?"

"Typical Burke, the classiest place possible. Fuck everyone else, they're only a bunch of eejets."

"Did he mention it to anyone in class yet?"

"Not that I know of. Probably because he knows well that people don't want the hassle of going out to Mac Tíre."

"He must have mentioned it to some of the class reps, give O'Brien a bell."

"I don't have his mobile."

"Me neither. I'd say Toland'll have it. Give him a shout. He has the car as well, he might drop over for a break."

We gave Toland a buzz and filled him in on the craic. He tried calling Conor O'Brien, but couldn't get through. Our interest in the Debs got the better of us and with Toland having the car, we decided to take a spin to O'Brien's house out the Turlough Road.

"How's the study going?"

"Cuntish, fucken honours maths is a bitch," says Toland.

"How's the brother getting on?"

"Sound enough, rag week is coming up soon."

"Sáváiste cabáiste."

"Yeah, I'm going to head down for a night out, should be a good laugh."

"That'll be us next year. College birds. On the lock. No more Leaving Cert," says Collins.

"It'll be great to have it over with."

"It'll be great to get a few women. It's like scraping the bottom of a tub of butter round here," says Collins.

"A fine-woman famine," says Toland, as he swings a right at the top of Marrian Row.

"Where you going?" Collins asks.

"Have to get petrol, Casey's is the cheapest."

"Did ya read that Cockburn article yet?"

"The Beat the Devil one?" says Collins.

"Yeah, it's a good piece."

"It's hard to read anything sometimes with all the fecking study."

Toland's mobile vibrates from a text message.

"Here he is. I texted O'Brien and told him we're dropping out."

"Nice one."

O'Brien plays GAA for the Ballybar Crokes and the school. He's a fairly handy mid-fielder, but his ego is way too inflated for his ability. I get on well enough with him even though he's a bit of a fool, he's one of these GAA footballers who thinks he's an Irish rebel, yet he's often down the pub with an Arsenal jersey on him watching the Premiership. That's something I can't understand. These people who sing rebel songs and talk about how great it is to be Irish but support English soccer teams. Baffling to me. If they in fact hold such contempt for the Black and Tans and proclaim the unshakable, unwavering and undeviating pride in their nationality, are there not plenty of League of Ireland teams to support? There are hardly any real rebels anymore. A rebel now is a celebrity who gets drunk in a nightclub and has their picture taken by the paparazzi. Most people like to talk the talk and sing the songs, but really they're just trading on other people's names.

We pull into O'Brien's driveway, the gravel crunching underneath the car's tyres. The Micra lights, on dim, fade to off. We step out of the car and wait for himself. The glass door glides to the right. O'Brien rears his ugly head and struts over to the car like the hard man he wishes he was.

"Howye, lads?" asks O'Brien.

Collins and I give him a howya-nod as O'Brien stands before us in his Ballybar Crokes track-suit top.

"Alright, Conor," says Toland.

"What's the sca?"

"Were you talking to Burke about the Debs out in Mac Tíre?"

"I was yeah, I think we're going to have them out there."

"Conor, why are ye thinking of that? It'll be awful hassle having them out there," says Toland.

"Burke said he was talking to the Fáilte Inn and they said the sixth years left a big fucker of a debt there from last year."

"Ye should still ask the year what they want."

"Ah, sure, you can't be doing that, what you'll get is everyone humming and hawing."

"No. What you'll probably get is most people saying that they'd rather have the Debs in the Fáilte Inn."

"Arra, I don't know. Did ye call Burke and ask him?" O'Brien asks.

"Do you have his mobile?"

"Hold on, I'll text it on to you."

He searches his jean pockets for his phone.

"I have to run into the gafe," says O'Brien.

"Here, we'll take off. Text on Burke's number," says Toland.

"Sound job, ga'luck lads."

We give O'Brien the good-bye and good-luck nod combined with a thumbs up. O'Brien moseys into the gafe. Collins opens the car door and lifts forward the passenger seat for me. We cruise off as Toland's mobile vibrates once again.

"You get the number?"

He unlocks the phone and clicks into his inbox.

"Have it," says Toland.

He hands the phone to Collins.

"Try him now sure."

Collins hits send and waits...

"Voicemail."

"Do ye want to chance the Fáilte Inn and see if one of the McMahons is there? We can see how much of a hole the sixth years left us in."

"Fuck it, we can try it on the way in, sure I have to drop ye home anyways," says Toland.

Toland parks the Micra in SuperValu car-park at the rear of the Fáilte Inn. The owners of the Fáilte Inn are the Mc'Hale Family, we probably should have called ahead to see if the manager is there or not.

--Why go through this rigmarole?

--Anything to not go back to the books.

"What do you reckon we should say if they ask us why we're here?" Collins asks.

"Just say we're with the Student Council and don't let on otherwise."

"Yeah, we can't go wrong with that. It's not like we're trying to find out top-secret information. Besides, I'd bet it's under the Saint Pat's account."

We saunter over to the foyer, there's a manager sitting behind the service desk on the phone. She puts her index finger up and makes the hold-on-a-sec face.

"Yeah, no bother."

This manager is a rather orangie looking lady, me thinks someone has been using the oul spray-on tan a biteen too much.

"Okay, can I call you back after? Great. Bye."

She hangs up the phone and gives us her full attention.

"Hey guys, how can I help you?" the manager asks.

"Hey, we're with the Saint Pat's Student Council. We were wondering if we could just check and see what type of state the sixth year's account is in from last year's Debs?"

The fact that Toland still has his school shirt and jumper on him helps our credibility a fair bit.

"Can you hang on for a couple of minutes?" says the manager. "I just have to run down to the office."

"Yeah, no bother."

"We're in no rush."

The manager heads off down the hallway beside the hotel bar.

"Now bejezze, we'll see how far in the red we are," says Toland.

"Oh yeah, we meant to ask you, you worked out in Mac Tíre House during transition year, didn't you?" asks Collins.

"Yeah, I was like a porter."

"No, because I think the new owners are Burke's cousins."

"The new owner is this Bracken fella. I know him to see, but I'm not sure if he's a relation of Burke's or not."

"Right..."

"Sure let me give the oul lady a shout, she'll know for certain," says Toland.

"Go for it," says Collins.

Toland steps outside with the mobile to his ear. His oul lady knows everything about everyone out the Mac Tíre Road. A real gossip. It drives him mental half of the time, but it's dead handy when you need to know a bit of info about someone. The manager returns with a large thonged ledger by her side. She places it down before us and opens it up to the book-marked page.

"Now, this is ye here."

The manager moves her right index finger down the page lines.

"And there, ye have a bit of a debt carried over from last year. A hundred and ten euro."

"Is that all?" asks Collins.

"That's it," says the manager. "Some schools leave massive debts altogether, so you're in good nick."

214

"Right, well, that's a grand job," says Collins.

"Okay, thanks a mill."

"No problem."

We head for the door and give the manager a courtly wave good-bye.

"Well, that shed some light on the subject."

It has started to drizzle outside.

"Where's himself?"

We search around for Toland, there's a faint muttering just down the way.

"There he is," points Collins.

He's under the shelter at the Fáilte Suite keeping in out of the mist.

"Yeah, I know. I'm on the way home now. Alright, bye," says Toland into the phone. "I swear to God, the oul lady wrecks the head sometimes. Did your wan come back?"

"Yeah, we're only down a hundred and ten."

"What did your oul lady say?"

"Ye were right. That buck Bracken, Brendan Bracken, is Burke's second cousin," says Toland.

"Isn't Burke the fucker for lying about the Fáilte Inn," says Collins.

"Some schools leave way bigger debts than a hundred and ten."

"Dickhead," says Toland.

"Let's tell Burke not to book anything till the classes decide where they want to have the Debs. It's not that much trouble to have them write their preference down on a piece of paper. I'll count them myself, it won't take me that long."

"Yeah, good thinking. We can just tell everyone what the story is and at least they'll have a choice," says Toland.

"Sound," says Collins.

"Right, get on to Burke at assembly in the morning."

We traipse back towards Toland's car.

"The oul lady didn't even know I left the gafe, she ate the head off me on the phone," says Toland.

"Better get back to the bloody books."

I'm awful groggy in the fecking mornings. Collins and myself head inside to assembly. We had a brief chat about the situation and decided that I would go after Burke and tell him not to do anything until the classes decide. Why me?

--Because Carolan's loud as fuck, said Collins.

We sit down and wait for Burke to show his slimy face. Here he comes now, look at the cut of him in his Tommy Hilfiger coat. That makes me dislike him all the more. Why would anyone want another person's name on their clothing?

--Why yes, I wear expensive clothing to show how sophisticated and refined my tastes are compared to the peasantry fancies of the proletariat.

"Hey, Burke?"

"Carolan, what's the story with ya?"

"I was looking into the Fáilte Inn and they said they'd take the Debs there and that we only owe them like a hundred euro."

"Really? Yeah. Well, it's a bit late."

"What do you mean it's a bit late?"

"Already put down the deposit with Mac Tíre House."

"Burke, did you ask anyone in the year where they wanted to have the Debs? No, you just fucking plowed on and booked it."

"The Fáilte Inn said they wouldn't take us."

"That's bullshit and you know well it is. Why did they tell me that they would?"

"I don't know, maybe they made a mistake."

"You're fucking full of it! It's because your fucking cousin just took over Mac Tíre House."

"Honest to God, the Fáilte Inn told me they wouldn't."

"Collins, this fucking wanker already booked the Mac Tíre House."

"Burke, we talked to the Fáilte Inn, what the fuck are you at?"

"What do you want me to do? If we pull out, we'll lose the deposit," says Burke.

"Burke, you're nothing but a cunt," says Collins, under his breath so Miss Keogh doesn't hear him.

"What's the big fucking deal? Have you seen the new Mac Tíre

216

House? It's pure class."

"It's going to cost everyone way more. It's a pain in the hole getting out there, plus you didn't ask anybody. You didn't ask where we wanted to have the final class night, ya fucking wanker ya."

"Listen lads, it'll be grand. I'm telling ye it'll be a great night," says Burke, in his calming fake-earnest manner.

What a piece of shite. The bell sounds. Burke strolls off to his class, not an ounce of guilt for taking money off people and giving it to his cousin.

I tried talking to a few people in the class and told them about Burke's fucking cowboy attitude to the whole thing, and I was met with nothing but equanimity. They just said,

--Sure it's booked now what can ya do?

Why is the class just accepting this? Collins and I seem to be the only two who are pissed off at all. I'm on the way over to Toland to fill him in on the scandal and I know well he'll be ripping when he hears about this fucking travesty, yet most people are like,

--Fuck it.

--Let it be.

--It's done now.

--Sure what can we do.

They fucking voted for that prick Burke to do a job and he's doing what his relation out in Mac Tíre House tells him. Conor O'Brien and the rest of the class reps are nowhere to be seen. They just do what Burke tells them to do. The whole fucking thing is ridiculous and everyone just takes it up the arse. Are they all taking crazy pills? They'll complain on the night that the whole thing was a bad idea. They'll bitch and moan like fuck while they walk to town because there won't be enough taxis to bring everyone back. Burke and his cronies are probably laughing like mad because they managed to get everyone in their classes to shell out an extra forty or so euro without the least bit of resistance.

--What a fucking sickner.

Chapter 18

The Association of Secondary Teachers Ireland, or the ASTI, have been threatening strike action since the start of the school year unless their wage demands are met. Today the teachers are officially on strike. They've been trying to negotiate with the Department of Education, but the government hasn't budged a bit. We're sitting here in assembly, not a teacher in sight. The younger classes can be heard down the hallways acting the bollocks, unsupervised. I suspect we'll be sent home today. I doubt they'll chance leaving a school without teachers, although the Department of Education have said it was ready in the event of a union strike. Personally, I think the teachers deserve their increases. They haven't had a wage raise in ages, and as much as I think schools are merely tools to subordinate and indoctrinate the youth, it's not all the teachers' fault. It's the way the school system works. Despite the severe limitations of mind-numbing and spirit-stifling curriculum, most of the teachers here at Saint Pat's actually try and do the best job they can. It's hard fecken work dealing with people, never mind the twenty-odd daft teenagers like me they have to put up with per class. Students have no interest in school unless they're in an exam year. Even then, most of the work in exam years is done after school. People learn very little in class, teachers in a lot of cases are more like baby-sitters. How can you teach people who don't want to learn? It's impossible. When I think about how soul-destroying it must be to work as a teacher, the more I think they deserve every penny they get.

Here comes Brother Leary.

"Okay, as I'm sure most of you know, the teachers are on strike, so we're going to close up for the day. We've notified the buses for those of you out the country," says Brother Leary. "Anyone have questions?"

Collins puts his hand up.

"Is there going to be school tomorrow?"

"Yes, the Department was aware that this was a possibility and have made provisions."

Leary waits for a second, then marches onwards to the next class as we make our way out. I'm not going to lie, it feels great not having to stay in school. Students spill out of the main entrance happy as Larry to be off for the day. Well wrapped up on this blustery morning, the whole teaching staff stand outside the school gates. The never-ending line of morning traffic sits across from them on the Oldport Road, as the teachers picket quietly, ASTI signs in gloved hands, freezing their arses off. Whenever you see teachers outside of school it's a sharp reminder that behind the tight upper lip and leather elbow patches, they are people too. Regular Joe and Jane soaps, most with Arts degrees trying to get on in life. By the looks of things, it seems it wasn't just a few agitators playing up as the media have been yammering about for the last while. If they're out, then all the teachers in the country must be out.

The teachers are on strike again for the sixth time in two weeks. The Department of Education weren't bullshiting when they said they were prepared in the event of an ASTI strike. They've brought in scabs to supervise the classes, they pay them about eleven euro per hour to sit on their arses and baby-sit the kids. Every morning when the scabs march into school the students taunt and heckle them like mad.

--BOO!

--FUCKING SCABS!

Us and the third years aren't too bad, we have exams to prepare for. Unfortunately for the scabs, any class without serious tests coming up goes absolutely bananas. You can hear the classes hollering all over the school. The scabs have to leave the classroom doors open while Brother Leary patrols the hallways to keep classes under control. For the last two weeks, the detention lists have become ridiculously long. The scabs only way of enforcing law and order is to dish out sceal threes like it's nobody's business. I don't know why the government doesn't give up on this farce and give in to the ASTI's modest demands. The teachers are clearly not going to stop until the Department starts negotiating. How much must it cost the Department paying the scabs? Do they think they're going to break the strike by holding out? What about the students? Aren't schools supposed to be about educating people? Look at this fella monitoring the class, what type of a situation is he in that he has to scab for eleven euro per hour?

Time moves faster these days with all the different happenings. Strikes. Exam numbers. I still don't know what to put down on the CAO form for college. I zip up my jacket and amble out through the main entrance for small break. My chicken and brown sauce sandwiches have my gob watering. The two lads sit at the wee wall beside the flag pole.

"Howye, girls?"

"What's the story?" says Toland, jawing on some cream crackers.

"Not too much, warped with the hunger."

"How'd ye get on with that economics paper?"

"Grand enough, those elasticity questions are handy if you get them."

"Yeah, bang out the Q over P and you're away with it."

Down the slope, near the GP room entrance, a number of fourth years shout and yowl. A couple of them start strutting towards the gates, laughing their arses off.

"C'mon strike!" shouts someone.

"What the fuck is going on?" says Toland.

"Are they having a laugh?"

"I think they are," says Collins.

A load of people begin to head towards them. Toland, Collins and myself return our lunches to our bags and leg it over to meet the lads at the school gates.

"Everyone, STRIKE!" yells another student.

I check behind, half the school is following suit, gibbering and joking.

"This is hilarious," says Collins.

220

As we get to the gates virtually all the students are walking out, even the students in the back yard are marching, bags on backs. We step onto the footpath and head up the hill at the Oldport Road. Everyone is screeching and guffawing like mad whores. The scabs patrolling the yards are gobsmacked by the rumblings, a couple try to convince some of the students to stop, but their half-arsed pleas are totally ignored. I'm shocked myself, this is mental, it looks like the whole school has walked out. We scooch along the packed footpath up the hill. I gawk down on the studentless front yard as the bell sounds.

"We're on strike, we're on strike, WE'RE ON STRIKE, WE'RE ON STRIKE!" Almost the whole student body chants in time.

An older woman walking her chocolate Labrador across the road gapes at us.

"WE'RE ON STRIKE, WE'RE ON STRIKE!"

Out the front entrance of Saint Pat's, Brother Leary strides straight for the mob. Myself and Collins are farthest away from the gable. Leary is nearly at the gates.

"Collins, c'mon."

I skid down the grassy knoll and skip the wall. Collins is close behind, he hops down from the wall into the car-park.

"C'mon, c'mon."

I glance over, Leary's addressing the crowd. Collins and myself boot it over to the flag pole.

"Quick."

We unknot the rope and pull down the Saint Patrick's blue flag as fast as we can.

"This is nuts man," says Collins, giddy as a goat.

We take off the flag and turn it upside-down. Collins fastens the grooves to the grips. The flag's secured, we hoist it upwards.

"Savage."

"I know."

The crowd notices the flag jerking up the pole. They start cheering again. Brother Leary spots us and notices the Saint Patrick's Blue blowing in the wind upside-down as it stalls at full mast. Collins and I leg it. We jump up the wall and hike back up the slippery knoll to the footpath. Leary quickly returns to the school. Incensed so he is. Everyone chants,

"WE RULE SCHOOL! WE RULE SCHOOL!"

Dying laughing, Collins and me mingle among the crowd.

"WE RULE SCHOOL! WE RULE SCHOOL!"

Some of the lads make signs by taping A4 pages together. One student is boosted up against the large green road sign, he tapes his handmade banner to it.

It reads: *GOV KISS OUR ASTI*.

Burke, the prick, makes his way through the empty front yard and along by the crowd. He stops about half-way up the road.

"Lads, this has been a great example, but we need to head inside now," yells Burke.

People in the crowd jeer Burke.

"Lick."

"Suck."

"Ya wanker, ya."

He seems very shaken by the whole thing.

"Burke, what the fuck are you doing?"

"Seanie, we need to go in. Seriously," says Burke.

"No we don't. We need to stay out here and let people know we mean fucking business."

"Whatever, Carolan."

"What the fuck are you on about 'whatever?' Keep kissing Leary's hole, ya fucking suck. Go back inside and support your boyfriend."

The crowd begins to "BOO."

Burke looks around powerless.

"Fuck Burke. Fuck Burke."

He turns and heads back towards the school, but the volume of the booing and heckling increases.

"Fuck Burke. FUCK BURKE." "FUCK BURKE."

The gobshite goes back with his tail between his legs. Good fucking riddance.

The twenty past twelve bell sounds. Less than twenty students walk out and around to class. What are they thinking? How can they not support their fellow students? Are they so enslaved by the school that they dare not disobey orders? A Nissan Micra slowly rolls down the hill with the music blaring and a couple of students hanging out of the car.

"SCHOOL'S OUT FOR SUMMER," booms from the car's speakers.

Rolling past the mob, Toland honks the horn repeatedly. Everyone screams and taps on the car's roof, he parks at the bottom of the hill just outside the school gates. Every vehicle that passes out the Oldport Road must be in shock. Just as a truck trundles by, an egg flies at it and hits its rear door. The driver hasn't noticed and keeps on trucking. It came from somewhere in the middle of the crowd. I weave through the students to see who the perpetrators are and find out what's the what. There they are with a carton of eggs in hand. I know one of those young fellas to see. He's a third year that lives across the field from me in Rathbawn Avenue. I catch his eye.

"Howya keeping, what's the craic?"

"How's it going," says the third year.

"Come-here for a sec. I'm not trying to run the show, but I think ye should save the eggs for later."

"Ah, I don't know. Sure it's a great oul laugh."

"I know, yeah, but if we start egging people they're going to go nuts, and when we go back to school, they'll kill us, ya know?"

"Right, right."

"Look it, if you're that mad to do it, off with ya, but I reckon we'll be better off not blackening our names. They'll only say we're a bunch of knackers if we let them."

"Alright ya."

"Alright, man."

Big lunch arrives. A load of the lads are texting some of the girls in the Convent, we've decided to head up the Square to see if we can get the Girls' School to join us. A rake of the sixth year girls are standing outside the Convent gates across from the Square. This could end up

223

being a great day, we go on strike and who knows, some of the lads might pull a date for the Debs while they're at it.

"Hey, Saoirse."

Saoirse O'Rogha is on the sixth year Student Council, she used to be good pals with Chris' old bird, Fiona.

"Seanie, wow, this is crazy."

"I know, are ye going to join us?"

"I am, and a good few of the sixth years definitely will."

"Nice one."

"What did Leary do when ye walked out?"

"He tried talking to Ned Burke-"

"-Dickhead."

"I know. Collins and myself ran down when Leary was talking to the crowd and put the Saint Pat's flag up upside-down."

"Oh my God, ha, ha, deadly."

"It was gas."

Sister McAuley waddles down the driveway. She's the head penguin of the Girls' School and doesn't seem so pleased with our presence. The Sisters of Grace run the Convent, though I've yet to hear of their grace in Ballybar.

"Can anyone who doesn't go to school here please move away from the gates, thank you."

A bunch of our lads move away as asked. Sister Mc'Auley turns her attention to Saorise and her friends.

"And, if any student from here walks out on class today there will be serious consequences."

Some of the lads start booing Sister Mc'Auley and making penguin calls.

"Wa-wa-wa-wa-wa-wa."

"Down with this sort of thing."

"Careful now," shouts people in the crowd.

"Very funny, you're nothing but a shower of blackguards, the lot of ye."

"Sister, we should be supporting the teachers," says Saorise.

"Miss O'Rogha, there'll be none of that in here and I'm warning

224

you now."

--She's having nun of it.

"Sister, it's ridiculous the way things are going."

As the good Sister's about to retort the crowd starts jeering so loud that she can't be heard.

"A disgrace is what ye are."

God, she's pissed off. Let her go back and have a nice cuntsandwich the oul bitch. She returns to the Convent, the boos and catcalls chasing her up the path.

"Ye aren't going to let her stop ye joining us, are ye?"

"No way, who does she think she is threatening us? The oul strap."

"I know, same craic with Leary, they talk to us like we're two-year-olds, they should be trying to help so they should."

The bell from the Girls' School rings. It's two o'clock now. There must be around five hundred Saint Pat's students and about a hundred and fifty from the Convent lined up at the edge of the Square. We're going to march around by the County Council, down by the Bank of Ireland, down by Tower street and back to the Square. Saoirse and the girls have made huge banners for the front of the march. They read:

Up the ASTI.

Student Power.

Other students have made a range of different signs from:

Free the Weed.

To,

Fuck the Dáil.

Every car, lorry and van that drives by leers in fascination. Some honk in support, others stare at us with a sort of daft disappointment plastered across their pusses. I'm sure they hate the idea of young people organising and fighting for something.

--Upstarts. Upstarts the lot of them.

We march down Herbert Street, banners and signs held proudly, a high-spirited mixture of the Boys' School and the Girls' School. What a sight. The nuns must love the idea of their precious angels mixing

225

with pups the likes of us. Past the Bank of Ireland we march, I did them a favour by trying to burn that place to the ground, I gave the bastards an excuse to rebuild the place bigger and better than before. Some employees peep out the bank's windows. I wonder have they ever thought about striking? They rent themselves out to the bank for an hourly wage. They're wage slaves. What's the difference between renting yourself out to a master for a wage and being owned by a master? I suppose if you're owned, the masters would look after you because you're the property of the masters. They have a vested interest in keeping their owned slaves safe and sound. However, if they only rent the slaves, well then they couldn't give two shites about the poor fuckers. Sure, why would they? They can just rent another slave, a slave who isn't worn out from labouring away every day for a paltry wage, never once realising the fruits of their labour. I bet they don't allow any unions in the Bank of Ireland. You couldn't have that. It would interfere with their harmoniously run machine.

Up ahead at Parrish's Corner we have some fans waiting for us, Jim Beglin, the news reporter from RTE, and a camera crew. We're going to be famous ha, ha, ha. Swinging a righty tighty down Tower Street we wave and rave in front of the cameras. We continue on past the Imperial Hotel. Across from the Square we settle outside the Court House, we're flanked by the Guards to our left and Jim Beglin and his cohorts from RTE to the right.

"On the road, everyone on the road."

I heard somewhere that if you're going to protest you have to stop traffic to really make it effective. We'll probably piss off a rake of people. Sure fuck it. They can take the scenic route around town. A Guard moseys over towards us and up the steps of the Court House.

"Ye'll have to come in off the road," says the Guard.

"We, shall not, we shall not be moved."

Everyone joins in, "WE, SHALL NOT, WE SHALL NOT BE MOVED."

The Guard stands there like a fool for a second, then steps down.

"WE, SHALL NOT, WE SHALL NOT BE MOVED."

Jim Beglin must be creaming the cacks. I'd say this is ratings gold for the boyos in RTE. It's fecking mighty craic altogether. Everyone, in every school, work-place, or any place where people have to acquiesce to illegitimate authority should strike.

"GET UP, STAND UP. STAND UP FOR YOUR RIGHTS!"

I'm here at home waiting for the six o'clock news. Mam heard about us on her lunch break and is dying to see if I'm on the telly. The mob dissipated at four o'clock without major hassle in the castle. A couple of more Guards came out to greet us, it looked like they were going to do something for a while, but the girls stepped to the front. The Guards wouldn't dare lay a hoof on them. I'd say half the town is ripping with us, there were a couple of County Councillors watching from across the Square shaking their heads.

The news headlines flash on.

"Mam, it's on, it's on."

Mam takes a seat with her mug of tea and watches the headlines intently.

"There we are."

Jim Beglin stands in frame, half smiling, with the students shouting behind him.

"There's the red head," says Mam.

I'm standing next to Toland and Collins about half-way from the front.

"Ha, ha, ha, we're fecking legends so we are."

"You're famous now. I bet they'll have ye in the papers tomorrow as well."

"I wonder are more schools going to strike after this?"

"You wouldn't know, the crowd in Dublin might give in now after this."

"Do ya reckon?"

"You never know."

"Still, we could take it a step further so we could."

Since our strike, the Department of Education hasn't equivocated in

227

their stance to the ASTI's protest. In fact, they've gone out of their way to demonise the ASTI. Many politicians have come down on the side of the Department, staunchly opposing the teachers' demands. Big fecken surprise. They're trying to make out that the teachers are overpaid, it's absolute lunacy so it is. In the meantime, we've been trying to organise the students by doing more than plain protest. All the class reps have taken the email and mobile numbers of every student. Each rep meets with the classes every other day to discuss what they want to do instead of what the Department wants to do with the classes. Every policy idea is put forth by email and text so everyone knows what's cracking. The teachers are trying harder to get their way and still strike a couple of times a week. Since half of our time is spent with scabs in the classroom, we've put forward the idea of taking over the school and running it ourselves. We had the classes vote on the idea of organising the school democratically. The tallies came out at:

477 in favour of the motion.

108 against the motion.

18 spoiled votes.

Encouraged by this, we've decided to formulate a new school policy. We, the students are going to change the whole daft system, no more of the Prussian mis-education ruining our individuality. We're sending out a public notice through the school newspaper and email. We're also going to send a master copy with the signatures of all the students in agreement to Brother Leary.

23-12-2003

To the Faculty of Saint Patrick's Secondary School:

Schools are institutions of indoctrination and inculcation of irrational attitudes of submission to authority. We, the students, are treated as empty vessels to be filled with what the Department of Education deems appropriate; we are numbered, humiliated, stupefied and broken into acquiescence. The hierarchical structure of the school system is severely damaging to the developing intellects of young people, and We the Students seek to eradicate this tyrannical system.

Instead, We hope to ignite a flame that may illumine our minds and invigorate our hearts. We intend to create a school that epitomises enlightenment, fosters individualistic and creative thought, and typifies the principles of democracy, equality and solidarity. Once We, the Students, return after the Christmas break, policy at Saint Patrick's will undergo a radical shift in a new direction.

Democracy will be the tool We use to govern ourselves, regardless of year or class. Neither the state, nor the church, not even the parents, but the Students alone should decide what happens in the institutions they attend.

In light of these changes, school uniforms will henceforth be optional. Likewise with the formal address of school staff. It will be the prerogative of the Student whether he chooses to address a staff member formally or informally. Members of the clergy are welcome to participate in school activities, but only at the Students' discretion. All religious events, such as Mass and Confession, will become optional. No more shall religion be rammed down Students' throats, it will be up to the individual if he wishes to participate or not.

Classes will be organised by the students; the faculty's role shall be to aid the Students to teach themselves. In relation to discipline, detention shall be abolished. If a Student's behaviour should become problematic or disruptive, a disciplinary hearing will be held by the class, or, if necessary, by the year. The aggrieved will bring his case against the accused and the class or year will decide whether punishment is warranted. If the Students come to the conclusion that punishment is indeed appropriate, it will be enforced by the class, or year, itself.

Given that the only path to third-level education is by taking the Junior and Leaving Cert Examinations, classes in these years will be open to form voluntary study groups for each subject in preparation for the state exams. It is lamentable that students who desire to pursue higher education have to subject themselves to months of memorising that will be swiftly forgotten afterwards; however, for the time being, those who wish to go on to tertiary education will have to endure such nonsense.

Further details will follow in the coming days and weeks.

Students of Saint Patrick's Secondary School.

Chapter 19

The morning of the 7th, our first school day of 2004. A load of us are here at Pat's to intercept Brother Leary. We got a set of keys from the caretaker, he's well aware of our plans and agreed to give us a copy of the keys provided we didn't rat him out.

--Plausible deniability, as the man says.

"Game time," says Collins.

Brother Leary pulls into the car-park, he steps out, carefully adjusts his usual black cassock, and squints at us from his car. Seemingly unshaken by our presence, he makes his way over to us at the main entrance. We're all fairly nervous. My hand is trembling like fuck. It's one thing talking about saying whatever to whomever, it's another thing altogether when you're about to go through with it.

"Please remove yourselves," says Brother Leary, breast out, calm.

"Did you read the letter?"

He nods.

"Good, well, then you understand that you're welcome to go inside provided you agree that the Students will run things."

"Who do ye think ye are, hah?" says he, in his patronising manner. "I've been in this school for over twenty years, you're daft if ye think this type of carry-on is acceptable."

He tries to take a step forward, we don't budge a bit.

"I'm sorry, we don't care how long you've been in here. If you don't agree to what we've proposed, you have no business in here."

"This is the Brothers' school!"

"Not any more," says Toland.

"I'm warning ye now, clear out of my way."

Everyone stands rooted.

"I'm serious. Whoever doesn't move will be expelled."

"Listen, you can either support what we're trying to do, or leave. There are plenty of other schools that are run like tyrannies, so off with ya."

Again, he tries to pass. Nobody moves. We stand silently, unwavering in our conviction. Leary looks like he's about to have a conniption, he glares at us, his face flushed, his nostrils flaring.

"Move, I'm warning ye."

Leary knows we're not messing, he knows we're not going to give in to his threats. He takes a few paces back.

"Ye can't shut down the place."

"The school's open as normal, just people are actually going to try and get something out of their day for once."

"Fine," says he, in a low tone.

Leary tramps back to his car, turns with disgust and shouts across the yard.

"I warned ye, there'll be war over this."

He gets into his car, slamming the driver's side door. Leary pulls out and drives off fucking fuming.

"Wow," says Collins. "I can't believe we just did that."

"I know."

It's like a big weight has been lifted, it feels unreal standing up to the big dick himself.

The morning bell sounds, everyone makes their way to assembly unsure of what to expect from the day. About half the students are dressed in the school uniform. Some wear the shirt and jumper and don't wear the trousers. Some wear everything without the tie. Some dress casual like myself, no uniform at all. The scabs are in, the secretaries, the caretaker, Vice Principal Corley, everyone who is supposed to be here is here, except Leary. Before the break we had a sit-down with the administrative staff and told them of our intentions. I don't think they believed us, but they all have a funny face on them today. Vice Principal Corley had the same reaction when his son in fifth year informed him of our plans. Corley said as long as the ASTI strike continues, he will continue to do his administrative duties, which is fair enough. We've been emailing and texting the students on what's going to happen today. The basic plan for the non-exam years is that they use the school timetable so everyone knows what rooms are in use, then the lads can have a class on whatever they want. No need for small break or big break anymore, people are free to come and go whenever they like. If someone wants to go outside for fresh air or decides they want to head to the vending machine, they're free to do so. Same story with the bathroom. What type of place gives people the power to decide whether or not someone can use the jacks? When you think about the fact that you had to seek authorisation to take a slash or a shite, it was nothing short of sadistic.

Yesterday went grand enough, the scabs stayed within their bounds, like we thought they would, and there was no sign of Leary, thank fuck. That might change somewhat today. The teachers are in and we've decided to go to the teachers lounge for a word. We're anticipating some bother with a few of the teachers, in particular with the more tenured ones. After all, some of them have been in positions of power for yonks upon yonks. They're not going to just roll over and give up that power. No more automatic,

--Yes, sir. No, miss.

We had a discussion about how to approach them and decided that Toland and I should meet them instead of bringing in a large number of students like we did with Leary. One of the reasons we don't want an overly aggressive confrontation is that we really want the teachers' support. No matter how much independence We, the Students, want, a good teacher is an invaluable resource. The fourth years sent an email out last night about what should be done in the event a teacher tries to take-over a class, they recommended boycotting any teacher who might seek to regain their power. If a teacher truly believes in helping students to better their situation, then they should at least try and support our cause. Toland and myself enter the teachers lounge. Some sit with sleepy faces tasting tea and coffee, others chat amongst themselves. They immediately buck up and give us their attention. I'd say most of them foresaw that we were going to have a heart to heart after telling Leary to hit the bricks yesterday.

"Morning everybody," says Toland. "I'm sure ye all heard what happened yesterday morning with Brother Leary-"

"-A disgrace," says Mr. Kenny.

If there's one buck we knew wouldn't like the new set-up, it's Kenny. He has been a teacher for twenty-eight years, a power mad bollocks, who revels in making people feel thick.

"Anyways, we're going to say the same thing to you as we said to Brother Leary. I'm sure you're all aware of how the school is going to be run, and as long as you understand that, you're all more than welcome to participate. But, if any of you don't agree then we think it's best you leave."

"The cheek of ye, who do ye pups think ye are?" barks Kenny.

"Yeah, yeah, listen, if any teacher tries to take-over a class ye'll be boycotted. It's that simple, alright."

The teachers stand and sit and stare there silently. I'm sure this must feel awfully odd, especially to the oul ones.

"We hope you support us like We support you, the teachers. Thank you," says Toland.

The clock in the hallway reads half eleven. Collins, myself and Toland decide to take a biteen of a break. It will do the mind good to get a dose of fresh air before we go back to the books.

"Here's the prick himself," says Collins.

Kenny marches over to us like a bull.

"What are ye doing out here?" says Kenny.

"None of your business."

"Get into class now."

Nobody pays a bit of heed of the fucken jackass.

"Get in!"

"Here, we told you the way things are now."

"I've been here for nearly thirty years!" the prick shouts at us once more.

"I'm warning ya, if you shout again there'll be serious bother, alright?" says Toland.

Kenny backs down a bit with Toland's warning.

"Look, I think it's better if you clear off, because if you think things are going to go back to you bossing people and telling them they're thick every day, you're fucking dreaming, man."

Kenny starts marching to his car.

"Keep walking, ya cunt ya," says Collins quietly.

"The state of him, why does he think acting like a maniac is going to get him what he wants?"

Kenny gets in to his navy Volkswagen Polo, the same frowzled face on him that Leary wore yesterday. He speeds off.

"Another fucker gone."

During our English study group we asked Mr. Neill if he would tutor the class on our assigned play Red Roses for Me by Sean O'Casey. He loved it. It's a big change to have a class of eager attentive students who each had an essay for him to correct and comment on. I now see why he became a teacher. His knowledge of literature is astounding, plus he's a master of knowing how to answer questions effectively in an exam situation. He went through all the different ways they will give and take away marks when the examiners are correcting our papers and showed us the pitfalls to steer clear of on exam day. I've never seen him enjoy a class more. That's the big difference between Mr. Neill and that clown Kenny. Mr. Neill became a teacher to try and make a difference, to help young people. In all the years I've seen him take abuse, he never once tried to make a student feel like dirt, no matter how bad they made him feel by playing puc. He always turned the other cheek. Kenny on the other hand, Christ Almighty, Kenny is forever picking on students, usually the weaker ones in the class. That's why he became a teacher, he gets to feel like the big man telling people they're stupid and showing off his intellectual prowess to teenagers. What a fucking gobshite. People like Kenny could never learn to work in a system based on equality, he needs to berate and humiliate others in order to attain a feeling of superiority. I hope he never comes back, bastards like Kenny have no business around young people.

We got through the day, only just. Some of the older teachers walked out. They couldn't stand being on the same level as everyone else. Thankfully, the majority of teachers took to the change fairly well, especially the younger ones. I suppose they're not that long out of school themselves.

One of the things we have been fairly concerned about is how the wasters are going to get on. We knew there'd be some lads who wouldn't play ball no matter what. The type of lads who want to destroy everything. People like Skeff. They think mindless destruction is,

--Bertified mon.

In the old system, people who weren't interested in school sat at the back not paying attention or played hell for half the class. In our system they can do what they want as long as they're not fucking anyone else over. It's a frustrating thing, but if they don't want to try to get something out of their time, it's their loss. We cannot force them to partake in the new school, but we cannot allow them to wreck havoc either. And so certain ground rules must be laid down and agreed upon by the students, otherwise we know things would descend into chaos. It's the only way to organise the school from the bottom up instead of imposing order from the top down. One of the big arguments by the students who thought the change wouldn't work was,

--How is every decision going to be democratic?

We worked on the problem for a while and came to the conclusion that not all decisions need be democratic. If a student wants to have a picture of Angelina Jolie in his locker that should be his decision. Someone having a picture in his locker affects nobody else, it does not encroach on another student's freedom. If someone wants to leave malodorous gone-off brown sauce and chicken sambos in their locker and it's stinking everyone out of it, that's an instance where they are infringing on the freedom of other students. If held to a democratic decision, more than likely the gone-off sambos wouldn't be allowed to putrefy away in the lockers. One person's freedom ends where the next person's begins. We have to have basic elementary principles that are agreed on by everyone. Chaos has no rules, it doesn't take others into account, we on the other hand have an anarchic order, instead of chaotic anarchy.

A mother of a third year has dropped in, she's going mental about the state of things. The teachers are on strike today so the students in class tried to calm her down. She wouldn't listen to a word of it. Parents at times can be like that prick Kenny, they refuse to treat young people with the same amount of respect that they give to so-called mature adults. They think ruling with an iron fist will lead to model behaviour, when it oftentimes drives people daft in the head. Some parents live through their children by making them do things only they want them to do. It's very common within GAA families to try and force the children into football or hurling, even if the young one is interested in other things. I think some parents have a sort of god complex. Why do they think they know what their children want more then their children?

--Nobody knows what's for one's own good, except one's own good self.

What's wrong with letting people fail? Why not let people discover things for themselves? Inevitably there will be many false starts, but surely to fuck a great deal more would be learned from these experiences than by planning out every moment before someone comes bawling into the world. Collins is trying to deal with the indignant mam. He's the right man for the mam, his mellifluous voice is soothing to the lugs of distressed mothers.

"My child is in here and he's not learning a bloody thing."

"Your son wasn't learning before, now he actually is. He's learning to teach himself," says Collins.

"Arra, he is not. He's in here watching films for half the day."

"How is he not learning by watching a film? Can he read and write?"

"He can."

"Did you do the Leaving?"

237

"I did."

"What academic skills do you possess that he hasn't already attained?"

"Well..."

"Do you remember anything from those exams?"

This stumps the mam, her son stands beside her with the gob shut. She glances at him then turns her gaze back to Collins.

"But, you can't be at that, he has the Junior Cert in a year."

"Yeah, and I have the Leaving in a couple of months, that's why we have special study groups for those taking exams."

"Sure that's not the way things work."

"We'll it's time to move on," says Collins. He looks at her son and asks, "What else are you at in here?"

"I'm doing the guitar."

"Do you do that outside school?"

"Nope."

"What do you think will serve your son better in life? Memorising facts that he'll forget in a month or learning to play a musical instrument?"

The mam still won't change her stance. It's like she can't stand having someone who's younger than her make more sense, I reckon this is the way in which a lot of older people make themselves feel superior. They think that they are more intelligent or rational by virtue of their age. They think they should automatically get respect because of their age.

--Respect your elders.

Why? If you believe in equality you would respect every person equally. There are thick older people who could do with plenty of education. And why is someone a grown-up or knowledgeable when they finish school? Is it like a criminal, once you get out of jail you're supposedly reformed? Learning should go on forever, we should always be trying to improve our minds. The truth is, when it comes to things like rationality, age has little to do with it. Some people are more rational than others. Perhaps they're born that way or they're conditioned that way. Certainly, there are some things that can only be learned through experience. However, rationality and general cop-on rarely discriminates based on one's age, older people do as many dumb and thick things as any young person. Sure aren't they the people running the world, and what a mighty job they're doing. It's apparent that no matter how much sense Collins makes to this woman, he isn't going to get through to her. I suspect the only reason she's still arguing with him is to save face. She's blathering on about how great the Brothers are for educating people. Obviously it never occurred to her, or most people, that religious institutions have a great deal to gain by indoctrinating and brainwashing young people in order to keep them within the realm of the cult's influence. I'm sure this mam went to Catholic schools like most, hence the increased chances of her daftness. She probably never had a chance. Most people never have a chance. They're fed the bullshit of religion, and the irrationality that comes with it, from such an early age. They never learn to free their minds of the bollocks beliefs. They're told the book of lifted fairy tales is legit and authentic, sure most so-called Catholics have never even read the Bible. How can you call yourself a Catholic and not read the book it's based on? I suppose if more people did read it they wouldn't believe half of the bollocks for long. This mam isn't having any of it. She drags her son away by the school-bag righteously. Collins' attempts to appeal to her rational side have failed, like I'm sure they would with most parents. They're slaves to convention and conformity.

An interesting topic brought up at a meeting today was how to help the administrative staff get better wages. When you think of someone like a caretaker, why should they make less than, say a teacher? If both jobs payed the same, which job would you rather do? Caretaker or teacher? I'd say most people would prefer to be a teacher. Think of how much more a caretaker sacrifices themselves. That's not to say teachers don't make sacrifices. They do. Teaching is a difficult job, but janitorial work can be awful altogether. Cleaning up after messy, dirty people, it's fecking horrid. A teacher is a much more empowering job than a caretaker, I bet a teacher feels a lot better at the end of the day than a janitor, and that's not saying much, plenty of teachers must feel terrible at the end of the day. The administrative staff aren't allowed join a union, they have nobody fighting for better conditions and treatment. It's not fair on them. I suppose if they were allowed to organise, they'd soon strike and they'd be dead fecking right.

There was a bad oul skirmish today between two bucks in second year. Some of the lads broke it up, but as soon as the two fellas got free they went for each other again. I'm not sure what started the fracas. Apparently the two fellas are friends and have a history of fighting and making up. This time it got so bad some of the fourth years had to go over and mediate. They said that the two lads should figure out their differences and forget about the whole thing. One of the lads agreed to make friends, but the other fella wouldn't compromise at all. He just continued to threaten the other student. The year decided to suspend him from going into any class with his frenemy for three days. Why wouldn't that student agree to disagree? Was the quarrel that serious? Maybe he just wants to fight?

Something I'm sure some of the teachers are not going to be too fond of is that a couple of students have put forward the idea that we should decide which teachers get hired and fired. I wish I had another year left so I could put forth the motion to get rid of that bollocks, Kenny, although with his popularity he'll be getting binned for sure. The fourth years emailed the proposal around yesterday. Before the end of the year the teachers who are not going to be returning will be notified, then the offers will be put out for teachers that are needed to fill certain positions and any newly created classes. The students will have to meet with the prospective teachers and if they like them, they'll be hired. If they don't they won't. I'd say all the oul strict teachers will go running for the hills when they hear of such practices. I think it will embolden many of the younger teachers though. It's definitely going to get my vote.

Last night a motion was emailed about keeping the school open on the weekends so students could avail of the resources. A good number of students live around the town and it would be handy to have the school open for them. There might not be many official classes because the lads who live out the country mightn't be able to get lifts on Saturday and Sunday. Still, it's a good idea for those nearer to the school. I'll say a yay for sure.

We're two weeks into our democratic school now and virtually no one wears the God awful school uniform, thank fuck. At first it felt daft, too good to be true that we could run the school our way. We had planned for a lot of cock-ups and luckily there have been no difficulties we couldn't handle with everyone chipping in. We've shown, at least so far, that our way wouldn't immediately fall into chaos. The thing that feels most exciting is that every day more and more students are getting involved. Sure what else would they do? Sit on their arses bored to tears? Of course there are still the lads who think they're too cool for school, but at least their excuse that school is for holding people down is gone. Already a whole host of new classes have sprung up, there's a computer games class, a philosophy class, astronomy class, film class, and a rake of others. The art classes are designing a project to redecorate the whole school. Miss Lavelle loves it. The teachers are now human beings instead of task masters and supervisors. A good majority of the students actually want to learn for themselves and those who don't stay out of the way. It's not perfect, but it's a damn sight better than before, and it'll continue to improve if we really want it to.

Chapter 20

Clearly Leary isn't going to leave us be without a scrap. At Mass on Sunday, his oul flower Father Ussher warned all sheep in attendance, many of whom were parents, that what we are doing is an affront to the years of blood, sweat and semen the clergy have spent mis-educating the children of Ireland. Toland's oul lady was present and caught the whole holy spiel, he said she was fierce shook when she returned from Ussher's fear mongering Mass. It sounds like Ussher was doing the priestly righteous indignation routine above on the altar. Whether it's Protestants or premarital riding, the church's time-honoured 'scare people into doing what they want' tactic never ever gets worn.

--Do you understand what will become of your children if this type of carry-on continues? Hell, I tell you. Holy Hell!

At long last the Department of Education announced that they were finally going to give in to the ASTI's demands, we can expect the teachers to be back full-time next week. Thank God there'll be no more scabs. I think it will stand to the teachers that they got to make the transition to the new system slowly, never having to deal with the change five days in a row.

Studying on the weekends is a right downer, I'm here memorising French essays like a fecking automaton. The amount of stuff I've learned off by heart is criminal. Christ, if the shagging smoking ban doesn't pop up on the production écrite part I'll go ape altogether. The CAO change your mind window is closing by the day. I can't wait to have all this done and dusted. What to do? What to see? What to be?

Fmmmm. Fmmmm. Fmmmm.

My mobile vibrates. The caller ID reads: Bobby Cusack. He's one of the fellas in fourth year.

"Howya Bob, what's the craic with ya?"

"Carolan, you need to get down here."

"Where?"

"Pat's."

"Why?"

"Leary is here with a couple of Guards and some buck changing the fucking locks."

I race past the oul Hat Factory toward Pat's. A small number of students stand outside the front entrance. Before them is Brother Leary, beside him at the main entrance is a locksmith and a Guard. I jump off my bike and dump it on the tarmac, the back spokes spinning. Collins is at the fore of the group arguing with the Guard.

"What's the story?"

"Leary said now that the teachers are back full time, things are going back to normal," says Collins.

"Did you try the back?"

"No."

"C'mon to fuck."

We leg it around the back to check if the rear entrance is open, there's a Garda car parked in the back car-park outside the Sports Hall. At the rear entrance some bogger Guard waits with a big happy look of superiority. I dangle a set of keys to show that Collins and myself mean serious business.

"How's it going?"

"Sorry, lads," says the Guard.

I glare at him plainly and give him the shift-out-of-the-fucking-way eyes.

"I'm not allowed to let ye pass."

"Listen, we go to school here, we have the keys, so please, step aside."

"I can't. Orders are orders."

"Says who?"

"Says the Superintendent and Brother Leary."

"What authority does he have?"

243

"It's the Brothers' school."

"No. It's the Students' school."

"Not on paper it's not, it's property of the Brothers."

"Are you having a laugh?"

The Guard says nothing, he just stares over at the lake, his lips tight.

"You're going to go against the six-hundred and something odd students just because Leary tells you to?" says Collins.

"Listen lads, I'm just doing my job, alright."

"Fine, you fucking prick."

Collins and I begin to walk away.

"Be a sheep, you fucking lackey."

We bout it back around to the front, the locksmith is about done with the door. A dozen or so students shout and shove trying to get past the Guard. Leary, behind him, inserts the key into the lock. The Guard steps back and attempts to close the door.

"FUCK THE PIGS!"

"Don't let him."

One of the boys throws his body in the way.

"Come out let ya!"

A couple of more lads try to step between the Guard and the gap. One of the lads holds on to the side of the door. The Guard manages to peel him off and quickly back-steps as Leary locks the door from inside.

"Fuck them anyways!"

A student asks, "Is the back locked?"

"Yeah, the bastard has another shade standing guard."

The only light switched on inside the school is that in the teachers lounge. I bet the pricks are probably sitting down proud as fuck of themselves.

After the take-over we got a load of students together and discussed what we can do to try and get Pat's back. It's a pain in the hole trying to organise during the weekend, everyone is off doing something or they can't get a lift into town. We came to the conclusion that reaching out to the teachers is probably the best course of action. To have a real shot at getting the school back we have to get them on our side, there's no way Leary can stand up against us and the teachers. I gave Mr. Neill a shout this evening, he said he'd see what the vibe is off the other teachers and get back to us as soon as he's able.

I'm here in the studious silence of the library, across the road I can see the cop shop in all its glory, twisted and warped, through the grains of the etched glass windows. Fucking pawns is what they are. The automatic doors part as Mr. Neill, nervous as ever, enters the library foyer with his battered oul brief-case by his side.

I nod hello and whisper,

"Let's talk outside, don't want to cause a racket."

"Yeah, yeah."

We step outside and head over near the section of the building opposite the astro turf and swimming pool.

"Well, sir, what's the verdict?"

"I'm awful sorry, Seanie, but I don't think the teachers will support ye."

"Really. Why?"

"Well, there's a couple of reasons. The ASTI are after winning a big battle, they're not going to put themselves out over a small school in the West."

"Yeah," says I, while inhaling.

"And worse again is that Brother Leary called around this morning, he warned every teacher that anyone who dissents won't be coming back next year."

"Are ya serious?"

"You have to remember, it's the government that pays our salaries, and you know, teachers have bills to pay like everyone else."

"The bastard! I mean seriously, what a fucking prick..."

"I know, it's a bad spot you're put in."

"There must be something ye can do."

"Not at this time, I don't think. The year is almost half-way done and no teacher is going to risk their job, especially after all the acrimony with the ASTI."

"I know. You're right, what are they going to do? It would fuck up their whole career. They wouldn't be able to go anywhere if they pissed against the wind so they wouldn't."

Mr. Neill adjusts his horn-rimmed glasses, his eyes seem sad with acceptance, that poor fella will be going back to trying to keep the attention of students who couldn't be bothered. They'll just take the mick out of him day in day out.

"Ye should be proud of yourselves though, it's a testament to ye, the way ye organised."

"Yeah. Well, either way, thanks a mill, sir."

"Oh, not at all, no bother. I was actually thinking if ye wanted, I'd be happy, ya know, to keep the grinds going after school."

"You don't have to do that, sir."

"No, no, no. I'd be glad to do it, honestly I would."

"Alright. I'd say there'll be a good few showing up, the mocks are soon enough."

"That's grand, the more the merrier."

On Monday morning, there were a fair few more uniforms than I had seen in a while. Leary got all the members of the School Board to back his return and contacted some of the more vocal members on the PTA. The parents, frightened by the PTA, made sure their sons wouldn't make trouble and toed the line. Anyone not in full uniform was not admitted to school. Leary and Kenny stood at the main entrance while Vice Principal Corley waited at the rear. They even had the Guards on hand to deter any ideas we might have had of protesting on school grounds. Some of the parents nearly fainted upon seeing the squad car parked in the middle of the school car-park, a couple even drove their sons home to change into the full uniform. The majority of the student resistance came from the fourth and fifth years. The first and second years were cowed with relative ease by the teachers enforcing Leary's law. One class of fourth years tried staging a demonstration in the foyer, Leary quelled them immediately by having the Class Head call their parents to come in and collect them. In one fifth year class they turned all the desks facing the back wall and ignored the teacher for forty minutes, another class continually set off their mobile phones throughout the day. Similar tactics to disrupt the classes were met with only marginal success. There have always been people rebelling, and the teachers for the most part are well able to manage it so long as they have strong backing from Leary and the staff. By Wednesday the students, although still rowdy, were more or less back to the old way.

--Yes, sir.

--No, miss.

The Guards continue to patrol every day, I don't know for how much longer Leary will keep them around. The teachers are back to their old selves as well. This week alone there's over sixty students on detention, it must be some sort of school record. Whenever a teacher does something the students don't like everyone whispers,

--Traitor. Traitor. Traitor.

It's disappointing that not one of the teachers will stand up for us, even the younger teachers who were really supportive during our democracy just follow orders. Still, I can understand why they don't, as Mr. Neill said, if they did they wouldn't be coming back next year. The whole fucking thing is so maddening, I can't believe how easy it is for Leary to get everything back to the old way. It's as if our two week experiment never happened at all.

This morning I'm meeting up with Toland and Collins at the library, we're waiting to see what action the Brother and the School Board are going to take. Even though Mr. Neill isn't on the Board he got wind that we were in the shite, he reckons there will be some sort of disciplinary hearing.

"Howye, bucks?"

"Hey," says Collins.

"How's the form?" asks Toland.

We stroll across the road to the Square. It's clear enough out today, for once the steel benches aren't dripping with dewy wet. The lads seem a bit on edge.

"What do ye think will go down?"

"It's hard to know, isn't it," says Collins.

"Maybe they won't do anything, I mean, there was an awful lot involved. They'll hardly go picking on people at random," says Toland.

"The PTA or School Board mightn't do much, but I wouldn't put it past Leary. Think about the type of fucker he is. You think he won't be looking to make an example of a few people?"

"The parents really fucked us, hah," says Collins.

"I know. You'd think they might look at things different because they were in our shoes before. But no. They had to go along with the bastards," says Toland.

"They've been through the system, then they probably went working a shite job. Doing what they're told every day. What do you expect, the only thing they know how to do is obey. Do what the boss says, sure it's drilled into them so it is."

"Makes you sick to the stomach," says Collins.

"What servile people we are," says Toland.

"Speak for yourself, I don't ever want to be one of those people."

"That's almost everyone well," says Toland.

"Then, I'm not everyone, no way."

Toland, fiddling with his fingers, gazes across at the Court House, then turns his face to the Garda Station.

"Can you believe he brought in the boys in blue? I never thought he'd go that far," says Toland.

"When you think about it, what else could he have done? Nobody would have listened to him if he tried to get us to go back on his own."

"He had to stop us going in, force us back to the uniform, to the oul way," says Collins.

"That, plus getting teachers and parents to clamp down. It makes my blood boil to think of the parents. You can understand the teachers, but the parents are as fucking thick."

"I know, my oul lady went mental. She told the oul fella and he asked what type of carry-on were we at? I said running the school for the students. To which he said 'I'll student ya!'" says Toland.

"I hate when oul fellas do that, like if you say I'm going in to get a video and they say something stupid like 'I'll video ya,'" says Collins.

"In their heads, deep down they must know they're wrong. It's easier to go with the old ways instead of looking in the mirror. Easier to get on so it is."

Mam and I are on the way to the dreaded disciplinary hearing now. Brother Leary singled Toland, Collins and myself out of everyone in school. He punished plenty of others by finding absurd reasons to put them on detention, but he's actually suspending us. We're easy targets after all. There has been a fair bit of an after-shock around the town from our democracy. The Convent and Moore College have become way stricter and clamped down on any act of dissent. No school tie? Give cheek to a teacher? Detention, or worse. They can't have the threat of a good example, that's why they had to crush us and vaccinate the surrounding schools like Moore and the Convent. Run tight ships, as rigid as can be so no one will get any ideas of challenging their rule.

Outside the teachers lounge myself and Mam wait for our show-down with the School Board. Mam is fierce nervous. I don't blame her, confrontation isn't easy. I haven't spoken to Toland or Collins yet, so I don't have a notion of how the proceedings are going to go down.

"You could do with smartening yourself up. Did you brush that hair today at all at all? It's like a bird's nest at the back," says Mam.

Mam has been on to me a fair bit lately to trim my fine mane of unruly red waves. I'm fond of them though. Everyone here has the same haircut, a one or two grade on the back and sides, trim the top, then spike up the fringe.

"I don't know, this look is kinda growing on me. Wink, wink."

A pudgy female face pops out from the half opened door, a member of the Board. Here we go. Game time. Mam and I stand up and make our way inside. On one side of the room around ten PTA members and some prominent people from around the town, such as big shot Barry Ennis, sit at a long table consisting of two smaller ones pushed together. Leary is bang smack in the middle, to his right is Ussher, like a spare prick.

"How are you? Thank you for coming in," says Ussher, trying to be affable.

The other gobshites, including Kenny and that quisling Vice Principal Corley, give their various nods and greetings as Mam and myself take a seat before them.

"I'm sure you're aware as to the reasons for this meeting today," says Leary.

Mam sits, wordless, her hands resting on her lap.

"No. Actually, I'm not entirely sure why you called this meeting, would you care to explain?"

The Board members shoot looks between themselves. Leary clears his throat and takes a sip of uisce.

"Where to begin... Mr. Carolan, your behaviour at this school has never been stellar, but your involvement in the class strikes and resulting disobedience was especially potent-"

"-How was it potent?"

My interruption flusters Leary, he really can't stand the sight of me.

"Ya think you're a tough fella rocking the boat."

--I'd rather sink it.

"Well, it's time you learn this won't be tolerated."

"Why? Because we don't follow you're dogmatic delusions and rules?"

"Weren't ye doing the same thing when ye were trying to run the show?"

"No, we weren't, for the simple reason that we don't believe in believing in any system that doesn't allow for that system itself to be replaced, so it's hardly doctrine or dogma as ye eejets understand it."

The Board are speechless, it's safe to say they're not used to being challenged. One of the flock pushes a pen and a piece of paper before me.

"Either way, we need you to sign this contract, assuring us that you won't cause any more trouble for the remainder of the term," bleats some sheep.

Look how smug they all are. Ussher there, on his path of righteousness. The parents, Christ, the parents are simply helots serving their sire.

"If ye think I'm signing anything ye put in front of me, you're all out of your fucking minds."

They all gasp.

"Seanie," says Mam.

"Sorry, Mam."

"There's no need for that type of language," says a member of the kakistocracy.

The state of them, they're offended more by a word than my non-compliance.

"C'mon, Mam, we're going."

Mam and I rise to our feet.

"Are you sure you want to do this?" asks Mam.

"I am."

"Alright so, you're eighteen, if this is what you want to do," says she, concerned and uneasy.

"It's alright, I do."

We step back from the table.

"You're burning bridges, you never know when you might need a reference from the school for something," says Baz Ennis.

"If it's a bridge between me and the likes of ye, I'd burn it down before ye knew it."

Myself and Mam make our way out. I leave the door open to show as much disrespect as possible, and don't bother my bollocks at all to look back at them. Mam wears a worried expression. I can understand. Then again, I'm sure she understands. She never finished school. She got treated disgracefully in school, and didn't she turn out a lot better than most.

When I got home the first thing I did was call the two boyos to see how their meetings went. Toland and Collins both signed the contract. I thought they might. I don't blame them a bit for trying to get on, both of their oul pairs are wicked strict. Whatever about my Mam, I know deep down she supports me and agrees, but if the two lads didn't sign that bit of paper there would be war in the Toland and Collins camp. As far as I know, other students got a slap on the wrist, while us at the newspaper received the lion's share of the blame. They more or less said to Collins and Toland,

--After your suspension you can show up for school, but don't worry about it.

In other words, they don't want to officially expel anyone. We're sixth years and it would make them look bad to expel people who will be finished in a few months anyways. In relation to the newspaper, the fourth years will be allowed to print an end of year edition as long as it receives Brother Leary's thumbs up. The nuns don't even allow the girls in the Convent to put out a student periodical. They might have reclaimed control for now, but the students have a had a little taste of freedom and I'm sure this won't be the last of it. A set-back is different than a failure. When I think about it, it's only a matter of time before people wake up. Change always takes ages. It takes a few times to get it right and we just have to keep pushing the bastards until they fall off the edge. Even with all the clamping down in the Girls' School, Saorise was saying they're working on a plan to turn it into a democratic institution. I read in the Connaught the other day that some of the students in the Galway-Mayo IT branch here in town are getting together with other colleges to fight for more student power. It has to start somewhere. Most of the parents and older people are never going to wake up. They're too enslaved. They've been standing up, sitting down, kneeling and heeling for too fecking long. Most of them are a lost cause. Clodhoppers. It's Us who can make the big difference, it's only a matter of time until we're the older people. We have to keep on going and try to get people to snap out of it. We have to stay true to ourselves, and that's fucking hard in this day and age. I will never wear a uniform again. I'm sick to my stomach of all the nonsense. Why bother playing their game? If I do the Leaving Cert, I'll have to genuflect to the same bullshit in college. Is that what I want? Why do I need them to tell me what I should or shouldn't be allowed to do? I'm going to be a writer come hell or mass slaughter. Why do I need them to certify me as an artist? Everyone can be an artist in some manner or other. Peeling a spud can be an art if one cares enough about it, having people over for a cup of tea can be an art if it's what one truly enjoys. I have to write to be a writer, not go to school so they can kill the creativeness in my soul. No more class. Done and dusted. I can't stay here though. I need a change. I need the freedom of anonymity. Maybe I'll move to Toronto, sure Chris has been haunting me to go and visit him since he left, we could get a couple of people together and open a pub. We'd have the whole of Ontario socialising in no time. Or maybe I should move to New York and be with my lovely love, Sonny emails me every week about going to New York so she can show me the City. That's it. I'd be an ex-pat living the artist's life in the Big Apple. I could befriend and hang out with all the artists in Greenwich Village. A working bard, playing hard when I need a break. What a life I might live. Will I or won't I? Won't I or will I? A thousand years as a sheep or a day as a Lion?

Chapter 21

R^{OAR!!!!!!!!!!!!!!!!!!!!!!!}